Seeing Double

A Nerd Boy/Popular Girl College Romance

Mj Hendrix

D1518502

Mj Hendrix Publishing Co.

for my babies, m and m. you've made every hard decision I was
forced to make this year worth it.
I love you five.

Contents

Also by MJ

Seeing Double is book two in the Good Ol' Boys Series. It can be read as a standalone, but the best reader experience would be to start with **Falling For Temptation**. Here is the blurb and link to the book on Amazon.

The tattooed vixen in my first college class is everything I shouldn't crave if I want to stay on the straight and narrow path.

My family expects me to find a sweet, innocent girl. Harley Kain's questionable past and skin-baring clothing definitely don't fit the bill.

I think she might be the temptress my momma prayed I would resist, but I can't look away. All I want is to get an Agriculture degree and go back to the cornstalks and dirt. It's the only life I've ever known, and I'm perfectly content on the farm.

Until I see her.

She's guarded, but my protective instincts kick into overdrive when I find out she's been walking home alone at night. When she finally confides in me, I start to realize the dangerous life she's running from.

I want to protect her. I want to do more than that. But if I give in to my overwhelming desire for her, I'll be throwing away my future. My family will never approve.

Even if I am willing to sacrifice it all and fall for temptation, convincing Harley she's worthy of love could be impossible.

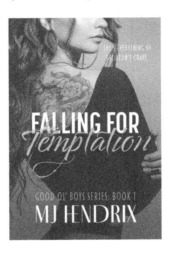

She's a million miles out of my league.

But when I find out that Kenna is my online student, the fake name I used to become a tutor gives me the confidence I need to talk to her.

I don't know anything about women, but it sure seems like she's flirting with me. This would never happen if she found out I was just that nerd who couldn't stop staring at her in the cafeteria, unable to speak in her presence.

If she wasn't dating my best friend, maybe I wouldn't feel so guilty for being desperately in love with her.

But Kenna is the girl every guy wants, because she lights up every room she enters with her perfect smile and addicting laugh. I can't focus on anyone else when she's nearby.

So I let myself flirt with her, and it somehow happens in real life, not just through our late-night emails.

The real hang-up is that she doesn't know there are two versions of me, the quiet guy I am on the outside and the real me beneath the surface.

When she inevitably finds out, I don't know how she'll ever forgive me for lying to her about my true identity.

Prologue

I smell charred flesh and smoke. I try to open my eyes. They're stinging, like I'm too close to a fire. A warm liquid is gathering under my cheek. The rest of my body is numb, slowly awakening from a slumber, like when you get up and realize you were sleeping on your arm and it's now tingling to life. The nausea, similar to a bad stomach bug, is crawling over me, and I need to retch out my breakfast of bacon and waffles.

"Lia...Lia..." I choke, starting to cough.

Shouts of alarm are getting louder, and I hear the creaking of metal. Raised voices are ringing in my ear. I can't make out their words. I want to beg them for help, to find my sister.

"Lia...Lia! Can you...hear me?" I cough through the searing pain in my throat.

An unknown voice speaks from far away. "I hear someone. Hey! Are you okay? Can you move?"

The shrill voice reaches me through the haze, but the energy to respond has left me. I just want to know if Lia is okay.

"The paramedics are on their way! Try to stay calm." The voice is still high-pitched, not at all calming my thundering heart and gasps for breath.

Other voices join in. I want to scream at them to find her and tell me that she's okay.

"Lia...Lia..." I whimper, but no one hears.

1

Kenna

Three Years Later

First Semester

I bypass the endless line at the Ole Tex University café, eyes on the barista. His name is Jared, and I met him last Friday at an off-campus party. He asked me for my number and has been texting me since then.

"Jared!"

His head turns from the latte he's making. A smile curves across his freckled face. "Kenna. Hey, beautiful."

I lean my elbows on the counter. "What's a girl got to do to get some caffeine before class?"

He laughs, eyes roaming over me. I offer a tiny smirk, inspecting my nail beds.

"Anything in particular?" He sets the latte down. "Hazelnut with no whip for Cassie."

A girl squeezes up to the counter through the mass of students to retrieve the cup.

"I'd love one like that but with oat milk and also a black coffee."

He nods. I count six cups lined up for him to make, but he grabs a new one and starts on my latte.

"Are you rushing?" I push back a strawberry-blonde curl that fell into my eyes.

"No, ma'am. I'm a proud Lambda Alpha. This is my sophomore year." He winks at me as he pumps the hazelnut flavor into the cup.

In light of this information, I try to look at him with new eyes. Lambda Alpha is *the* fraternity to be in, but frat boys typically don't do it for me. The over-the-top self-confidence and entitlement turn me off.

Is Jared an exception?

He continues crafting my latte, adding in the steamed oat milk and espresso at the lightning speed of a barista with now eight empty cups currently waiting to be filled. He takes his special time to form a heart with the foam, even with the line of students about to be late for class. He pushes the lid over it before handing it to me, and I wonder why he bothered with the design. He adds the black coffee to the space.

"Wow, you're literally salvaging my entire morning! Thank you so much." I take a sip and experience a burst of foamy deliciousness. "Mmm, immaculate."

He chuckles while hurrying to start on the orders piling up. "Text me later, babe?"

I cringe internally at the term of endearment as I nod with a smile. "Sure. Have a good one."

I turn to leave, ignoring the irritated glances being thrown my way. I hand the other cup to my roommate, Harley, with a smile. She gives me her own brand of a thank-you. I knew almost immediately after we met that cracking her tough exterior wasn't even going to be a challenge. She's all tattoos and attitude, and I'm half in love with her already.

We are going to be besties.

We make our way to the science building, a ball of dread forming in my stomach. Chemistry is my worst subject, and I'm already regretting the choice to take it my first semester. I should've waited until next year—or my next life, maybe.

I make plans with Harley for lunch before we split ways.

The classroom is only half full. I don't want to risk getting called on, so I take my seat in the back row. My goals are to blend in and pass. If I can sit beside a smart kid willing to share notes, even better.

I take out my MacBook, settling in and saying a prayer for invisible waves of knowledge to somehow float toward me. I turn around to see if I recognize any of the students walking in from the party where I met Jared.

My breathing halts when I spot a guy I met on Monday at the library walking through the door. He's a head above the other students with inky hair and black-framed glasses. He resembles Superman's nerdy alter ego in the absolute best way. I stare at him as he sits in the same row a few chairs down, keeping his eyes down to the ground.

His T-shirt has a Rubik's Cube on the front. It looks like it's been washed a hundred times, faded and hugging his broad shoulders. He doesn't speak to anyone as he pulls out his notebook and pen.

I bet this class won't be a challenge for him.

"Kenna. Hey, babe."

I jolt at the sound of a female voice, turning around to see the redhead I met at the pre-semester party and became friends with immediately. "Maya. Hey, girl."

She smiles, sitting down next to me and blocking my view of the sexy, smart boy. "I'm so glad I met a few people over the weekend, so the first week of class isn't so awkward. What were you looking at?"

"Oh, uh, nothing. Praying for a natural disaster, so I don't have to sit through this class."

She laughs. "Girl, yes. I would give anything to find some nerd to cheat off of."

The professor takes his place at the front of the class and begins the lecture. My hands cramp from speed-typing. By the end of the hour, I'm already overwhelmed.

"Okay, this is going to be horrible. Let's find a study partner right now. Someone who looks unfazed by what we just heard," Maya suggests.

I nod. My confidence to survive is crumbling. I'm a smart person, but college chemistry is on a level I don't quite comprehend.

Maya stands up, eyes on the crowd of students filtering up the staircase. I hope she can find us a savior. My eyes drift to the guy I saw coming in earlier. He's packing up his bag and his head is down.

Maya follows my gaze. "Oh, perfect." She waltzes past the two empty chairs separating us from him. "Hey. How's it going? Love your backpack."

He stands up before looking down at her. He doesn't say anything.

"Um, so, yeah, we were wondering if you'd like to study with us." Maya gestures back at me.

I try to act natural as his eyes—a freaking gorgeous bright blue—look up. His eyes burn over me, taking in my frame from head to toe. I blush for no reason at all. His calm inspection makes my skin heat. It doesn't feel like he's checking me out for salacious reasons. It's more like he's observing a house on the street or a car he might want to drive. I'm not offended, simply confused. Men typically look at me with much more suggestive eyes.

When we met Monday, he acted like my existence was irrelevant. All he said was his name.

Levi.

Maya keeps talking. "We were going to meet in the library to go over the notes later this afternoon, around three. Are you down?"

His eyes are still on me as he silently nods.

Maya turns to me with a smile. "Great. See you then."

When I get to the library after my last class, I'm dressed in a pale-pink sundress. The ruching between my breasts and over the hips gives my body emphasis in all the right places.

Maya texted me a few minutes ago to say that she reserved a study room. I find her easily enough, with Harley following behind me. We claim our seats as I sling my backpack onto the table.

"Um, you look nice," Maya says, her left brow lifted.

"Thanks." I take out my MacBook, positioning it on the space in front of me.

We chat while we wait for thirty minutes before Maya sighs. "I can't believe he isn't showing up. We're way out of his league."

I don't agree, but I am disappointed. I was hoping to strike up a conversation with him this time. I'm dying to get inside his head, and I can't put my finger on why.

"Oh well. Maybe we should try reviewing the notes to see if we can help each other," I say.

"What's up with the party on Friday?" Maya changes the subject.

"Beach theme. Bikinis, denim cutoffs, that sort of thing. My cousin Lexi says we definitely need to make an impression."

To my left, Harley snorts.

I turn to face her. "What?"

She shakes her head, looking up at me with a smirk. "Didn't say anything."

"Have you seen that guy?" I blurt out.

Her dark brows come together. "What guy?"

I lean a little closer. "Adam, the sweet, sexy farm boy you met."

She shrugs. "No. Wouldn't matter if I did."

I detect a faint sense of discomfort, and I can't determine why. Adam was hot and sweet, a rare combination. He seemed to like my roommate when we met him and his friend. I don't really know Harley yet, but I know we're going to be friends, whether she wants to be or not.

I almost don't feel bold enough to ask, but curiosity wins over. "What about his friend Levi?"

She finally looks up at me from her notebook. I'm starting to wonder if she owns a laptop because I haven't seen her with one.

"Nope. You?"

I shake my head. "They were kind of...different." I stare at my roommate as I wait to hear her opinion.

She laughs. "Uh, yeah, you think? What kind of guys don't have swim trunks? Also, the smart one looked at you like you were the first beautiful girl he'd ever seen. My guess is he's from a religious convent or some kind of cult."

My belly clenches at her words. "You think he noticed me? I felt like I was nearly invisible. He wouldn't even look up at me when I tried to introduce myself." I look at Maya to see her reaction.

Her mouth gapes open before she throws her head back, laughing. "I gotta say, I'm with Scary Barbie on this one. You're the first blonde with tits he's ever encountered. Guy has no clue how to react."

I lean back in my chair, slightly stunned. *He's intimidated?*

This isn't the news I was expecting to hear. "Well, what should I do then?"

Maya taps her pen against the table. "I would just make it obvious you're into him, and that'll give him the courage to come around eventually. Invite him to parties, like you did yesterday, and he'll start to catch on."

Harley is studying her notes as she answers, "Yeah, can't say I disagree. Give him time to get used to your big, bouncy hair and all that, and he's bound to make a move."

2

Kenna

Second Semester

"I've never been friend-zoned in my entire life." I drop my tray onto the cafeteria table.

My butt follows suit, plopping into the red plastic chair. The sad fruit cup and deli sandwich look completely unappealing.

Maya's copper head pops up, her amused face barely containing a snicker. "Nerd boy still isn't giving you the time of day?" She sticks a cucumber slice into her mouth, smiling as she chews.

I hate to say it seems like she enjoys my unrequited crush, but frankly, I think she does.

One of the girls I've become friends with, Raelynn, is sipping on her water, and her eyes meet mine as I begin to explain. Of the two of them, she's the only one I really feel like actually likes me.

"I'm sure that sounds egotistical, but it's a simple fact. At this point, it's just a *wanting what I can't have* issue." I sigh, leaning my elbow onto the table, cheek in my palm. "But it didn't start that way. I saw him in my chem class on the very first day, and I was hooked by his *gentle giant lumberjack mixed with Clark*

Kent vibe. A big, yummy dream wrapped up in an old T-shirt and black-framed glasses."

I shiver, and it's not for show. I wanted to sit in his lap, hoping he'd study and cradle me like he does that thick genetics textbook. I've done all I can to make my interest known for the entire first semester of classes, but the man has yet to show me even a shred of attention.

My friends laugh. Maya is completely bent over, gripping her stomach. She finally recovers, and I feel a bit self-conscious about my confession. I should really start journaling instead of baring my soul to people. At least I held back the part about being jealous of a freaking textbook. Maya is still catching her breath.

"You—ah, ha. You really have it bad for the guy who couldn't be odder if he tried." She shakes her head, spearing a cherry tomato with her fork.

"It's...he's not odd. He's quiet and reserved. There's a difference." I don't know why I'm defending someone who's spoken exactly one word to me, which was his name. "I can't put my finger on it—why I'm so into him—but I honestly find it hard to believe y'all don't at least think he's attractive. He's clearly got an athletic body. He's just not full of himself, like the athletes."

I indicate the group walking by us now. The one in the lead winks as he passes by with a confident strut. I wonder if I really do see Levi differently for some reason.

Raelynn shakes her short blonde hair. "No, you're totally right. He's got a body for sure, and I even see a little of that guy from that old show...about Superman when he was a kid?"

I snap my fingers at her. "Yes! *Smallville*! I totally forgot about that show. The episode where they tie him up like a scarecrow out in the field without a shirt on? That was my sexual awakening."

The pieces are falling into place, and I finally think I understand where my enormous crush originated from. Some of the tension eases from my shoulders.

"Okay, whatever, he's attractive, but can you even imagine how awkward it would be to have sex with a virgin at our age? I'm not interested in having to teach a freaking college-aged male how to go down," Maya states as she flicks her red hair over her pale shoulder.

I'm about to pipe up with my teacher-student fantasies, but it probably wouldn't go over well.

I wonder if I could still see well enough if I was wearing his glasses.

My roommate walks into the cafeteria, flanked by her boyfriend, Adam. Of course she landed the first guy she wanted almost as soon as the year started.

The hot nerd in question—Adam's roommate, Levi—is trailing behind them. I stand up to wave at Harley, and she nods at me, waving back.

I just saw Levi before my last class, but he's as delicious as ever. Broad shoulders, ebony-black hair, and vampire-pale skin are my kink. Square glasses that he should be modeling for an eyewear company complete the look that gets me all fluttery and weak. I almost forgot how tall he is—a few inches above all the rest of the miniature-looking students walking by. His gaze stays focused ahead, like I don't exist in his world.

What could I possibly be lacking to Smallville?

"He has to be gay," I mutter to myself.

Raelynn lets out a tiny gasp. "You think so?"

She leans toward me, observing him as he towers above most of the students in line for Monday's chicken Parmesan.

"Only one way to find out." Maya stands up and winks at me. She adjusts her bra so that her boobs are nearly falling out of her scoop-neck sweater. She struts toward the drink station as Levi exits the food line.

My stomach is uneasy as I watch her sway in the same direction he's headed. They reach it together, and he waits for her to go first. From across the room, I can see her smile at him before bending over to get a cup from the crates on the floor instead of the stack on the counter. She turns back to face him, her mouth moving as she speaks. There's a shorter blonde guy stepping up behind Levi, but I can't tell which one she's talking to.

"What's she saying?" Raelynn leans in, blue eyes wide.

All I can do is shake my head, chewing on my fingernail.

Maya tosses her copper head back in a laugh, and my stomach drops.

Did he really say something funny to her?

It didn't look like he spoke at all.

"Is she talking to the other guy?" I whisper.

Raelynn nods. "He's in her brother's fraternity, I think."

I blow out a sigh, but my heart rate spikes again as she drops the cup and bends over to get it, tits on display for Levi's face a few feet away. The blonde guy's eyes leer like it's the last show of the night at a Vegas strip club.

My gaze flits to Levi's face. He never strays from staring a hole into the top of the drink station. I can't help the upward curve of my lips as Maya rights her posture, finally turning to fill up the cup with water.

"Gross. Why wouldn't she get a new cup?" Raelynn is disgusted.

I burst out laughing. She's adorable, but always a step behind what's really going on. I feel better as Maya makes her way back to us and sits down. Harley, Adam, and Levi are getting closer, so I lean in to hear the report.

She shrugs. "You're right. Must be gay." Her voice betrays her casual posture, and I think she must be a tad bit hurt that her pricey silicone sisters didn't earn their usual approval.

I match her shrug. *Maybe he is gay. Or maybe he doesn't like redheads.*

Even as I observe him walking toward our table with my best friend, Harley, he only looks up occasionally to watch where he's going. He avoids eye contact with me like it's the green plague.

He sits three chairs down from me, past Harley and Adam, and I slump a little over my tray.

"Hey, how was the rest of your break?" Harley asks, turning to me.

Her blue eyes and ebony hair perfectly complement her petite frame and tattoo-covered body.

"After you left, it was pretty meh. We went to the lake house for New Year's, so that was nice."

Harley stayed with me for the first week of winter break because her foster mom is an abusive bitch. Adam's family doesn't really accept his choice of girlfriend, which outrages me on my best friend's behalf.

"What about you guys? Please tell me you didn't actually go *camping*." I say the last word like it personally offends me because it does.

Adam laughs out loud. His handsome face has grown a little scruff since I last saw him. "Kenna, camping is a great American pastime. Have you ever tasted campfire food?"

He has one hand curled around Harley's waist, and he raises the other to his mouth, sipping on a glass of sweet tea. They're a ridiculously hot couple. I'm thrilled for my roommate. She deserves a nice guy like Adam.

"No, I have not, and I've lived a very full life the past nineteen years, sleeping on comfortable mattresses with real sheets instead of the cold, hard ground."

I pick up my fork to poke it into a squishy strawberry. *Oh, how I miss my mother's chef.* Rosie always had the best fresh produce, sliced and ready for me when I woke up.

"Well, if you go with someone, you can find lots of fun ways to stay warm," Harley says casually.

Adam chokes on a bite of chicken. He's still such a sweet, innocent little farmer. They started dating last semester. With his upbringing, Adam is naive, and Harley is the first girl he's ever been with.

I raise my eyebrow at her, and we both laugh. His face is tinged pink, but he recovers quickly, clearing his throat. Levi is silently eating his lunch. I want to crack open his skull and read his thoughts as they scroll across those baby-blue eyes.

Last semester, I invited him to four parties—one where I wore a scandalous bathing suit, just for him—and he didn't show up to *any.*

Maya and Raelynn stand up, bidding us good-bye as they head to class.

Harley eyes Maya disapprovingly before giving me a look that says, *why are you still friends with her?* Harley has never liked Maya's pretentious attitude and her tendency to dish out backhanded compliments.

Adam's brother Dan walks up to the table, sitting in the vacated seat across from me with a flirtatious smirk on his chiseled face. He's the darker-blonde version of Adam.

"Hey, Kenna. You coming on the camping trip?"

His tray is piled high with carbohydrates and fat. Male metabolism is a universal injustice.

Harley laughs, shaking her head. "Kenna is too prissy for a tent." She bites into a bowl of chocolate ice cream, pushing her salad aside.

"Hey, no one has even invited me! Who all is going on this trip?" *That could possibly affect my decision.*

Adam looks around. "Anyone is invited...but so far, it's just us and Silas."

Silas is their other roommate, a baseball player. The four of them moved from the middle of nowhere, basically an unofficial religious convent, to go to college. They're all surprisingly outgoing, except for Levi.

"Who's...us?" I ask, hoping I don't sound pathetically obvious. I'm pushing the fruit around on my plate to appear nonchalant.

Adam's face scrunches up in confusion, but Harley knows exactly what I'm asking.

"All the guys in the apartment, plus me, and I'm hoping you won't leave me hanging as the only one who has to sit to pee."

Levi is casually eating his side salad, probably doing equations in his head. My face heats a little with unjustified annoyance.

"Okay, I'll come."

He freezes for a split second before continuing his chewing. I suddenly realize he doesn't talk to me because he actually *dislikes* me. As far as I know, I've never been disliked for no reason, especially by a guy. I pride myself on being friendly and outgoing to everyone. I even cracked Harley's rock-hard exterior in a matter of weeks.

What is with him?

"Awesome." Dan grins at me.

Harley squeezes me into a side hug. "Yay! We can cuddle to stay warm."

"Who's going to keep me warm?" Adam teases her.

"When Kenna goes to sleep, I'll come share my body heat with you, babe," she says, leaning in for a smooch.

Levi suddenly stands up, his tray cleared. My heart sinks a little as I realize we probably don't have a class together since it's a new semester.

I have got to get over this guy. *Maybe I need a distraction.*

"You got class?" Adam asks him.

He nods, lifting a hand before turning to walk away.

"You should work out with us tomorrow. Adam is destroying me in the gym, and I need moral support," Harley says, drawing my gaze from the retreating set of broad shoulders.

"Okay." *I've got to get some endorphins from somewhere.*

3

Levi

"Levi, wait up!"

I hear footsteps quickly gaining on me, and I recognize them as my childhood friend Dan's without turning.

"Bro, I think I'm in love," he admits.

Blood begins pounding in my ears. I think I know who he's referring to. My friends know they don't have to wait on a response for me to be listening.

"She's like...the prettiest girl at this school."

More like an ethereal being in human form.

"I'm hoping she asks me to the sorority thing they're having at the end of the semester."

He turns to look at me, so I nod.

"Okay."

I have no idea how to read women, but Kenna seems to like Dan. She smiles at him a lot.

Why wouldn't she like Dan?

He can talk in a group setting, and he's a nice, good-looking guy. I'll work on being happy for him just as soon as I find a trash can to throw up in.

"Silas says half the baseball team is batting for her. The competition is stiff, so I've got to come up with a plan. The camping trip would be the best place to make a move, but it's too far away." He's half-talking to me, half-musing to himself.

He knows I'm helpless when it comes to females. You have to be able to talk to one before you can ever hope to actually...date. Being sheltered at home wasn't something I ever had a problem with growing up. My social anxiety and introverted personality agreed well with being a hermit. My only friends were the textbooks in my room and the guys a few miles away from the farm.

"You have to help me. You're smart," he pleads.

I gape at him, unsure if he's joking or not. She's not a science test, so I'm pretty sure that moves me out of the *smart* category and into the *big idiot* one.

"Maybe...talk to Adam?"

He's the only one of us who managed to get a girlfriend in the first semester of college, away from our sheltered lives in the country. At least he and Dan learned about women growing up with sisters.

All I really know is that one of them is so gorgeous that I can't breathe when I look at her.

Dan shakes his head. "No can do. He would definitely tell Harley, who would tell Kenna. I'd be better off just asking her to dinner."

I guess that means information isn't safe from one female companion if you tell the other one. I try to log away any valuable facts I hear on the subject of women.

We're walking toward the building we both have a class in as my steps falter.

"It has to be more special than that," Dan says.

His bravery and self-confidence astound me.

I let myself imagine for a brief moment what it would be like to spend time with Kenna—alone. What if she wanted to sit and talk to just me? The emerald depth of her eyes would put me under a spell, and I'd lose the ability to form coherent thoughts. If she even got within arm's length, my brain would short-circuit. Actually, it has. The first time I met her, she sat beside me at a table in the cafeteria and introduced herself, and I nearly had a panic attack. All I could do was stare at the blurry shapes in my textbook, inhaling her scent of cherry vanilla.

I've wondered if it came from her skin or her curly blonde hair. I've fantasized about how soft it would be if I were to reach over and touch it. I've spent too many nights awake, wondering that.

"We have to find out what she likes. Maybe I could ask her friend, the nice one. What's her name?" Dan asks, reaching the door to his classroom and turning to face me.

I clear my throat. "Raelynn."

He snaps his fingers. "That's it. I'll ask her what Kenna likes, and maybe that'll help me come up with something. Thanks, bro. See ya later."

He walks into the room, and I continue on to my biochemistry class.

While my weakness is talking to women—really, just people I don't know in general—biochemistry is one of my strengths.

I sit next to the only new friend I've made since moving here, thankful he's also in this class. Melvin's curly fire-red hair looks shorter than the last time I saw him.

He beams up at me, freckles peppering his pale skin. "Levi! Hey, man. How was your Christmas break? Did you get my emails?"

His glasses are actually somehow thicker than mine, with dark-red rims.

"It was fine. Yes, I did. Here are my notes."

I pull out the sheet of paper I scratched the equations on. Melvin hungrily reaches for it. His eyes skim over the complex formulas.

"Why are you cloning...squirrels?" I ask.

Talking to Melvin is simple because it's always about subjects I feel comfortable with.

He looks up at me, excitement sparking in his eyes. "My grandparents outfitted my lab with brand-new equipment for Christmas. It's all..." He trails off as a girl walks by with a bright-pink backpack.

She's got a full head of curly, dark hair. Melvin's eyes couldn't possibly get bigger, and I know exactly how he feels.

His Adam's apple bobs as his eyes move over her as she sits a few seats down from us.

He finally turns back to me, clearing his throat. "Anyway, yeah...it's pretty great."

His eyes look over me, observing the old T-shirt I'm wearing as I take off my jacket. I'm about to pull it back on as his intense inspection of me continues, but he snaps out of it.

"How are you so in shape? You're, like...smart and fit. How?" He leans in toward me, and I remember that personal boundaries are something he lacked in our chemistry class last semester.

"Uh, I work out with my roommate." I self-consciously scratch my head, wishing he would stop looking at me.

Silas used to push me to work out with him, so I wouldn't stay in my room the entire day studying, but I've grown to enjoy it. I contemplate whatever topic I'm studying while I lift weights.

Melvin gapes at me like I grew a set of horns.

"Can you...can you help me? Help me get in shape?" He's staring at me like I solved the origin of the molecule.

"I, uh...sure." I'm not sure if I want to take on an apprentice with such skinny arms in the gym.

Some people have the genetic makeup to work out, and it makes a difference in their physique. My dad is a big man, as is my grandfather. I've never met Melvin's family, but he's a scrawny little guy. We'll have to start with the smallest dumbbells.

He grins, looking over at the girl with the pink backpack.

"I drink those Ensure protein shakes every morning, but I feel like I could use some bulking up, you know?"

He flexes, but nothing happens. I nod. At least one of us should get the girl we want.

"Yeah, definitely. We go every morning at five."

If teaching Melvin how to work out can land him a date with the pink-backpack girl, I'll do what I can.

He leans in to whisper as the professor steps into the room. "I wanna ask Vivian out. Isn't she stunning? She's smart too."

He does nothing to conceal the longing in his gaze, and I marvel at his ability to look at a girl he finds attractive for such an extended amount of time. The beautiful girl suddenly turns to face him, and he jolts as his cheeks burn.

Well, maybe not.

Before turning away, I notice her smirking. All women completely mystify me, some more than others. She doesn't seem offended.

Isn't staring considered rude and even offensive sometimes?

"Have you ever had a girlfriend?" he whispers, even as the professor begins his introduction on a topic we both know better than he does.

We get along well, partly because we devour textbooks relating to science, like some people indulge in parties, sex, and normal college student activities at an unhealthy rate.

In my first semester at Ole Tex, I realized my intellect was several levels above what was taught in my classes. My extensive homeschooling and the advanced online classes my mom enrolled me in put me miles ahead of a normal college student. I should be in grad school, but to get there, I have to get my bachelor's degree. I also need to figure out how to handle the social aspects of college and life with people my age.

Who knew lunchtime would be my biggest challenge?

"No," I whisper back.

I almost laugh at the probability of such an absurd notion. Again, I'll have to figure out how to talk to a female before I can keep one around long enough to label as mine. A bouncy head of strawberry-blonde hair with an angelic, immaculate face appears in my mind, but I force her to get out of my head.

Kenna Davis is the last girl on this planet I could ever be with.

"You could get one easier than I could. At least you don't exactly look like a science freak."

I don't really know what he means, considering my shirt has a pi symbol on it and my glasses could start fires if the sun hit them just right.

I don't know what to say, so I remain silent.

"We should help each other. Who would you date if you could?"

His question surprises me, but I'm definitely not answering it. Even pretending that I'm capable of dating *her* seems like trying to figure out what's at the bottom of a black hole. It gives me a headache.

"You should try talking to that girl over there. I think her name is Lexi."

He points to a girl with white-blonde hair and unnaturally dark skin appearing orange. I have no interest in her, so I shrug noncommittally.

"My uncle is really smart like us, and you know what?" he whispers.

I wish he would at least pretend to listen to the simple lecture.

"He's old and cranky and completely alone—always has been. On my eighteenth birthday, he gave me a subscription to *Playboy*. He said it's the closest I'll ever get to a real girl because I'm just like him. I don't think he knows about online porn."

I turn to stare at his profile, and for the first time, I consider the possibility of never being able to communicate with the opposite sex. *Surely I will eventually get over it?*

I'm finally around more women, not just in a church setting. Most of the girls here seem nice, and only one truly terrifies me. Maybe I should try to find one who's not so completely out of my realm.

I start to look around the room for a girl who seems shy like me, preferably one interested in the lecture, so I can have at least one thing to talk to her about.

"What do you mean by help each other?" I whisper back.

My chest feels a little tight at the possibility of spending forever in isolation. I'm sure I could at least find a roommate like Melvin, but there's no doubt in my mind that my close friends Silas and Dan will find girlfriends sooner or later, like Adam has. For them, it's only a matter of finding one who doesn't care that they're college-aged virgins. My issues run much deeper.

"You can help me get muscular, and I'll help you...well, we can help each other think of ways to talk to the girls we like." He chances a quick glance at Vivian.

I remember Dan and his plan to ask out Kenna. I start to feel sick again when I think about his ability to be charming and flirtatious. Even back home, he was the boldest with girls.

"I don't...there's no one I want to talk to," I whisper back, scribbling nonsense on my paper to appear to be paying attention.

He squints at me. "I know we aren't, like, best friends or anything, but don't just lie to my face like that." His tone is incredulous.

Guilt tinges my cheeks pink.

He hesitates, clearing his throat. "Look...you obviously don't have to tell me who it is, but you should at least try to talk to her even if you think she'll never go out with you. You never know until you strike up a conversation. My grandma told me that after I cried on my birthday." His willingness to admit embarrassing moments will never cease to amaze me. "The alternative is a lifetime of regret and wishing you'd just gotten over it and said hi to her."

I debate his words. All I've ever said to her is my name. *What would it be like to attempt a greeting?*

My imagination runs wild throughout the next forty minutes. In my head, I say hi to her, and she says it back. We end up sitting next to each other at lunch, and twice, our elbows touch accidentally. The next day, she smiles at me, and my heart nearly beats out of my chest as Kenna stands on the tips of her toes to wrap me in a hug. She's wearing a pale-yellow dress. She looks beautiful as a figment of my imagination, but I know in real life she's unmatched in her appeal.

Once the class ends, I slowly gather the notebook I never wrote anything legible in. Melvin is waiting for me, and I stand to walk out with him.

Vivian starts to walk by us with her pink backpack, and I'm shocked to hear him squeak next to me.

"Hi."

She pauses, turning to him with her lips curving upward. "Hey. What's up?"

She actually stops next to us, and he's a frozen ice sculpture, staring at her.

An extremely awkward five seconds crawls by. Her smile begins to falter. I muster some courage, taking pity on my friend.

"How was your break?" I say, my voice a little higher than usual.

She smiles at me, clearly relieved. "It was pretty good. I went skiing. What about you guys?"

She turns back to Melvin, whose open mouth is nearly drooling. I clip him on the shoulder, praying he finds the courage to continue what he started.

He does—finally.

"It was...so pretty," he sighs, and I wish there was a portal that could swallow me.

She laughs, throwing her head back. "Yeah, snow is just magical, isn't it?"

He grins, seeming to gain courage with each passing moment that she engages with us.

"Oh, yeah. Isn't it fascinating that each snowflake has its own individual pattern?"

He begins walking toward the door with her. Now I'm the one frozen in place.

Surely, if Melvin can do it, so can I.

4

Kenna

"Harley..." I blow out a labored breath. "I'm about to die. How much longer?"

I pant, my arm weakening and dropping the ten-pound dumbbell. My hands reach out to rest on my knees. I really might vomit. It's coming up any second. My skin is flushed when I look in the gym mirror. I'm suddenly thankful it's only six a.m., and there's not a horde of students here to see my embarrassing lack of stamina.

She's breathing just as heavy as me, her dark hair sticking to her cheeks. "Dude...I told you. He's killing me."

She stands up straighter as Adam makes his way back over to us with a kettlebell.

"No, absolutely not. I can't lift another thing," Harley says, folding her arms over her chest.

We're both in sports bras and spandex. Hers is an olive-green set, and mine is royal purple.

I lean over to whisper in her ear. "Try not covering the distraction zone." I cough.

She obliges instantly, dropping her arms. Then she lifts them up in a stretch over her head.

"Come on, babe. We're almost done. You guys have...one more...set." His words trail off as his eyes blaze over her tan skin.

Bingo. I knew we'd get out of this earlier if she just used her assets to our advantage.

Ten minutes later, I'm stretched and moving toward the cafeteria. I'm absolutely starving. The sweat is cooling on my skin in the January air. I pull my hoodie over my head as we reach the entrance.

"So, about this camping trip..." I begin.

Harley spins toward me, her hand sealed in Adam's. Dan joined us after he crawled out of bed late. *Lucky jerk.*

"Yes?"

"Are we really going to sleep on the ground? Can't we bring an air mattress at the very least?" I try to form the puppy-dog face that usually gets me the things I want.

"Do you want to be a wuss?" Her voice is incredulous.

"I have one I can bring for you, Kenna. There's no reason for you to be miserable," Dan pipes up, smiling at me.

"Wow, thank you! What a kind thing to offer." I punch Harley's shoulder.

She shakes her head.

We shuffle through the line, and I pile my plate high with eggs, sausage, biscuits, and gravy.

"So much for working out. It always just makes me hungrier than an elephant." I groan, stepping up to the coffee station.

Dan is next to me, his face always cheerful. "You're building muscle, though, and that's what matters. You need protein to get stronger."

He fills a cup with coffee, handing it to me.

"True. How are all of you guys so fit?" I'm thinking of Levi's broad shoulders with the corded biceps pushing through the sleeves. A chill runs over my arms.

"We've worked outside our whole lives, baling hay, fixing fences, moving rocks and tractor equipment. There's always work to do on a farm."

I start to mix sugar and cream into my coffee as he continues on.

"Once we got older, we wanted to work out more. Silas was always doing stuff with his baseball team, and we wanted to get stronger like those guys. I guess you could say it became a competition."

He's reminiscing at this point, and I start to slowly walk back to the table. He trails behind me.

"So...it was you and Adam, Silas, and Levi?" I ask, always careful to keep my tone casual when discussing the latter.

My enormous crush is embarrassing enough, considering he acts like I don't exist. I don't need anyone to realize I'm always asking questions about him to satisfy my overwhelming curiosity.

Dan nods as we claim the seats across from Adam and Harley.

"Yeah, the four of us have been friends forever. When you're homeschooled, it's awesome to have kids your age living close by."

Talking to Dan is easy. He's sweet and outgoing. Some things he and Adam say are a little odd, and they sometimes make a face that lets you know that whatever was just said by someone else strikes them as offensive. They both adjusted remarkably well over the first semester at Ole Tex. I get the feeling that coming from a large family helped them with the aspect of living in close quarters with a bunch of young people their age.

I can't say the same for their quiet friend. Levi emotes as much as the statue of *David*.

"Kenna, will you come to Adam's with me after this to help me look for a car online?" Harley asks.

I nod. "Sure. I don't have class until eleven today."

I want to cry, thinking about the precious sleep I missed this morning. Maybe I'll get a nap later. "You have to let me borrow some clothes to change into. My boob sweat will never dry."

Having double Ds isn't the greatest for working out. Adam and Dan both stiffen at the mention of breasts, and Harley and I smirk. We're helping them acclimate to life in the real world, however gradually.

The three of us separate from Dan, who's headed to his first class at eight.

Harley has unofficially moved into Adam's apartment. I think they are trying not to sleep together but failing most nights. The dorms really suck after the initial excitement of the first semester, so we spend most of our time at the on-campus apartment the guys got for the second semester. Adam's nearly twenty-two, and they all came into the university with credits they'd earned online.

We walk into the boys' apartment, the minimal decor screaming that it's a male-dominated space.

"I'll grab you something to wear," Harley says as she and Adam walk into his room.

I'm assuming they'll try to shower separately but end up under the same stream. Oh, what it must be like to be in love.

"Here. You can change in Levi and Silas's room. They're both in class."

She hands me a pile of clothes, nodding at the closed door. I stare at it for a second before stepping closer.

I will absolutely resist the desire to search for his diary. There's no way he writes about anything interesting. Probably just fancy equations and notes about hating me. The thought of him even thinking about me long enough to scribble my name seems unlikely, and I let out a sigh of defeat.

I am not vain, but I am used to having my pick among the guys I've known. I dated the quarterback at my private school. We split amicably after high school because he went to an out-of-state school, and we both knew the relationship would never survive through the drunken haze of college parties. It was a relief, honestly. He was nice arm candy. A *pretty but dumb* type of boy who bored me to tears.

Levi and Silas's room is neat, to the point that I feel a twinge of guilt in my stomach when I remember my mountain of dirty laundry that has found its home on Harley's unoccupied mattress.

I thought boys were supposed to be all messy and unkept.

Silas's bed is right in front of me, made up like it belongs to a soldier. I know it's his from the Nolan Ryan poster hanging over it. I'm afraid I'll break out in a sweat again if I see where Levi lays his perfect head down, so I refuse to turn and find out what color his pillowcase is.

My hoodie comes off first, followed by the sweaty sports bra. My breasts feel immediate relief from the cold air in the room.

Okay, I'm not a slut, but the thought of rubbing them on his sheets suddenly intrudes into my head. I think I would actually feel sparks from such an obscenely inappropriate action.

He would never know. The little act of rebellion would stay between me and my removable showerhead. I shift my topless torso toward the wall I know his bed is on, and my entire body locks up as I make eye contact with Smallville.

Levi's cobalt-blue eyes are wider than I've ever seen them. He's sitting up in bed, shirtless, his entire upper half exposed.

He doesn't have his glasses on, apparently having just woken up.

My gaze burns down his body, reveling in the expanse of male chest and the dusting of dark hair decorating the thick, defined muscles. He's ripped to shreds, which is completely unexpected for such a smart, reserved type. It's not *absolutely* unexpected, considering that I knew all the guys worked out together.

But hot damn, if I had a crush on this guy before I saw his body, it's only increasing to an unhealthy, obsessive level.

I want to pour strawberry syrup on his abdomen and lick it off. *That's it. I'm doing it.* I'll tie him to the bed and force him to let me objectify him if I have to.

His mouth is open, jaw nearly brushing his comforter, which is selfishly concealing his lap area. I would give anything to rip away the navy-blue blanket his knuckles are hanging on to for dear life.

He hasn't moved a millimeter since I turned toward him, and for a moment, I wonder if he's breathing.

Then I notice the rise and fall of his beautiful, pale pectorals and realize he is very much alive and well.

He must be in shock. My generous breasts are on display, and there's a very good chance it's his first time seeing any salacious female anatomy.

I take a bold step in his direction, almost against my will—*almost.*

5

Levi

I'm having the best dream of my entire existence. I try to keep my body still, relaxing my mind so I don't wake up from this glimpse into utopia.

She's slightly blurry, but I can barely make out what I know is the tantalizing form of Kenna Davis. Her upper half is all skin, and I want to thank the dark recesses of my mind for this moment.

If I can force myself back into a deeper sleep, maybe I can convince the dream Kenna to walk closer to me, enhancing the image.

Miraculously, that's exactly what happens. I physically jolt as her slow, deliberate steps begin to draw her toward me. Each second that passes by feels like my chest is being impaled by a large, cold object. I'm in heaven and hell. A brief thought of how degrading this dream is to the real Kenna flits across my mind, but I dismiss it immediately. It can't end now. I have no choice but to let it play out.

She's close enough now that I can see the gentle sway of her breasts, magnificent pink nipples pointing straight at my eyes. I have never even dared to imagine a scenario like this, but apparently, my subconscious is taking over. I gladly relent. Hot coals are pressing everywhere into my skin, and my arousal is becoming more prominent with each second that ticks by. Sweat is gathering on my lower back.

How is this so real? I dream all the time, but I've never in my life been so engaged in one that felt like it could be actually happening.

But this could never—would never—occur in my world.

I should stop it and wake myself up. That's the gentlemanly thing to do. I'm objectifying her, and she doesn't deserve to be the focus of my perverted fantasies.

I'm weak and pathetic because I can't force myself to do it.

Kenna's erotic shape is directly in front of my face now, finally in clear focus because I'm nearsighted. Her chest is the most delicious, lavish image my eyes have ever seen. Her breasts are full, and they look succulent and soft. I never knew they'd appear so supple. I'm overheating, and I have to get some relief. I sound like I'm having an asthma attack.

I glance up to confirm that my subconscious created her face to its full, stunning design. I've only allowed myself brief glances before, so I'm not even quite certain what her exact features look like in such close proximity.

Her image in my dream is clear and distinct. I can make out every tiny freckle on her nose and each individual eyelash. The emerald green of her eyes is actually rimmed with a lighter, pale olive around the iris. Her lips are the ideal shape, slightly full and parted, the pink of perfection.

The thought occurs to me that I should kiss her, since this is only a dream. It's probably my one chance to experience what that would be like.

Suddenly, she moves, her hand reaching out to grip my shoulder.

I suck in a harsh breath. *Dreams can't touch you.*

My body turns to stone the second she connects with my heated skin.

Kenna Davis is standing in front of me—topless.

Her immaculate breasts sway as she climbs onto my bed, straddling my hips. The embarrassing stiffness between my legs touches the delicate spot between hers, and I jump backward in complete shock.

Is this real?

My quick movement causes her to gasp and reach both hands out to steady herself on my shoulders. Her bare nipple brushes against my chest, and I'm literally about to explode from that sole touch. My hand reaches up to graze against her side, right below her waistline. The skin is surprisingly rough and uneven.

Does she have a scar?

I don't have time to dwell on it because her mouth drops open. The sensual gasp that escapes her lips sends me into cardiac arrest, and my body responds against my will. My head rolls back against the wall, and she leans into my tense shoulders, causing unexpected friction between us.

"Levi..." she rasps, her warm breath on my neck.

It's the ultimate high, and I'm lost to the sensations coursing through me. She's straddling my lap, silky breasts pressing into my bare chest. Her flawless body is wrapped around mine, but I'm frozen in place.

She leans in to press a tiny, gentle kiss to the bottom of my right ear.

My body contorts, sending electric shocks straight down and out. The friction occurs again, and this time, I lose the battle of wills. I've never felt anything like it, and I call out her name on instinct. I experience sensory overload as I have my first orgasm with another person in the room.

"Kenna..." I whisper hoarsely, gripping on to her trim waist through the last pulse.

She leans closer to me, gripping me even harder, her breath on my ear.

The sheet between us is now very wet, humiliating me to my core. My lack of experience with women has never been so apparent. This is my first time seeing a bare female chest, let alone touching one that belongs to a woman I've fantasized about for months.

She looks down at the stain on the sheets, her open mouth turning back up as she gapes at me. I'm mortified beyond belief. A sick feeling begins to rise inside of me.

I always stick to the shadowy corners of the room, letting my outgoing, good-looking friends take the spotlight. I don't go to parties, and I don't talk to girls or look at female bodies, even on a screen.

"Levi," she says again.

This time, her voice is more audible, and I know without a doubt that it's real. Her hooded eyes are looking down at my chest.

My ultimate fantasy has become an absolute nightmare. The worst possible scenario I could fathom is actually happening.

Kenna begins to lean forward, her pink lips puckering toward mine.

Is she crazy? How is she not disgusted...or laughing at me?

Voices begin to speak outside of the room, and I realize Adam and Harley are talking. They're home, and Silas or Dan could get back and come in here at any moment. Panic licks through my veins at the vulnerable position we are in. I don't want anyone to see her like this. They'd never guess in a million years that she could be in here without a shirt on.

Kenna's eyes are watching me, her faultless body still half-naked and exposed to my perverse gaze. She's so far above me in experience, beauty, and every other category I can fathom.

Is this some kind of game to her?

She's not cruel, so I can't imagine what her motive must be. My mind can't comprehend that this could possibly mean anything to her. I need some distance from her before I make some other blundering mistake.

"Levi, can we talk, please?" Her voice is low, and she begins to slide off of me.

I need her to put a shirt on. I lift up the throw blanket from the foot of my bed, gently covering her chest and shoulders. She reaches up to hold it on, and I release a sigh of relief. I can think marginally clearer.

What could possibly be said after a moment like that?

Even if I could form words that would make this better, there's no way I'd be able to get them out of my throat.

All of a sudden, the door to the room opens as a feminine voice speaks. "I'll see if she's done. Kenna, did you trip and fall —oh."

Harley's eyes are dumbstruck as she assesses the situation we are in on the bed, and I immediately shift the sheets so that she can't see the worst of it. Thank heavens Kenna wasn't still on my lap.

She jumps up, still pressing the blanket to her tantalizing front. "I, uh...I was...I'm almost done."

She walks back to the front of the room, where she stripped down earlier, retrieving her shirt from the floor.

Harley is inching back out the door. "Okay...Silas is home from practice and wanted to come in and shower, so...I could tell him to use Adam's?" she offers, looking from me back to Kenna with a question on her face.

"Tell him I'll be done in a minute," I choke out, thankful that my voice is much steadier than I feel right now.

She nods before looking back at Kenna. I've heard the guys talk about girls having their own language, and I would bet anything they're silently talking about me right now. The humiliation can't possibly increase from this point. I've already plundered into the darkest pit conceivable.

I stand up from the bed, the sheets awkwardly wrapped around my waist because I'm only wearing boxers, which now have a sticky spot. Thankfully, Harley has shut the door, and Kenna drops the blanket to pull a T-shirt over her head. I avert my eyes.

"Can we talk about this?" she says quietly as I walk to the bathroom door.

My eyes dart back up to hers, and she's folded her arms over her chest, legs twisted over each other. Her face is pinched in concern. She's pleading with me.

I barely shake my head. "Please, no."

Then I walk in and close the door.

6

Kenna

"Okay, yes. I didn't exactly cover myself right away, but part of me was still wondering if he really was gay or not," I explain to a very curious and shocked Harley.

She crowded me back in Adam's room the second I emerged, banishing him to the main area.

She bites back a smile, barely containing a laugh. "What's the verdict?"

Okay, so, yeah, I'm pretty sexually experienced, but that was a first for me. I can't say my ego isn't hurting.

"Definitely not."

Harley claps a hand over her mouth, snickering into it. I can't laugh with her, not when he dismissed me so coldly afterward.

Her amusement dies down when she realizes I'm not even smiling.

"I don't see the problem here. If I hadn't interrupted—sorry about that, by the way—you guys might have messed around. You've wanted him since day one."

So, obviously, I left out the part that could potentially embarrass Levi. He's got nothing to be ashamed of—he basically gave my tits the greatest compliment they've ever received. I'll never forget that moment. The humiliation on his face certainly isn't something I'll be able to forget easily, either.

I sigh, defeated. "I mean, he wasn't really even making a move toward me. I sat on his lap, and he pretty much froze up." *After completely melting.* "Did you and...what was it like with Adam when he first saw your boobs?"

Adam was a virgin when he met Harley, but it didn't take too long for her sexy, inked body and spunky personality to steal his heart.

She looks away sheepishly. "Uh, the first time he saw me topless was the first time we had sex, so..."

My palm meets my forehead, and I collapse on the bed. She sits next to me, wrapping me in a hug.

"Don't be so discouraged! We had time to get to that point. We made out a lot before then and slept in the same bed. He saw me in a bikini at the beach party that first week of school. You just...I mean, you gotta remember these guys have hardly seen girls they aren't related to, and the ones they knew dressed like nuns. Then you walk up, all hot and—you have great tits, but you can't just shove them in his face and expect him to suck on them like a normal guy would."

I realize she's totally right, and I'm a complete idiot.

Levi is nothing like the guys I've known or dated in the past. That's part of the attraction I feel toward him. He seems so steady and...mysterious.

"I can't believe I actually expected that to happen. I just thought, *Hey, all guys like boobs. This is a great way to get him to finally make a move on me.* I could not have screwed this up any worse."

I fall backward on the bed, staring up at the ceiling. She lies on her side next to me.

"Look, you didn't screw it up beyond repair. You might just need to take a step back and try to be his friend first. He's going to need some adjustment time before you can pounce like that again." She covers a smile. "You're like a sexy lioness, going in for the kill."

She pets my wild strawberry-blonde curls, and I know it's all meant in love. Harley's that girl with a tough exterior and a marshmallow middle.

I groan. "Ugh, I just hope he doesn't think I'm a whore, walking around flashing people."

She waves me off, rolling back up into a sitting position. "Oh, psh. I bet he'll be too busy replaying it in his head for that. I think you finally made him see you as the hottie you are, and he's definitely going to remember the twins." She pauses, playing with the ends of her long hair before going on. "He's a super shy guy. That sentence was the longest one he's spoken to me since I met him—eight months ago. Keep giving him little hints about how you feel. Flirt with him in ways that are subtle but easy enough to interpret." She pats my leg.

I slowly ease into a sitting position, starting to feel a tiny bit better with her reassurance.

"I just wish I had an idea of what he's thinking. He's said exactly four words to me since I met him—*Levi, Kenna, please*, and *no*. Like, what am I supposed to do with that? Since the beginning of last semester, I've invited him to every social event possible, and he never shows. I'm honestly embarrassed at myself for trying so hard."

"Kens, you are missing the big, glaring part about how he was essentially raised in a convent. That guy's, like, crazy intelligent. Adam told me he has a photographic memory, and his parents wanted him to be this super genius, so they made him study all day, every day. He only ever left his house to help them work on the farm." She shakes her dark head.

"I swear, he was even more sheltered than Adam and Dan because all he had was an older sister, who apparently ran away from home when she was seventeen. She met some older guy online. After that, his parents cracked down hard on him. His parents completely disowned her, going so far as to claim Levi as an only child."

I'm absorbing all this new information, my heart squeezing with concern. I had no idea he wasn't from a loving family. My parents are actual saints sent down from above.

"Why did they finally let him come to college?" I ask.

She shrugs. "I don't know for sure, except that all four of them basically had to beg and plead to be allowed to. Levi's drill sergeants probably just wanted him to get smarter, so it would make them look better. All the guys had to room together, and they're definitely not supposed to be dating girls or going to parties." She smirks again. "Oops."

We both crack up, realizing we've instigated most of that in them. I force air out of my lungs, trying to get over the churning I've felt since his cold rejection.

"Well, jeez, I honestly had no idea it was that bad for him. I figured even if he was a virgin, he'd seen online porn or at least a *Playboy*."

She shakes her head again. "Nope, I'd bet he's literally never even seen a bra. I send Adam dirty pictures, and he can barely handle it."

She wiggles her eyebrows at me, and I try to douse the spark of jealousy that lights up inside my chest. I'm obscenely happy for them—I am—but I want it too, and I want it with Levi.

My best friend stands. "Come on. Let's go out there, and you can practice some tamer flirting while helping me find a clunker to drive around that's not too clunky."

I don't get a chance to practice the tame flirtation on Levi because he never joins us in the main room. Thankfully, Dan gets home, and he's easy to get along with. Adam and Harley smooch on the couch the whole morning until I have to leave for my next class. The air is pretty chilly, and I'm stuck walking across campus in Dan's Carhartt jacket because my hoodie was trapped in Levi's room on the floor.

The classroom is overcrowded, and my heart sinks at the sight of so many somber, dejected faces. This class is going to kill us all with slow, torturous stabs.

"I just know I'm going to fail. I am literally incapable of understanding biology. It's completely ridiculous that it's a required course for a communication-sciences degree," I mumble to myself, sinking down in the cushioned chair next to a smart-looking kid.

I'm hoping his brain waves will somehow waft toward me in the stiff air. He has bright-red curls and thick glasses. His eyes turn to me like I must be lost.

"Uh, you...are you sure you're in the right class?" he asks quietly, fidgeting with his MacBook.

I set mine out next to him. The slim pink design was a Christmas Eve gift from my grandmother.

"Yes, I begged and pleaded with the advisor, but she forced me to do it. She's sadistic." I sigh, observing the others around me.

I think I picked the ideal seat for success. If I joined my sorority sisters, waving at me from the back, I would never pay enough attention to pass.

The guy next to me clears his throat.

"There's an online tutoring program you could sign up for. It's kind of pricey, but it offers the best help and twenty-four/seven support for test prep, studying, anything you need," he kindly offers.

I turn to face him with a grin. "Wow, that sounds perfect! Could you text me the info?"

I pull out a pen, leaning over to write my name and number on his notebook.

"What's your name? I'm Kenna."

I smile at him, and he reaches out a bony, pale hand, lips turning up.

"Melvin. Nice to meet you."

7

Levi

"If I'm being honest, I'm not completely sure she likes you. She's friendly with everyone," Silas says to Dan, grunting as he presses a weighted bar up from his chest.

He's only supposed to do moderate workouts without the baseball team, but I'm not his mom. Our lifting together has always been a tradition, even though Adam bailed to teach Harley and Kenna how to do it. Thankfully, the guys have stayed a safe distance away from the trio by the dumbbells. Dan still keeps checking out Kenna in her pale-pink spandex, and I'm unjustifiably irritated with him for it.

"She flirts with me all the time. I'm not saying she's in love with me, but I know there's something there," Dan replies, taking over the bench as Silas stands.

This conversation is basically a repeat of the same one we've been having almost daily since we got back to Ole Tex after winter break. I'm leaning toward Dan's side on this, but I'll never admit it.

I lift up the bottom of my workout shirt to wipe the sweat pouring into my eyes. It's max-out day, and I've been hitting the weights like a maniac the past week. I've thought of *that moment* incessantly. The nervous energy that surrounds me every time she's at the apartment—which is pretty much always—is unbearable.

"What do you think, Levi?" Silas asks as he spots Dan.

Shit, I was hoping I'd get left out of this conversation. I've been sticking to noncommittal answers up to this point.

"Uh, about...if she likes him?"

I glance over, catching a sliver of glorious cleavage as Kenna bends over to pick up a weight. My gaze snaps back to Dan's strained face.

Why can't she put on a shirt to work out?

I'm going to have to face the corner to do stretches to avoid seeing her from that angle again.

Silas stares at me. "Yes. Haven't you been listening to this whole conversation? I think she talks to me the exact same way she talks to him...and Adam, for that matter. You're the only one she's quiet around."

"That's only because he's quiet," Dan interjects, standing up to let me go.

I gratefully take the bench, eyes on the ceiling. They can't force me to talk when I'm maxing.

"Add twenty," I say.

They both grab a ten pounder for one side. Silas continues talking to Dan while watching to make sure I can push the bar up.

"Harley talks to Levi even though he's quiet. Kenna just stares at him. Now that I'm thinking about it, I think she might have a thing for him."

I nearly drop the bar on my throat, but thankfully, Silas is holding on to it.

"Whoa, man. You got it?" he asks.

I nod, straining to lift it. I grunt, finally pressing it all the way up.

"Damn, Levi, you're a maniac," Adam bellows from across the room.

I sit up to see him and the girls watching me, and if I wasn't already flushed, I would be now. Kenna's eyes trail over me, increasing my already-high temperature.

We haven't spoken, but we've silently established that looking is okay.

Dan is leading us toward the pull-up bar now. "Are you serious? You really think that?" he questions Silas, glancing from me to Kenna with her high, messy bun of tangled curls.

She's chatting away with Harley, who's laughing at whatever she says. I look away before my mind can replay last week's fiasco for the millionth time.

Too late.

DO NOT get a boner right now.

Silas shrugs. "I don't know, man. You're just gonna have to ask her out." He jumps up to grab the bar, repping out his usual twenty reps.

Dan turns to me. "You have to be honest with me. You think she has a thing for you?"

I am beyond thankful Kenna hasn't told anyone about what happened. If she did tell Harley—and therefore, Adam—I wouldn't be able to look his brother in the eyes right now. Adam would have definitely questioned me about it and possibly told Dan.

"I don't—"

"Hey, y'all. Wanna go eat pancakes at the apartment? We need to plan out the camping trip." Adam saves the day as he approaches.

The girls are still over by the dumbbells, now stretching. I watch her for a second until she makes eye contact with me. Then I force out a breath, tearing my gaze away.

"Sure." I jump up to grab the bar after Silas lets go.

I'm fueled by frustration and need, cranking out twenty-eight pull-ups in a row before my arms give out. I jump back down, oxygen shooting in and out of my lungs.

Looking up, I see Adam and Silas staring, both squinting at me.

"What?" I pant.

They look at each other and then back at me.

"You good?" Adam asks, always the protective older-brother type.

"Fine." *Definitely not in the mood to talk about it—ever.*

"Brother," Dan says, clapping Adam on the shoulder, "you have to swear your secrecy, okay?"

His gaze bores into Adam's eyes, and Adam nods slowly.

"What?"

Dan glances over at the girls and then back at his brother. "What do you think about me and Kenna?"

Adam's brows shoot up, his light-brown eyes jumping to my face.

Why is he looking at me?

He hesitates. "I, uh...man, I don't really...I should ask Har—"

"No way! You swore secrecy. She'll tell Kenna, and you know it." Dan lets go of his shoulder, pulling his sleeve up to wipe sweat from his face.

"Yeah, I just think...I think she likes someone else...or she did last semester."

His eyes flit to my face again, and I bend over to stretch my hamstrings, avoiding his gaze.

What is happening?

I was just gaining control of my breathing before this.

"Who?" Dan questions. He's not letting him off the hook.

"It was in the beginning, right when I met her, so I don't know if she does anymore," Adam says, shifting his feet.

Silas is smirking at me when I stand up again, and I give him a quizzical look.

Why is everyone staring at my face?

"Oh, who cares? That was forever ago. If he hasn't made a move already, she's probably sick of waiting." Dan jumps up to do more pull-ups as the girls start walking toward us.

I allow myself three seconds to watch her before turning to Silas and Adam.

Does she know that pink spandex makes her look naked? I draw in two big gulps of air, forcing my lungs to open up.

"Yeah, you should go for it, Dan. She's probably sick of waiting," Silas says, still staring at me.

Adam looks from him to me, and I wish I knew what they were thinking.

Kenna and Dan would be great together, and I suddenly need to hit something.

"Yeah, I'm doing good. Sticking with the guys," I reassure my mother over the phone.

She calls every Monday evening like clockwork.

"Well, are you sure you don't need any money? Even for toiletries or some clothes? How are you paying for gas?"

She's worrying, and I don't know how to convince her that I'm fine.

"I'm fine, Mom. I never go anywhere." I pause, debating my next words. "Are things okay there?"

I hold my breath, waiting for her reply. I look up to see the door open as Silas pokes his head in.

"He's fine. I'm fine. Don't worry about us."

Her typical answer doesn't ease the tension in my shoulders. My father isn't an easy man to live with. He runs his home like a drill sergeant.

"Well...I love you. Talk to you later, okay?"

"I love you too, honey. I'm so proud of you."

I hit the End button.

"Hey, come hang out with us," Silas says, tapping his fingers on the frame.

"I think I'm just gonna—"

He steps fully into the room, shutting the door behind him.

"You've got to be kidding me with this shit, Levi." He gapes at me, shaking his head.

"What? I—"

"You're a pussy—that's what. Get your head out of your ass," he shoots at me, folding his arms over his chest.

I stand up from the bed because I know I'm an inch taller than him, my frame the biggest of the group. "What was that?"

My mood has been steadily declining over the last seven days.

He starts to chuckle. "Ah, I see. Pissed you don't have the balls to go after what you want, so you take it out on your friends. That's a great way to handle it."

He shakes his head, walking back out into the living room and shutting the door before I have time to form a response.

Is that what I'm doing? Is it that obvious that I want her?

I take several long, steady breaths before deciding that Silas has never lied to me and he's always had my best interests at heart.

Turning the knob and pushing open the door, I see the group sitting around the living room, playing a card game and watching *The Office*. Harley is nearly in Adam's lap on the recliner. Silas and Dan are on either end of the couch, and Kenna is cross-legged on the floor. Boldly stepping toward her, I seat myself a few feet away, matching her Indian-style pose.

Her green eyes flick up to mine, and the corner of her mouth curves up. The look of acceptance sends a satisfied rush through me, and I relax a little despite my rushing pulse.

Harley leans forward, shuffling the deck on Adam's kneecap.

"Okay, the game is called King's Cup. Every card means something, usually a little competition to find out who has to drink."

The coffee table has a can of White Claw on it. There's an open white box on the floor, and I notice each of them has their own can. Dan reaches in and tosses me one. I stare down at the mango-flavored drink.

"It's barely alcoholic. You won't feel a thing," Harley says, smiling at me.

She and Kenna have slowly been acclimating us to college life, and the transition has been easy for all the guys, except me. I nod, determined to step out of my comfort zone. I'm not a pussy.

She smiles. "Okay, I'll go first." Her Northern accent is prominent among all us Southerners.

She grabs a card from the stack, flipping it over. "Okay, six is dicks. The guys have to drink."

She leans forward to shove the card under the tab of the can. We all take a sip.

"When it pops, whoever makes it happen has to chug the can," Kenna pipes up as she reaches for the next card. "Ace—is that waterfall?" she asks Harley, who nods. "Okay, so I start drinking, and everyone has to do it until I stop. Then the person to my left can stop and so on until it's back to Harley."

She looks around the group, eyes glazing past me. She starts to chug, and we all follow suit. The fuzziness burns down my throat, but I ignore it until she stops a few seconds later.

I grab the next card, expelling the air in my lungs.

"Jack." I look up at Kenna.

She's watching me, but Harley answers, "That's Never Have I Ever."

I stare at Kenna as Harley speaks. When Harley doesn't elaborate, I look up into her blue eyes.

"I don't know how to play that."

"So, everyone holds up five fingers. You start and just say something you have never done that you think the rest of us—or at least, some of us—have done. When someone says something you've done, you put a finger down. Loser is the first person with all the fingers down."

She smiles at me sweetly. I like Harley. She's great for Adam. They've had their ups and downs, but they're well suited for each other.

"Um, okay...I've never been to a beach-themed party," I say, knowing they all went to one last semester together.

I was invited, but the mere thought of a crowded party makes me sweat.

Silas scoffs. "That was dirty."

The game goes around the room, and I'm the only one left with all five fingers.

They all drink, and I smile. Kenna's perfect face is frowning.

Dan lifts up the next card—an eight.

"That means you pick a mate to be your drinking buddy," Kenna elaborates.

He smiles at her with charm. "Then I pick you."

She laughs, leaning forward to toast him. My chest feels tight.

Silas draws a three and has to drink.

I'm starting to realize how drinking games are meant to work.

When it's Harley's turn again, she draws a ten.

"Hm, this one is Categories. I choose one, and you all have to say something that relates. This is too easy. Sexual positions." She looks at Kenna.

"Reverse cowgirl."

Her emerald eyes focus in on me, and I'm wildly curious about what she just said. A smirk plays on her lips. I'm betting *alone in your bed* wouldn't count for this.

"Doggy," I say, my eyes never leaving hers, a loud drumming in my ears. It's the only one I know.

I'm almost done with my first alcoholic drink, and I'm already feeling braver. She blushes, eyes trailing down my torso.

Is she remembering the same thing I am?

I listen attentively to the entire round, my brain trying to form the picture correlating with the names, especially one that's only a number—sixty-nine. I can't fathom how that would logistically work.

When it gets back around to me, I don't hesitate to take a drink. My first contribution was all I had on the subject. No one laughs. They just move on with the game. I had no idea how much my friends had learned in the last few months away from our isolated home.

It's Dan's turn, and he draws a jack. Harley has to remind him what it means, and he breaks into a grin.

"Ah, yes. Never have I ever"—he makes eye contact with his brother—"had sex."

Silas chuckles, and Harley smirks. Adam just tips his drink back, chugging the last of his second can.

Harley and Kenna both drink, but Dan, Silas, and I don't. I know he just wanted to mess with Adam, but I wish he hadn't dragged me and Silas into it. It's embarrassing enough that I'm probably the only one who's never even kissed someone. Realizing that Kenna is far more experienced than me brings up all the feelings of inadequacy and humiliation that ravaged me when she saw me lose control.

After my second drink, my head is getting fuzzy. Kenna grabs another drink from the box on the floor.

Is it my imagination, or did she scoot closer to me?

It's definitely not in my head. She was farther back when we started, but now she's only an arm's length away. My heart rate is increasing as my skin feels hotter.

Could it really be a possibility that she isn't disgusted by me?

Dan takes every chance he can to flirt with her. After his fourth drink, he plops down on the floor between us. There was plenty of space, but I still feel the urge to shove him out of the way for the intrusion. Kenna looks over his shoulder at me, biting into her lower lip.

I want her more than I can comprehend, but now Dan is leaning in to whisper in her ear. She smiles, lashes brushing her cheeks as she nods at whatever he said.

He's so confident, going after what he wants, even when it's someone as unattainable as Kenna. She laughs at something Harley said, and he sits even closer to her. Their arms brush up against each other as they lean back on the couch. I'm jealous of the innocent contact.

I could've sat closer to her. I shouldn't have been a coward and taken a place with space between us.

As we finish up the game, Dan is the one who has to chug the can with the cards on top. They all holler as he downs it without stopping. I shake my head at his loud burp at the end. He grins as he looks over at Kenna.

"They'd better have White Claw at the party we're going to next weekend. These things are awesome."

I try not to let the way my body instantly tenses up to show. My eyes dart to Kenna's face as she laughs at him.

"They'll probably have them. There's always a million types of beer at sorority parties."

A curly strand of golden hair has slipped down in front of her face, and he lifts up a hand to brush it out of the way, stopping my heart in the process.

She doesn't seem to notice, hopping up as Harley stands to go to the bathroom. I attempt to keep breathing as both girls disappear into Adam and Dan's bathroom.

When did things progress to this point with her and Dan?

"What party are y'all going to?" Silas asks.

Dan smiles, looking up at him. "Her sorority is having a thing, and she has to bring a guy. I volunteered, but I could tell she was so relieved."

He can't seem to stop smiling about it, and I can't look at his face anymore. I'm beginning to resent my childhood best friend.

I stand up, and Adam's eyes follow the motion. "Where are you going?"

"Bed. I have work tomorrow morning," I clip out, not in the mood to be questioned by my well-meaning friends anymore tonight.

They've always pushed me out of my comfort zone, but lately, it's getting to be too much.

8

Kenna

From: McKenna Mae

To: Mr. Taylor

Mr. Taylor,

Thank you for responding so quickly to my inquiry. Basically, I suck at biology. I barely passed in high school, and to be honest, I cheated a lot. I'm only telling you this now to let you know I need as much help as possible.

The semester just started, but I would like for you to be with me every step of the way, so I don't get behind.

I'm willing to pay you whatever you charge for your best services and unlimited help with homework and preparing for tests. Please name your price!

Desperately,

McKenna

I type out the email and hit Send before reading over it. If this guy isn't willing to do these things, I'll just be on to the next. He seems to be the most qualified and available on the tutoring site Melvin suggested. My parents literally deposited an obscene amount into my bank account to pay for the tutor, but I'm eternally grateful because Lord knows I need it.

My email pings with a response several minutes later.

> **From:** Mr. Taylor
>
> **To:** McKenna Mae
>
> Miss Mae,
>
> I can comply with your terms. Whatever help you need, I am ready to provide it. I attached my pricing below.
>
> You won't have to cheat through this year. I'll make sure of it.
>
> What is your next assignment? Let's get to it.
>
> Sincerely,
>
> Mr. Taylor

I gotta say, I like the way Mr. Taylor sounds. I appreciate when people get right to the point. Why waste time? Life is short. I know that for a fact.

Someone knocks on the door to my dorm.

"Come in."

Maya pops her red head in. "Hey."

She's not exactly my favorite person to be around because of her judgmental attitude, but I wave her in. "Hey. What's up?"

My phone pings with a message from Dan.

Dan: hey beautiful, any preference on where we have dinner? I was thinking that place with the good queso. what do you say?

I wish I could be excited for my date with him. I should definitely stop wishing it were with his roommate.

Kenna: hey! that place sounds good.

I know I shouldn't have said yes, considering I barely like him.

Okay, fine, I one hundred percent view him as a friend. But he's a good friend because he offered to go with me to the sorority party. I was grateful because I still hadn't found a date who wouldn't try to sleep with me. Then he asked me to dinner. What was I supposed to say? *No, but you can pick me up at eight for the party?*

I let out a sigh, and Maya perks up as she sits down on the edge of my twin bed.

"Ooh, that sounds like it has a story behind it."

She's such a gossip. I always feel like I have to tell her about all my dirty laundry because she pries.

"Nothing. Just worried about my biology class. It's my worst subject."

She cocks a brow at me, clearly thinking I'm holding back on her. "Have you found a date to the Kappa Beta party?"

I know Maya wanted to join the Betas with me, but she didn't get in. I can't help but feel like she resents me for it even though I had nothing to do with it.

"Yeah, I'm going with Dan."

"Ooh, Farm Boy 2.0." She calls him that because he's Adam's younger brother. "If I was gonna go for one of the four male maidens, it would be that one." She snickers.

I'm truly not sure how much longer I can maintain this friendship. My sister, Lia, was everyone's best friend and the life of the party. She never met a stranger. People clamored for her attention.

When she died as a sophomore in high school, my entire world crumpled. All the pricey therapists didn't do much for me until one suggested I fight to keep her memory alive. That's what I'm doing by being friends with a bitch like Maya and being active in a sorority. I've essentially adopted parts of Lia's ability to get along with anyone and never stir up trouble. Well, I'm trying.

Lia never got her chance at life and college, but she deserved it more than I did. I'm doing my best to live it up for her while I can.

Maya gets up from the bed when I don't reply, walking over to inspect herself in the full-length mirror.

"Well, I have a date coming up too. His father is a podiatrist. He has a three-point-nine GPA, and he's going to be a veterinarian. He's in a fraternity, of course." She turns around, smiling.

"Do you like him?"

She shrugs. "Yeah, sure. You should ask Dan to be the DD for a girls' weekend. That way, we can all get wasted and have nothing to worry about." She starts to laugh. "I wonder if he could even assault someone. Would he know where *it* goes?"

How does she always find a way to insult someone in every conversation we have?

My sister would dismiss her without causing friction, but at this rate, I'm tempted to use physical violence.

"I really need to figure out a tutoring plan for my class. Can we talk later?"

I look back down to start typing out a response to Mr. Taylor.

"Okay. Can't wait to hear how it goes with Dan." She chuckles as she walks out and closes my door.

I breathe a sigh of relief and start typing.

From: McKenna Mae

To: Mr. Taylor

Mr. Taylor,

The next assignment is a quiz—already! I swear these professors enjoy inflicting pain on poor, unsuspecting students. I have a study guide, and I attached a picture of it. You are a lifesaver.

Can I double your rate? My father insists on it to ensure I get the maximum benefit of your skill set.

In addition, if I get an A, you will get a bonus equal to the cost of the tutoring. He likes to throw money around to show appreciation. I hope you are not offended! (Don't worry, though. I know I won't get an A even if you're Albert Einstein.)

Appreciatively,

McKenna

Five Years Earlier

"I can't believe I am finally in high school. I need an upperclassman boyfriend by the end of the week." Lia tosses her pale-blonde hair over a tan shoulder, smirking at me as we walk up to the front doors of the school.

"You're too young for anyone older than a sophomore."

We're Irish twins, born in the same year, eleven months apart. Our mother chose to hold me back so we could be in the same grade. Even so, I take the role of big sister seriously.

Mom always said she raised us as twins and that we're lucky because having a sister with you in life is like having a bodyguard and a best friend rolled into one.

"Kens, don't act like you wouldn't date Chase Colson if he even *glanced* in your direction." Lia rolls her eyes as she opens up her locker. "And you're a freshman, just like me."

My cheeks heat as I look around to make sure no one can hear her. "Shut it, Lia," I say through clenched teeth.

She laughs, tossing her head back. "Relax. You could get him easy."

My eyes widen at her unfounded confidence. Chase Colson is the pitcher of the baseball team and the hottest guy in the senior class. His last girlfriend graduated a year before him and is now an Instagram influencer.

"I appreciate the vote of confidence, but there's no way."

She smiles and waves as a group of older girls pass by us and each one remembers her name.

"Kenna, it's all about confidence. Go for what you want like you deserve it, and most of the time, you will get it. It's that easy."

She is the prettier sister with her long, straight hair and bright blue eyes. She's suddenly engulfed in a hug by one of the varsity cheerleaders.

"Lia! We are so excited for you to be here." The girl turns to me, a giant smile on her face. "Kenna! I've heard so much about you from Lia. You're trying out, right?"

I form a smile, trying to appear as confident as my younger sister. "Yes, of course. I'm stoked."

The girl grins, sauntering past us. Lia grabs her textbook before slamming her locker, so we can stop by mine.

"You have all the tools. You just need to learn how to use them."

My sister landed a coveted position at the local high-end boutique all the most popular upperclassmen work at. She made friends fast, but it also gave her confidence an enormous boost for a freshman. I've had the same gig as a lifeguard at the city pool since I turned fourteen.

We start walking down the hall to find our classes.

"I just want to make a few good friends and form a solid group. Cheer could be fun, though." I'm thinking of the cute outfits and getting to be down on the field for the football games with a front-row view of the players.

Lia nods as she recognizes some more faces, smiling at everyone. No one has ever denied the chance to return Lia's electric smile.

"We are not settling for a solid group. We're going to be *the* group, okay?" She loops her arm through mine. "Selena! Wait up, babe!"

Present Day

Dan steps a few feet ahead of me to open the door as we leave the restaurant.

"Thank you," I say with a smile.

"Of course." He walks beside me out to his red pickup, opening my door again.

"Well, your mama sure raised you right."

He laughs. "Dad is the one who always told us to open doors."

"Ah, I see."

He shuts it and goes around to the driver's side. Right before he opens it, I blow out a breath.

I can do this. I can like him. I've got to focus on all his great qualities—handsome, tall, funny, easy to talk to, a perfect gentleman.

Hopefully, if I do that long enough, I'll forget about his even taller, better-looking, mysterious, and impossible-to-talk-to roommate. My thoughts bring on a sickening swirl of guilt in the pit of my stomach.

"Are you cold?" He fiddles with the heating knob on the dash.

I shake my head. Each act of sweetness has only made me feel even worse for not really liking him.

I've tried seeing him as more than a friend. All evening, I have *really* tried.

But sometimes that spark just isn't there, and no matter how badly you want it to be because it would be nice and convenient, it's not.

His brother dating my best friend doesn't help the scenario.

"Thanks for dinner. I had a really nice time."

I force a smile on my face as I turn to him, and he returns it weakly.

"Yeah, of course. I've been wanting to take you out for a while now." He parks the truck in the lot by my dorms.

I swallow, debating how to respond. I study the green Prius in front of us.

Would Lia be happy about this? Would she want me dating guys I don't like just because I can't have the one I want?

"I—"

"Do—"

We start to speak at the same time, and we both pause.

"You go ahead," he says, always a gentleman.

I clear my throat. "Okay, so I don't know exactly how to say this, but...I don't know if we should...I guess I have decided I'd like to stay friends." I hold my breath, not looking at him.

He laughs. I swing my gaze over, unsure if he thinks I'm joking or not. His head is thrown back as his chest shakes with laughter.

"Man, you sure know how to break hearts, don't you?" he says through a smile.

I'm not entirely sure what's happening.

He doesn't sound mad, considering he's still chuckling and shaking his head. I keep staring at him, relieved he isn't upset, but...I'm confused.

"Okay, well, if you're going to destroy me like this, you at least have to tell me who it is." He smiles over at me, relaxed in the driver's seat.

"Are you—are you serious? Can we stay friends?" I start to smile, almost unbelieving that he really isn't mad about my rejection before our first date has even ended.

He nods. "Yeah, of course. I'm not going to say I'm thrilled to hear it, but you're cool. Plus, you're Harley's best friend, and between you and me, I think she'll be my sister before long."

That doesn't surprise me at all.

He looks back out at the growing darkness. "Are you gonna tell me who he is or what?"

I shake my head. "I don't know what you're talking about."

The tension in my shoulders slowly releases. I'm beyond thankful that he's a nice guy who can take no for an answer without throwing a fit.

He scoffs. "Okay, yeah, whatever. I'll find out sooner or later, I guess. So, are we still going to the dance party thing or—"

"Oh my gosh, yes! Please, *please* come with me. If you don't, I might just quit altogether."

I won't. I'm in a sorority because Lia always wanted to be, but it's truly not my thing. Most of the girls aren't very nice, and the entitled frat guys are ten times worse.

I look over to see Dan's smile drop.

"Okay, well, I'd be happy to. I still don't see why whoever this guy is that you're pining over won't take you. He'd be nuts not to want you on his arm." He opens the door as he says it, and I follow him out.

"Like I said, don't know what you're talking about."

I'll die before admitting to my unrequited love.

He puts his arm around my shoulders.

"Yeah, yeah, whatever. They'd better have White Claw there if we're only going as friends. Also, can I make out with another girl in a dark corner?"

"Hmm, I guess, as long as it's not Maya."

"Deal."

9

Levi

This must be what torture is like. When I was a little kid, I loved to read suspense novels about secret agents. I would spend hours envisioning myself as the spy who would get captured, but would always resist the torture and eventually escape.

Now, I know if the punishment was anything like this, I'd crumble like a sand castle under a wave.

"Turn to the right a little bit and put your hand on her waist."

Harley's playing the part of the photographer in our apartment living room. Dan obeys, his hand curling around Kenna's slim waist. I feel the churning of the greasy cafeteria dinner inside my stomach.

"Kenna, stick your leg out a little farther, so we can see the full slit."

Watching this is like experiencing someone slowly prying my fingernails off. She extends her long, tan leg through the high-cut slit of her gray-blue dress. The color makes her eyes look like the Texas sky before a storm. I thought they were green before tonight, but I guess they're sort of hazel.

I should go back into my hovel and do some homework or plan a bank heist that I'll hopefully get caught during. Then I can safely be put away before causing serious bodily harm to my handsy best friend.

I can't make my legs move. I'm standing in the kitchen, frozen in place, as I watch the scene unfold.

"You guys look so great together," Harley says, moving around them as she takes enough pictures for an entire album.

Is this absolutely necessary, right here in our apartment?

"I just hate that we have to do it inside because of the stupid rain," Kenna says, her smile never faltering as she leans back into Dan's chest.

She's the embodiment of perfection. Being in her presence reminds me of the one vacation I remember my grandparents taking me on to Niagara Falls. I stood in awe that God could create such an incredible sight, much like I am now.

"Is my hair okay, Har?" Kenna brushes a pale strand out of her eye, tugging on the top. It's piled high on her head, a massive curly mass of light-red-and-blonde hair. Her full lips are the perfect shade of a delicious raspberry.

"Yes. You look flawless, as always." Harley smiles at them both.

"Let's get to it. My cheeks hurt." Dan adjusts the white collar of his shirt.

Kenna turns her back to him, giving me an uninhibited view from the kitchen. I suck in a breath, realizing the entire dress is held together with thin straps, revealing her back all the way down to the top of her butt.

Why can't she have some kind of flaw literally anywhere?

"Hey, can you tighten the straps a little? It feels loose around my waist," she asks Dan.

"Sure, if I can...figure it out."

He starts to mess with the crisscross fabric on her golden skin, and I force my eyes away, demanding that my body move. I stalk to my room with wooden steps, so I don't vomit all over the linoleum.

I have to make myself get over her before I do something violent and permanently damaging.

Once a wall of safety is between us, I pull out my laptop. I should be catching up on emails and getting work done. Before I open the campus email account I set up for tutoring, I go to the private one I have under Levi Taylor. Ever since I left home, I started going by my mother's maiden name. I haven't told my friends yet, but I want to legally change it. I don't want to have any connection to my father.

The response I was looking for is in my inbox. A shock wave cuts through me, and I click on the name to read the message.

To: Levi Taylor

From: Samuel Rogers

Mr. Taylor,

I haven't had any success with locating Sarah Wright, age twenty-five, who looks anything like the photo you sent. Her official records stop five years ago in Bonnet Valley, Texas. Is it possible she's living under another name?

—Samuel Rogers

The spark of hope I was feeling fizzles out.

Is Sarah going by another name? Maybe she got married.

I close out the email, frustration inching through me.

Unfortunately, if I'm going to pay the private investigator, I have to keep up with tutoring. I click on the campus email icon.

I have seventeen unread messages, so I start to work through them. Who knew so many students needed tutoring? I'm trying to tutor enough to make a full-time income.

Several messages are from students needing me to check over their assignments before they turn them in. It takes me about two hours to work through them all, making corrections as I go.

I go back to my inbox, clicking on a thread with two unread messages. The first one is about an upcoming quiz with the study guide attached.

The second one stops my heart.

From: McKenna Mae

To: Mr. Taylor

P.S. I just sent the first installment for this month's tutoring. Thanks for your help! Also, you don't have to call me Miss. I usually just go by Kenna. When I made my student email I accidentally put my middle name in the last name spot!

The oxygen is suddenly removed from the room, as if I were in space without a proper suit to keep me alive.

Kenna's real name is McKenna. She's hired—and already paid me—to teach her biology. I sign everything as Mr. Taylor because Melvin told me it was more professional as a college science tutor. Considering my education and intelligence level are significantly greater than most college freshmen, I didn't feel it was misleading. I haven't made it public knowledge that I'm not using Levi Wright anymore.

Is this wrong? Am I morally obligated to tell her who I am?

I'm definitely overreacting. It could be another freshman named Kenna at OTU. Even if it is her, we can maintain a perfectly professional relationship with me as her tutor.

I try to relax as I type out a response.

From: Mr. Taylor

To: McKenna Mae

Kenna,

That sounds good. I am not offended. Your dad must really care about your success to be so generous.

You should start going over the study guide every night, trying to ingrain it into your memory. Make some flash cards and look over them when you're in bed, watching TV.

Do you have specific concerns for the quiz or topics you don't quite understand? A big part of success is making sure you get the concepts. Acronyms can be very helpful. I'll go over your study guide and make some notes to help you get started.

—Mr. Taylor

I type it out several times, rephrasing things over and over, which does nothing but make me feel crazy.

It feels obscene to be sending her a long message after what happened between us. I've spoken exactly four words to her in person.

The fact that she's out on a date with Dan gives me a twinge of guilt, but I remind myself that I'm only helping her with her class and it's completely innocent.

I click on her study guide, pulling up the picture.

My throat constricts as I read the topic typed out in bold.

REPRODUCTION: SEXUAL AND ASEXUAL

The guide goes on to list the differences between the two types of reproduction. It even has a small segment on arousal being a part of sexual reproduction.

My face burns as I read it. Not only do I have to talk to her... but I also have to teach Kenna about sex.

What have I gotten myself into?

I slowly close the computer. It's wrong to be thinking of her this way. She's out with another man as I sit here, recalling the scenario of her in my room touching me.

Why did she do that? I still haven't worked it out logically. Her actions that day don't line up with her normal behavior toward me.

Silas is right. She doesn't talk to me, but we stare at each other constantly. Plus, she likes Dan.

Why is this so confusing, and why don't I understand women at all?

I can't help myself from thinking about her on top of me as I work out my physical frustration with the palm of my hand.

"Do you really think this is all necessary?" Adam asks Kenna as she totes yet another bag up to be loaded into the cherry-red Jeep.

Her car is massive and the only one we can all fit into to go camping. It's got a top rack that most of the luggage and tents fit on, but we don't have any room left for the last bag she just deposited into the stack.

Her mouth drops open as she gapes at him. "Adam, I don't know what you want me to do about it. I can't sleep if I don't do my skin care routine, and I totally forgot to pack my Hunter boots, and—"

He holds a hand up in frustration, rubbing his eyes with the other one. "All right, I'll see if I can"—his voice drops lower as she smiles and begins to walk away—"create a portal to the campsite," he mumbles to the ground.

I try not to laugh out loud as I see if I can help him come up with a method of squeezing everything into place.

We finally pile into the vehicle. I crawl into the far back, and I hear Silas and Dan arguing about who has to ride back here with me. I'm sure it's more about who gets to ride in the middle with Kenna since Adam is driving and Harley is riding shotgun.

"Oh, y'all are such boys." Kenna starts to crawl into the back beside me.

It seems odd to me that Silas wouldn't let Dan sit by her, but I'm not questioning it.

Her sweet cherry scent wafts toward me as she finds her place in the seat, pulling the buckle across her chest.

I watch her from the corner of my eyes, trying to drum up the courage to talk to her. It's been over a month since the incident of premature ejaculation in my room, but I still haven't spoken to her since then.

Except for the emails. The messages we send back and forth have become the highlight of my day. I survive on them like a camel in the desert with no water in sight. The thought of pulling them up on my phone and reading over them with her next to me sends a thrill through my veins, and I can't defy the urge.

I click the screen to life and tap the email icon with our thread of messages.

From: McKenna Mae
To: Mr. Taylor
Mr. Taylor,
These acronyms are killing me. I wrote up the pros/cons list, like you suggested. Did I miss anything?
—Kenna

Kenna,
Your list looks fine, although I don't know about number three. That doesn't factor into the differences between sexual and asexual reproduction. How did you do on the quiz?
—Mr. Taylor

Mr. Taylor,
Even if the book doesn't say so, don't you think that enjoyment has a factor in the amount of offspring produced sexually? Surely, the plants don't get to it as much as the animals.

I made a 79 on the quiz. I didn't even cheat! I'm so happy. THANK YOU!

—Kenna

Kenna,

Are you asking what I think personally or scientifically?

That is wonderful. I'm glad you were able to do it on your own. That was all you. I merely guided you a bit. Keep reviewing the flash cards and notes for the upcoming test.

—Mr. Taylor

Mr. Taylor,

Personally, what do you think? I don't care what science thinks.

I've reviewed these flash cards so many times that I'm dreaming about them. Nightmares, actually. I'm having nightmares that I can only asexually reproduce, and it sucks.

—Kenna

Kenna,

Personally, I think it's physically impossible for a human female to asexually reproduce, so don't worry about that.

I believe enjoyment in sexual reproduction is a

major factor for humans, yes, but we make up a very small percentage of the organisms that reproduce sexually for enjoyment.

—Mr. Taylor

Mr. T,

What about the dolphins?!

—Kenna

Kenna,

The belief that dolphins have sex for pleasure is a theory that has not yet been proven. They have found that female dolphins have clitorises, but the studies are not conclusive about whether or not they have orgasms.

—Mr. T

My last message was sent on Thursday, but she didn't respond until late last night. I touch the new message and read it a foot away from her. Guilty pleasure is becoming a familiar, delicious sensation to me.

From: McKenna Mae
To: Mr. Taylor
Mr. T,

You have got to be kidding me. A dolphin gets a

study about sexual pleasure, and they hardly know anything about female human pleasure?! That's so messed up. What's up with the priorities of these scientists?

Also, I have another quiz on Tuesday, but I'll be out of town for the long weekend. Is this study guide okay for me to look over on the road, or should I add something to it?

—Kenna

The burning in my cheeks has to be obvious, so I turn to face out the window at the passing trees. This email is my first confirmation that it's her—my Kenna. I guess it's still not a sure thing, considering how big OTU is, but the chances seem almost certain now.

Stop. Calling. Her. Yours.

The moral gray area is only getting cloudier the longer I talk to her under my last name. I'm fairly certain she has no idea it's me. Also, I am her tutor, talking to her about sex...

But it is the topic of her class—or at least, it was at first. They've moved on to mitosis now, but *technically*, I'm still teaching her biology.

Before I can talk myself out of it, I type out a new email.

From: Mr. Taylor
To: McKenna Mae

Kenna,

I was not aware there was a lack of studies being done on the female orgasm or that there was a need for such studies. Is there a reason this concerns you?

Yes, the study guide looks like a good overview, but here are a few more things to keep in mind.

(Attachment)

—Mr. T

I don't even read over it before I hit Send. My heart is beating hard enough to start an earthquake. I count to one hundred, looking out the window before allowing myself a glance in her direction.

Her bare legs are curled up underneath her, wild hair in a tangled mess around her shoulders. She's swallowed in a giant tan hoodie. Her face is tilted down as she stares at her phone.

I adjust my dark-framed glasses as I turn to look toward the front of the car. Adam and Harley are murmuring and giggling as usual, while Dan and Silas bicker about who's going to win the next MLB game. My phone lights up in my lap.

From: McKenna Mae

To: Mr. Taylor

Mr. T,

It concerns me because sex has always been focused on the pleasure of males, and it's way too easy for them. Some women struggle to climax, especially with a partner, and they're wasting time trying to figure out if dolphins squirt. It's just annoying.

Okay, I will study that one. Thanks!

—Kenna

This doesn't clarify anything for me. It seems like the more I learn about sex, the less I know.

Women struggle to climax? Does that mean Kenna does?

I don't even want to begin to unpack her statement about it being "way too easy" for men. I can't decide if it would be worse or better for her to be referring to me or another guy. My stomach starts to cramp up as I stare at the screen, debating my response.

Talking about things isn't my strength, and it never has been. I'm better at ignoring them until I can eventually escape the situation and dwell on it excessively.

Nine Years Earlier

I wish my family had forgotten about it being my eleventh birthday. My mom is humming the hymn we sang at church last week as she scrapes my birthday cake off the kitchen wall. Every few seconds, I can hear her hiccupping as she stifles her sobs.

"The next one will be made by Mrs. Haines. I bet she can get the space shuttle to look just like the Challenger. I'll pay her extra to get it just right, okay, honey?"

She doesn't look at me, and I know it's because her face is red from crying.

"Why is Dad mad at Sarah?" My voice is quiet, and I don't think I really want to know. At the same time, it must be pretty bad, so I couldn't help but ask.

She stills slightly before continuing with the scraping.

She isn't going to answer me.

I'm about to voice it again, but I hear the heavy steps of my father. My stomach cramps as he enters the kitchen.

"I said I would clean it up." His mouth forms a hard line as he stares at my mother's back.

She slowly turns, a practiced smile on her face. "It's okay, honey. I don't mind at all. The icing could have stained the wallpaper."

She bustles over to the garbage, dumping in the soggy mess of vanilla cake and blue-and-green icing, as if when it goes into the waste bin, we can forget about the whole incident.

My father looks at me, and for a split second, I think he might actually apologize for ruining my birthday by angrily smashing the cake into the wall, but he does no such thing. My heart sinks into my stomach as I realize yet again that having hope in him is a foolish waste of time.

I want to ask about Sarah. I want to know how long she'll be grounded in her room. I know whatever she did must have been really bad because I've never in my life heard my father curse. He yells, throws things, and makes threats, but cursing is a line he doesn't usually cross, except for today.

"Two months. Only water, tuna, and crackers for the first one."

My mother's eyes widen, but she manages a stiff nod. My father thumps out of the kitchen, and I hope I never have to suffer through another birthday ever again.

I want to speak up in defense of my sister. I want to say that it's cruel and mean and horrible to lock her in her room for two months. But in our house, silence is not golden.

Silence is safety.

Present Day

I send the email to Samuel Rogers. I've finally earned enough money from tutoring to pay him to start looking again.

> **To:** Samuel Rogers
>
> **From:** Levi Taylor
>
> Mr. Rogers,
>
> I have enough now for you to begin the search again. Can you see if you can find any Sarah Taylors, age twenty-five?
>
> The same photo I sent before is who you're looking for.
>
> —Levi Taylor

From: Mr. Taylor
To: McKenna Mae
Kenna,
I'm sorry to hear that. I wasn't aware of these troubles. I wonder if a study on this problem should be started. I'll look into it and get back to you.
Have a nice weekend.
—Mr. T

I smile at the message, boldly typing out a response.

From: McKenna Mae
To: Mr. Taylor
Mr. T,
The fact that you are unaware of it does not

surprise me, as most men are. I'm sure a smart guy like you will have no trouble finding a woman to perform "studies" on. Maybe someone you work with?

You have a nice weekend too!

—Kenna

Flirting with my tutor is maybe—a tiny bit—how I'm fulfilling my unrequited crush on another intelligent man. Why am I pretending Levi is the one sending me *barely* salacious emails with underlying meanings?

I don't usually feel weird talking about sex with anyone, and I shouldn't with him, especially in light of the fact that he has been tutoring me on the subject.

Now that I'm sitting right next to Levi, I feel strangely guilty. I'm hopelessly obsessed with him, but he still acts like I don't exist. There's absolutely no reason for me to feel even a hint of guilt considering his apathetic position toward me.

The tension between us is palpable, and I'm ridiculously aware of every movement he makes. He's got a sexy five-o'clock shadow going that makes my toes curl. His eyes are glued to his phone.

How did I never realize how hot a smart, silent type could be?

He's got me squirming in my seat with lust over his veiny hand resting on his book in the seat between us. He's simply *touching* a book, and I'm literally jealous of the fate of a dead tree—again. I'm a simpering mess.

"Ugh," I groan, barely audible.

Levi's dark head whips over to me, and his sky-blue eyes make contact with my gaze.

Is he going to play the staring game with me?

I expect him to look away after a few seconds, but his eyes don't stray from my face.

His pale skin and messy, dark hair flopped over his forehead are the perfect shades to complement his dusty-pink lips. I want to taste him. His eyes dip down to my mouth as I lick my bottom lip, and I know he wants it too.

Why does he deny himself? Am I not being clear enough about what I want? You'd think walking up to a guy in bed and straddling him—topless—would be a bright enough green light.

Apparently not.

I lean forward a fraction, and his eyes widen, lips parting as he sucks in. His hand on the seat moves toward mine. I stop breathing, anticipation and want the only two things I can feel in this moment.

His fingers brush mine, little bolts of electricity shooting through me. I blink slowly, my eyelids drooping down.

Kiss me. I try to connect with his brain through telepathy.

"Kenna..." he whispers, a handful of breaths separating our mouths.

I love hearing my name on his lips. His deep voice makes my generic name sound sexy. I feel the sudden craving to hear him growl it while on top of me.

I reach farther over on the seat, our fingers intertwining. He plays with my hand, the heat from his skin spreading through me.

I'm fifteen again, feeling all fluttery the first time I held a boy's hand at the movie theater. My body is growing warmer, and I can't even imagine what it will feel like when he finally kisses me.

I need it *immediately.*

I press closer to him, but at the same time, he jerks back. His head nearly smacks the window, and his hand is white-knuckled around his book. I lean back into my seat, the rejection pouring over me like a bucket of half-melted ice after a lawn party.

"Hey, Kenna," Silas says, sitting in front of me. "Are you—" He breaks off, eyes flicking from my face to Levi's.

Dan turns around to smile at me. Levi could be mistaken for a sculpture.

"Am I what?" I ask Silas. My cheeks are slightly warm, but thankfully, my voice is controlled.

"Uh...I was gonna ask if you were an only child." He swallows awkwardly, looking back at Levi, who is staring out at the passing foliage again.

I relax a bit, smiling. "Oh. No, I'm not. I have a little brother, and I had a sister who passed away."

It's not hard to talk about Lia, but I think it makes some people feel uncomfortable. They don't know what to say.

"Oh, that's terrible. I'm sorry you had to go through that." His voice is kind.

I nod and mumble a thanks.

"So...how are your classes going?"

"They're good, mostly. I absolutely love the ones that pertain to my major, communication science." I lean back in my seat, stretching my legs out. "But the worst thing ever is biology. I don't know why they're forcing me to take it, but it makes me want to die."

"You should get a tutor," Dan suggests.

Our friendship, surprisingly, has only grown since I told him I didn't want to be anything more.

"Actually, I did get one. He's been helping me a lot." I pause, debating how far I want to push this. A split second later, I make my decision. "Actually, I kind of have a crush on him."

Levi squirms in his seat, and I turn to look over at him. His blue eyes are wide as he gapes at me. He looks at Dan with a question in his gaze.

I feel a sudden urge to simply talk to him directly, right in front of his friends, to see if he'll ignore me then.

"So, Levi, are you good at biology?" I say, my tone conversational.

He reaches for the textbook on the seat. He stares back at me through his thick lenses, knuckles gripping the book in his lap.

He doesn't speak, only nods.

Dan pipes up. "Levi is a super genius—always has been. We used to do giant sums with calculators to test him, but he would get it right faster than we could type it in." He grins at his friend, whose brows are furrowed in confusion.

Silas joins in with another memory from their childhood, and he and Dan bounce back and forth with recollections. I lean my head back, gritting my teeth in irritation.

What is Levi's deal?

I close my eyes, willing myself to take a nap since it's doubtful I'll sleep much at all on the hard ground over the next few nights.

My phone pings, and I pull up the app notification. A trickle of excitement runs through me as I see who it's from.

From: Mr. Taylor
To: McKenna Mae
Kenna,
Smart guys like me have no trouble with studies in biology or any scientific subjects. When it comes to

the female anatomy, I'm afraid my experience is yet to be had. I wouldn't know where to begin.

I hope you don't feel this conversation has breached any borders of impropriety. If you become uncomfortable, please let me know immediately.

—Mr. T

I bite into my lip. I really want to know how old he is. I'm hoping he's at least somewhere *close* to my age. Even if he's not, I have no intention of ever meeting him.

What's a little harmless email flirtation? I'm pretending he's someone else anyway.

From: McKenna Mae

To: Mr. Taylor

Mr. T,

I am not offended. We're just talking. I was bored until I got your message. The guy sitting next to me is pretending I don't exist.

Don't start with the main attraction. Look up the seven erogenous zones. Start at number one and slowly work your way up.

Then, study those anatomy charts we looked at to understand number seven. It's really not complicated if you know where to focus.

Happy studying!

—Kenna

I smirk to myself after I hit Send. Maybe I'll help Mr. T find himself a nice girl, and she'll owe me one if he takes my advice. Levi sucks in a breath next to me, and I look over to see his face is pink as he reads his book.

I'm sick of trying to figure him out, so I turn over and close my eyes again.

The sun is starting to set as we reach the campsite.

"We'd better hurry if we're going to set up the tents before dark," Adam says.

Everyone begins unloading the Jeep and taking stuff to the tiny dirt pad next to a rickety picnic table, a rusty grill, and a sad rock circle with ashes in it.

"Um, is there a bathroom?" I ask.

I've had to pee for the last hour.

"We passed it coming in," Harley tells me.

She's got a cooler bag over one shoulder and her duffel on the other.

"You're kidding. That building way back there? I'm bursting."

She shrugs. "We got this one because it's a discounted site since it's on the edge of the park. I usually just go number one in the bushes over there. Here's some biodegradable toilet paper." She fishes around in her bag and hands me a squished roll.

"Okay...I'll be back to help in a jiff."

She waves me off. "The guys will get it all."

I nod, watching Levi hoist my giant suitcase over the rocky ground and deposit it by the picnic table. *Muscles, muscles.*

I turn around, ambling into the darkening forest.

"I am so going to get eaten...or bitten by something poisonous," I grumble.

I'm here to have fun with my friends, not to connect with the wildlife.

I finally find a spot that seems secluded. I glance around to be sure I'm alone before pulling down my workout shorts.

"It's a good thing I've been doing more squats lately."

After finding a position that feels okay, I start.

"Oh shit! Shit!"

Pee goes all the way down my leg before connecting with my shorts.

"Oh...gross."

I go ahead and finish the job since I already started.

I'll just find a little stream to wash off in.

I pull the disgusting shorts back up and keep walking in search of a stream. I know Harley said there's a lake out here somewhere.

I get extremely lucky a few minutes later, coming upon a tiny little brook. "Yes!"

I cup the water in my hands to wash the urine off my leg, but I can't get the shorts rinsed good enough. Once again, I look around for any Peeping Toms.

Satisfied that I'm alone, I pull the shorts down and around my sneakers, stepping out. I quickly dip them into the water.

"So far...camping trip: one, Kenna: zero," I mumble under my breath.

This is why I should stick to sorority parties.

I hear the snap of a twig right as I finish rinsing and I bolt upright.

"Who's there?" My voice is trembling, and I slowly turn to see a man's tall form in the darkness. My shorts are still in my hand, dripping wet. "Who—who are you?"

"Shh," he whispers.

I raise my trembling voice. "I'm here with friends. Four giant dudes wi—"

"*Quiet.* Don't move," he says sternly, and I immediately recognize Levi's deep voice.

Is the universe playing some kind of sick, twisted game on me?

He's now seen me completely naked, top and bottom.

"I—"

A sound from the other direction draws my attention. I slowly turn around to see the still shape of a very large cat.

I suck in a breath. *Oh no. No, no, no...*

"I'm right here," he whispers, closer to me now.

I'm frozen in place as the shadow of the animal that must've been enjoying a nice evening drink by the stream watches us.

"Is it going to attack?" I whisper.

His hand connects with mine, grasping my fingers tightly. "Probably not. We need to stay standing up, so it knows we're bigger than he is." His deep voice is low as he speaks into my ear.

"Why don't we just run?"

"It could ignite his hunting instinct."

My breath starts coming out in faster bursts as I stare at the motionless cat, envisioning the possibility of bloody scratches and my veins being sliced open.

I'm nearly hyperventilating as I realize we could actually *die* out here. My parents would never survive another loss like that.

Levi's fingers begin brushing up the inside of my forearm, distracting my panicked thoughts with the sensation of his touch.

"Where are your pants?" he whispers.

Right then, the mountain lion begins to move ever slightly toward us. A low purring sound can be heard above the noise of the gently flowing brook.

Levi immediately steps in front of me, raising his arms up. He's a big man.

The cat stops, barely visible in the ever-darkening night. I try holding my breath, sending up a prayer for safety. I absolutely *refuse* to die without pants on in the middle of the woods.

The beast surveys us for another few moments before slowly turning around and jogging into the brush. I let out the breath I didn't realize I had been holding.

Levi watches for another few seconds before pivoting toward me. His head reaches at least a foot above mine. His eyes look down over me before quickly moving back over the top of my head.

"Um, do you—"

"Oh shit, turn around!" I screech.

He gently shushes me, turning back in the direction the feline predator ran off in.

"Sorry," I whisper, tugging the wet shorts back over my bum while his back is turned.

"Okay, I'm good."

He pivots again, and I'm almost glad I can't make out his expression in the darkness.

"We should get back," he says.

He reaches out to grab my hand again, sending tiny fireworks up the nerve endings in my skin. We start to walk in—I hope— the direction of the campsite.

"My clothes just won't stay on around you," I joke, feeling self-conscious that he's seen it all now.

He doesn't respond.

Okay then...

A few moments pass before I speak again. "If you had not shown up when you did, I legitimately would have freaked the f —"

"Kenna!"

I hear my name being called from what sounds like pretty close by.

"Levi!"

"We're here!" I yell back.

I halt my steps, pulling on his hand. I don't want this moment to be interrupted by anyone else.

"Thanks for...coming to the rescue."

I wish I could see his face.

"I'm glad I did."

I can barely hear him, but I'm ridiculously happy that he's finally speaking to me. A flashlight shines on us from the direction of the voices.

"Oh my gosh! You scared the hell out of me!"

Harley and Dan walk up to us from behind the trees. Levi releases my hand.

"You didn't come back, and I was scared out of my mind. What happened?"

She engulfs me in a giant hug, and I return it with a nervous laugh.

"I peed on myself."

Dan reaches for me, pulling me close for a hug and keeping his arm around my shoulders as we start to walk.

Harley laughs out loud. "Were you just going to stay out there until it dried or what?"

"No. I walked to find a stream to rinse off in, but there was a mountain lion right beside it!"

She gasps. "That's so scary! What did you do?"

"Levi got there just in time. He literally jumped in front of me, and the thing ran off into the bushes."

Dan claps him on the back. "Wow, man. I'm glad you were there. Sorry, Kens. Adam and I were getting firewood. Maybe we should only go up to the restrooms from now on."

"Uh, yeah, definitely so," I agree. "No more peeing in the woods for this girl."

We make it back to camp, and Adam and Silas have a fire going. Both the tents are set up now—a big one for the guys and a smaller one for us girls.

We eat cold sandwiches, drink warm Cokes, and laugh about my *urine and mountain lion* catastrophe.

Levi silently watches me from across the fire for the rest of the night, but we don't speak again.

11

Levi

The guilt plaguing my every thought is going to crush me.

I'm a sick, twisted scumbag. I saw my best friend's girl almost completely naked, and I held her hand.

Does this qualify as an affair?

That doesn't even take into account the salacious, perverted thoughts that won't get out of my head, mostly about the seven erogenous zones I now have memorized.

Ears. Lips. Neck. Breasts. Butt. Inner thighs. Vagina.

I didn't know skin could be so smooth. I knew in theory that women were generally less hairy than men, but I wasn't the least bit prepared for what I saw in the woods.

I knew it already, but it's confirmed now that she's flawless, every last inch of her.

"Levi, you're kidding me. You'd never seen a mountain lion, and you handled it exactly right?" Adam says.

Adam and Silas have heard the story several times now from Kenna.

I shrugged a response. Protecting her was an instinct. I didn't really even think about it.

Dan keeps looking from Kenna back to me. I know I should tell him about her state of undress in the woods...and the hand-holding.

I debate how to bring it up the entire next day of fishing and swimming in the crystal-blue lake.

She is wearing a tiny pink bathing suit. The girls back home in Bonnet Valley only ever wore T-shirts and shorts to swim in. Kenna's and Harley's suits look like a bra and panties.

I sit as much as possible to hide the physical response my body has to seeing hers.

"Levi! Come get in!" Silas yells from the lake.

He, Dan, Kenna, and Harley are bumping a water volleyball back and forth.

"I'm good."

I have no interest in claiming a seat closer to the constant flirtation between Dan and Kenna.

Adam comes back from the campsite with a cooler, restocked with drinks, and sits beside me. He pops open an off-brand cola and hands me one.

"So, I bought a ring."

My head swivels over. He takes a long sip, releasing a sigh afterward as he watches his tattooed girlfriend laugh in the water.

"She's everything I never knew I wanted."

A small smile is stuck on his face, and I shake my head in disbelief.

"What about your family?" I hate to bring it up, but it seems like a pretty big issue.

"They rejected her for unfounded reasons. She has a past, but it doesn't define who she is now."

I'm envious of his confidence. He's giving up the only life he's ever known to be with the woman he loves. It's inspiring, and yet I can't fathom the dedication it requires.

"I'm happy for you, man. She's a lucky girl. You're both lucky."

His smile is blinding as he claps me on the shoulder. "At first, I thought it could never work. The obstacles seemed insurmountable, but now I see that a lot of it was in my mind. I had to leave home for good, but that's a natural part of life. I think my parents will eventually come around."

I consider his words as we watch the others splash around. The sun is shining, and it should be a perfect day.

Kenna laughs as Dan picks her up and spins her around over his shoulder. My stomach roils as I watch them.

At the end of the day, if Dan is happy, I can be happy for him. No one needs to know about the misery I face internally.

From: McKenna Mae
To: Mr. Taylor
Mr. T,

I am not offended. We're just talking. I was bored until I got your message. The guy sitting next to me is pretending I don't exist.

Don't start with the main attraction. Look up the seven erogenous zones. Start at number one and slowly work your way up.

Then, study those anatomy charts we looked at to

understand number seven. It's really not complicated if you know where to focus.

Happy studying!

—Kenna

I reread Kenna's email an embarrassing amount of times with my Google search page open on my laptop. I'll need to remember to erase my browser history after this. All the information I'm finding is brand-new and extremely interesting. Memorization is my forte. I already know the zones, but I can't help myself from studying further into each one.

It's Monday evening, and we just got back from the camping trip. Kenna and I didn't speak again after the mountain-lion incident.

I was dying to get home so I can talk to her, because I'm a coward and a cad. The signal out at the site was nonexistent, so I couldn't send any emails.

Her relationship with Dan confuses me. They talk and flirt with each other, but sometimes, it almost seems platonic. He didn't even sit next to her or kiss her once.

What kind of man could be with her and not shower her with affection?

I'm starting to think they aren't an official couple yet, which means I might still have a chance.

I finally begin to type out a response to her last message.

From: Mr. Taylor
To: McKenna Mae

Kenna,

I trust your weekend was safe and enjoyable.

I've been looking over the charts and studying the seven zones. It doesn't seem too complicated—on paper. I'm surprised so many men aren't familiar with it.

Maybe the guy who was sitting next to you was just intimidated. As a man, I can say that we often act in foolish ways because of our own personal insecurities. Either way, I am truly sorry that it seemed like he was ignoring you.

How are you feeling about the upcoming quiz?

—Mr. T

I reassure myself for the millionth time that there's nothing wrong with this.

I'm her tutor.

We are discussing biology.

The uncomfortable, tight feeling hasn't left my chest since she and Dan went to the dance.

Silas opens the door to our room. He barely made it back in time for practice, but he's arguably the best player on the team. Even if he was late, the coach would probably look the other way.

He's already showered, and he tosses his baseball bag on the floor before collapsing on his bed.

"Dude, did you know Adam is going to propose?" he asks me.

I nod, eyes trailing back to my inbox as I hear a faint ding, indicating a new message. My pulse jumps but slows again when I see it's another one of my clients.

"That's insane to me. He's only known her...around eight months. He's jumping in the deep end."

My eyes are on the screen as I look over the student's failed quiz.

"He seems pretty confident that it's the right time." I glance up at my roommate.

"I would never in a million years propose after that short of a time. You don't know someone after eight months. It's *insane*." He sounds completely aghast that our friend would do something like this.

It really didn't surprise me at all. He and Harley are glued to each other every time I see them. There's no reason to drag it out once you know you've found the one you want to be with.

Unless they don't know you think they're *the one*.

"I think he's made up his mind, so all we have left to do is be supportive—unless you have some kind of objection other than the time frame."

He's staring up at the ceiling thoughtfully, and he doesn't respond for a few seconds.

"I guess we might as well plan a bachelor party," he muses.

The door opens unexpectedly, and Dan walks in. Knocking isn't something he's accustomed to unless it's on his own door when Adam and Harley are in their room.

"Hey, are we going to start planning a bachelor party for Adam?" Silas asks him.

Dan's face lights up. "Yeah, man. I want to go to Vegas. None of us have ever been."

My eyes widen at his idea. The four of us in Las Vegas sounds like sending a herd of newborn baby calves into oncoming traffic. Sin City isn't designed for three virgins and a man completely in love with his girlfriend.

"That would be awesome. We should. I wish we could ask someone along who's been before," Silas says.

Am I the only one thinking this is the worst plan possible?

My mind scrambles to come up with a place that has far less people. Bachelor parties aren't my area of expertise.

"What about...another camping trip? Just us guys," I offer.

Dan crosses his arms over his chest. "No way. We've been camping a thousand times. This is a once-in-a-lifetime party for my big brother. It needs to be special."

So special that it gives me a panic attack?

I look to Silas, hoping he'll be on my side.

He's typing on his phone. Finally finishing whatever he's doing, he looks up at us. "Yeah, I guess Dan's right. This should be something new we've never done. We could see if the girls wanna go on their own trip at the same time. Adam would love it if he got to see Harley."

Dan claps his hands together. "Yes! That's it. Kenna told me she's been a ton of times because her parents have some deal with one of the casinos. They stay at a nice one for free. I'll get her to help me plan it, and we'll bring the girls with us."

My body is completely still.

I have to confess to him what happened. He has to know what I did.

I'll tell him before the trip. I make a promise to myself to do it before we fly to Vegas—the last place on earth my introverted self ever wants to be.

The worst part of this is that I'll now have to watch Dan and Kenna together again. I was hoping after the camping trip, I could avoid them by staying in my room and eating at different times in the cafeteria.

"When are we planning it for?" I ask.

Dan reaches for the doorknob as he speaks. "He's popping the question in two weeks, and I have a feeling it'll be a short engagement. I say we go the first weekend we're out of school."

Silas agrees, and I simply nod.

I look down as my inbox pings, and I see a new message from McKenna Mae.

12

Emails

From: McKenna Mae

To: Mr. Taylor

Mr. T,

This guy is the most mysterious man I've ever met. I've never experienced anything like him.

It's like one minute he's saving me from the jaws of death, and the next, he pretends like I'm a ghost. Is there any scientific reason for this kind of behavior? Do you know anything about bipolar disorder?

Honestly, I just need to get over him. There's another guy who likes me, but I've been hung up on this one.

BTW, I know you said you were single, but I have no idea how old you are. You don't have to tell me if it breaches protocol or something. LOL.

—Kenna

From: Mr. Taylor

To: McKenna Mae

Kenna,

I do know some about bipolar disorder. I would love to share my limited knowledge to help you see if he is bipolar, but I'm afraid through secondhand information via email, I am not equipped to do so accurately.

I am twenty years old. I'm young to be a tutor, I know. I assure you, I have the qualifications. Even though I am a student at OTU, I have received extensive education in top-tier online classes.

I was homeschooled, but I technically have enough college credit hours to have received my master's degree.

I don't know your exact situation, and I'm sorry I can't offer you more advice.

Do you feel prepared for the upcoming midterm?

—Mr. T

From: McKenna Mae

To: Mr. Taylor

Mr. T,

Now that I know you're, like, barely older than me, I feel so much better talking to you about this! Maybe since you're an intelligent guy, you can give me insight. He's super smart—like, apparently a genius. Which I find *so hot*.

Is it possible that maybe he's just nervous that he doesn't have much experience with dating?

I don't care about that at all, but I'm afraid that's his hang-up.

Or he just isn't into blondes, or girls who go out or are in sororities? Hell if I know.

Sorry for bombarding you with my relationship drama!

No, I never feel prepared for tests, ha. Maybe we could meet in person to go over the guide this time?

—Kenna

From: Mr. Taylor

To: Kenna

Kenna,

That could be *exactly* his hang-up. I know for me personally, dating is very intimidating when I'm at a school filled with beautiful girls who have a lot more experience than me. It's emasculating in some sense. I know the only way to gain experience is to go out and get it, but intimacy for the first time at this age feels somewhat like jumping into ice water from the helm of the *Titanic*.

I'm afraid I can't meet up with you in person. I apologize for the inconvenience.

I have altered the study guide that the professor

gave you. I believe this one is more comprehensive and conducive to how you learn.

—Mr. T

From: McKenna Mae

To: Mr. Taylor

Mr. T,

That really makes me upset that you feel that way! I honestly think you'd be fine if you just took the plunge. Drink a little bit first, but not too much, and focus on her as much as possible—the seven zones! Truthfully, so many guys are terrible that she wouldn't even know if it was your first time.

Is there anyone you'd maybe feel comfortable being vulnerable with, some girl you like?

This new study guide looks phenomenal. Thank you so much.

—Kenna

From: Mr. Taylor

To: McKenna Mae

Kenna,

There is a girl. I like her more than I can express with words.

But she likes someone else. Either way, she's a million miles out of my league.

—Mr. T

From: McKenna Mae

To: Mr. Taylor

Mr. T,

You're breaking my heart over here! I'm so sorry. That sucks. We both want what we can't have.

You seem like a wonderful guy. I'm sure you will find someone else.

What is it you like so much about her? I bet I have a sorority sister I could hook you up with!

—Kenna

From: Mr. Taylor

To: McKenna Mae

Kenna,

I don't even know where to start. She's intoxicating. I'm hypnotized by her beauty, her laughter, her voice, just...her. Describing her is like describing what fresh rain smells like on a stormy night or the first touch of pink in a sunrise.

I wake up thinking of her. I both long to see her in passing and pray that I don't, because seeing her is just a reminder that she'll never be mine.

Guys like me don't end up with girls like her.

—Mr. T

From: Samuel Rogers

To: Levi Taylor

I found a potential for Sarah Taylor who's the right

age. Her last known address was just outside of San Francisco, California. If you approve the amount below, I'll book the flight and see if she matches the photo you sent me. Making direct contact from there will be up to you.

—Samuel Rogers

13

Kenna

Several months ago, I would've thought I was insane for saying this, but I think I'm getting over Levi. *Finally.*

I am *done* with his hot-and-cold act. He saved my life on the camping trip, but that was a month ago, and I've waited around for him to make a move for long enough. I'm invisible *again*. It's bullshit.

Also, I have a new crush. Mr. Taylor has been emailing me for weeks, and it's been so nice to have him to talk to.

I peer around my biology class in search of someone who looks like they might have the last name Taylor. I don't really know what I'm looking for other than some crazy-intelligent twenty-year-old male who's probably shy.

It's a little odd how similar he sounds to Levi, but I know it isn't him. Those types of lucky coincidences just don't happen.

However, Mr. Taylor is very forward and honest with me, whereas Levi acts like a mute in my presence.

My redheaded friend sits down next to me, pushing his glasses higher on his nose.

"Hey, Melvin. How are you?"

I smile at him, and he does the usual *blushing and looking down* routine before clearing his throat.

"Hey, Kenna. I'm great. I've had a productive week." He gives me a shaky smile.

"That's nice. I'm glad. By the way, thanks so much for the online tutoring program recommendation. I think you saved my sanity," I joke, getting out my MacBook and tapping until I'm in my class notes.

"Oh, yeah? That's awesome. I'm glad it's helped you."

I pause for a few seconds, debating how to broach my next question.

"I, uh, was wondering if you knew any of the other tutors." I try to sound nonchalant.

As I'm speaking, his phone beeps with a text.

His eyes widen at the screen in his hand. He begins typing away at lightning speed, eyes lit up with excitement.

"Um, everything good?" I ask.

He finally looks up, a blinding smile on his face.

"Uh, yeah, sorry. This girl just texted me." He looks like he's at the dentist, trying to give visual proof of how well he's been flossing.

I giggle, shaking my head at him. "I'm guessing she's a girl you find very attractive?"

He blushes deeper, the cherry color of his cheeks nearly matching his overgrown curls. "Yeah, I guess you could say so." His dimples are truly adorable.

"Well, I'm super happy for you. I hope it works out."

The professor is beginning the lecture, and even with the incredible help I'm getting from Mr. Taylor, I have to pay attention if I want to pass this horrific class.

"This is an amazing idea, but I can't believe you guys want to do it."

The four of them in Las Vegas of all places is an unexpected plan.

Dan is stretched out on the sofa in their apartment. He asked me to come over to discuss the bachelor-party plans tonight, so I stopped by on my way to the Betas' toga party.

The white fabric I bought from the local craft store crisscrosses over my breasts and wraps around my waist and hips to create a backless Greek goddess minidress. It looks pretty hot, and I didn't have to scour all the clothing stores in the universe. Thank God for Pinterest.

I fiddle with the dainty gold body necklace hanging down the front as he speaks.

"Kenna, it's Vegas and the best place to go for a night of excitement and preparation for a lifetime of being shackled to one woman."

I scoff. "Wow. Love your opinion on the institution of marriage." I cross my arms over my bare stomach. The body glitter I put on at Maya's insistence is sticky on my skin.

"Well, what do you think of the idea for you girls to meet us there?" he asks.

The door to Levi and Silas's room opens, and a tall, sexy body topped with a jet-black head of hair steps into the kitchen. He visibly starts at the sight of me in the living room. His eyes trail over my body, covered in a scrap of white fabric and shimmery skin.

I jut my chin out. "Yeah, we'll be there. I don't know who all you want to come. I'm pretty much Harley's only friend here, besides you guys."

I watch Levi as his dark-blue eyes continue to trail over my body before he turns away and walks into the open-concept kitchen. I guess he's back to the silent, burning stares he likes to torture me with. The itchy glitter seems to be getting worse.

"What about that girl she works with? Sally?" Dan asks, tapping on his new smartphone.

The guys all had flip phones when they first came to college, but they upgraded recently, all except for Adam.

"Sal. Yeah, I could ask her. I know she has a kid, though, so she might not be able to get away. Either way, it's fine, I guess. Harley won't care if it's just us two."

Levi is making himself a sandwich, and it's the most enormous thing I've ever seen. He piles every type of lunch meat and cheese you can imagine on it before following with pickles, lettuce, tomatoes, and jalapeños. I guess it takes a lot of calories to maintain a physique like that. I shift my feet, the tight straps of my makeshift dress suddenly digging into my sides.

"I thought you'd be more excited about the idea," Dan says.

I look down at my gold sandals. In truth, I'm a little nervous to be in close quarters with Levi again. My head is foggy around him, especially now that I've decided to forget about my massive crush. The only way I know how to do that is to put some distance between us. Three nights of partying in Vegas is just a recipe for me to forget my conviction and fall all over him *again*, only to be rejected—*again*.

I look back up at Dan, pushing my hair behind my ear.

"Sorry, I am. I guess it's just crazy to me that they're really getting married. I mean, I feel like that's a million miles away for most of us. As long as they're happy, I'm happy for them. It's just wild."

He stands up, coming over to pull me into a friendly hug. He's the sweetest guy.

"I know, right? It is crazy, but I think I'll go insane if they don't just do it already and let me have my room back." He chuckles, pulling back. "Where are you going anyway?" He looks down over my attire.

"I have a toga party to get to." I try to drum up some enthusiasm in my voice.

"Wow. On a Thursday night?"

"Sorority girls never sleep. Or study."

The whole sorority thing has really been grating on my nerves. I joined for Lia's sake. She'd always talked about being in one, and even though I knew the constant events and going out weren't my thing, I did it for her. I'm a homebody through and through. Give me a bottle of wine and a few close friends any day over a room full of handsy, intoxicated strangers.

Levi has finished his mountain-man sandwich and is chugging a glass of water. His bicep is flexed against the sleeve of his gray T-shirt, and somehow, I even find the way his Adam's apple bobs in his veiny neck to be sexy.

I have got to convince Mr. Taylor to meet up with me.

"Well, have fun. I gotta start working on a paper." Dan lifts his backpack off the floor and pulls it over his shoulder. He moves out the door a few seconds later, waving as it shuts behind him.

I narrow my gaze on Levi. He's washing his plate and cup at the sink, eyes down.

I know I should leave. It's the smart, safe thing to do. He's a lot of man, and staying could mean some emotional risk.

But I can't make myself move toward the door.

My feet slowly take me into the kitchen. The lighting is dim, the only source a lone bulb over the sink.

He mechanically turns the faucet off as he places the dishes in the drying rack. I step right up next to him, my hip pressed into the cheap Formica countertop. I can smell his fresh-shower scent, mixed with a spicy cologne that I wish I could inhale instead of oxygen, right from his skin.

I suck in a breath as he turns to me, eyes blazing with barely restrained desire. The depth of their blue speaks louder than any words he could say to me, and for a brief moment, all my doubts are erased.

He wants me—*desperately*—possibly as much as I want him.

His big hand grips the countertop, veins popping as his breathing tempo increases slightly. His eyes focus in on my sensual red lips. I'm breathless, waiting on the brink of anticipation, begging him to dive in with me.

Please, please put me out of my misery.

His head dips down, the slowest descent that could rival an overturned bottle of crystalized honey. He takes his time, but there's no rush. I'd wait forever to experience this moment with him.

Finally—*finally*—his forehead presses to mine, and he inhales deeply. I close my eyes, feeling his hand reaching up to cradle the side of my neck under his callous fingertips.

I force myself to wait for him to take my lips. It will be his first kiss. There's no good reason why he wouldn't take the opportunity to claim what I've been offering him.

Then he sighs, inching back a fraction of a step before I grab his muscular arm, trying to pull him back to me.

"No, please..." I whisper, opening my eyes to see him studying my face. I don't understand the pain in his pinched expression.

"Kenna...we can't." He swallows, struggling to form the words. "I can't. I'm sorry." His deep voice is laced with desire, clearly wanting it despite his denial.

"Why? Why not?" I demand, angry that I put myself here once again—this place of vulnerability—just to be crushed with disappointment.

He opens his mouth, closing it again as he shakes his head.

"Why don't you talk to me? I see you staring, but you never speak. You just *look* at me all the time. Why?" I'm in no mood to let him run away from me again, and I take another step closer. My stubborn spark has flamed up.

He closes his eyes, seeming to attempt to gain some control. I've never been so confused, hurt, and angry at the same time.

"I don't...I'm sorry for looking at you...so much," he finally gets out as he drops his hand from my neck.

My jaw hits the floor. "You think this is about you looking at me?"

I'm dumbfounded that a man his age—who could clearly gain experience if he wanted to—is so naive about women.

His cheeks tinge pink, and he looks down at the floor under our feet.

"I know it's rude," he mumbles, rubbing his hand across the back of his neck.

I want to shake him and scream at the top of my lungs, but I know that won't help the situation. *How could I possibly be any clearer about what I want with him?*

My phone starts to ring, and I angrily ignore the call.

His eyes suddenly lick over my skimpy toga, and he takes a step away from me.

"You're going to be late," he says quietly.

I shake my head, searching his face for another second before expelling a breath and spinning on my heel to leave.

Feels like a good night to drink a little too much.

Five Years Earlier

"Kenna, hurry up! If I don't get there in time for Shaun's birthday shots, he might take them with Jacy." Lia tugs on my hand, propelling me through the tall grass leading up to the little house in the middle of nowhere.

"Where the hell are we? What if there are rodents out here? Or snakes?!" I start to pick up the pace, much to Lia's approval.

"If you moved faster, it wouldn't be an issue. Oh my gosh, I can't believe my boyfriend is going to be a legal adult!"

I pull back on her hand, stopping abruptly. "Your boyfriend? Since when?"

She laughs, waving me off as she adjusts the sleek high ponytail in her hair, smoothing back any stray hairs. "It's not official, of course, but he definitely has been hinting at it."

I slowly trail behind her as the lights from the house become brighter and the sound of Texas country music begins to float toward us in the autumn breeze. It's still so damn hot.

"I can't believe you're dating a senior."

I'm still single, and it's almost Halloween. How embarrassing that my little sister landed such a hot boyfriend sooner than me. Chase Colson smiled at me on Monday, and I flirtatiously batted my eyelashes at him. Aside from him, I'm not interested in anyone else despite the many offers coming my way.

Lia claps excitedly. "Eek, I know, right?! He's the perfect first high school boyfriend. Just bad boy enough without being in detention every other day. *Obviously* an athlete, but not one without any brain cells. He's practically fictional."

"Okay...but do you like him? You sound like a thirty-year-old describing a job opportunity."

We're only twenty feet from the porch, where some of our classmates are gathering to play a game of beer pong.

Lia and I halt for a moment as she faces me. Her lips are the perfect shade of pink to match the strapless crop top she paired with a white miniskirt. I'm wearing the same thing but in blue and taupe.

"Kenna, yes, of course I like him. I'm also interested in the... social status he can offer me. If there was some guy I was just *super* attracted to and really liked for who he was, he would clearly be my first choice. But as a freshman in high school without an actual crush, why not date someone who can advance me into an ideal position for the next three years?" She looks at me like it's the most logical decision in the world.

Lia is the social butterfly, flitting around to every party, and always the center of attention. I'm not shy, and I'm not against socializing, but it gives *life* to Lia. I don't have nearly the same obsession she does with popularity.

I reach out to grab her hand, giving it a squeeze. "I'm here with you, and I'm super excited to go in there and dance to Whiskey Myers, but I want you to know that I love you for who you are, no matter who you're dating or what your social status is. Okay?"

She pulls me into a tight hug. "I know you do, big sis. I love you more than life itself." Leaning back, she grins at me, her beautiful face illuminated by the porch lights. "Let's go have a blast. And for the love of cheese crackers, will you *finally* flirt with Chase Colson?"

14

Levi

Present Day

From: McKenna Mae

To: Mr. Taylor

misterr T,

You shouodnt sell youselff so short smartty .some guys are really dicka but if she wont go out with yoou, Id love to be your sexx pracitic dummy ;)]

-keennn

I read the typo-filled email from Kenna several times over, completely confused. I'm sitting in the on-campus coffee shop with a steaming cup in front of me. The rain is pounding on the roof of the building.

Was she drunk when she sent this? I immediately feel an urge to call her and make sure she made it back to her dorm room okay.

What is she trying to get at with this message? Does she really want to hook up with her biology tutor?

My stupid brain tries to come up with some kind of way to try and meet her without showing my face, excitement spreading through me.

But then she'd still be cheating on Dan...and she just doesn't seem like that kind of girl. I must be misunderstanding her intentions.

The mass of discomfort in my stomach grows again as I realize I have no choice but to talk to him about this.

How can I bring it up without crushing him or revealing that I've been secretly emailing her for months?

I'm officially the worst person who ever lived. Self-loathing fills me to the brim.

Before I can make a plan to talk to him, I have to make sure Kenna made it home okay last night. I'll reply to her email first and see if she responds.

From: Mr. Taylor

To: McKenna Mae

Kenna,

Are you okay? Based on your last message, it seems like maybe you had a bit too much to drink, and I wanted to check in on you. Please let me know ASAP. I'm concerned.

—Mr. T

My fingers tap the table as I wait for her response, and more people begin filing into the little café. Silas walks through the door, joining me at the round table.

"Hey. Glad you got here early to save a spot." He pulls out his notes from the class I'm tutoring him in, flipping to the most recent lecture.

I clear my throat. "Before we start...can I talk to you about something?" I ask, nerves causing me to rub my sweaty palms over my jeans.

He looks up and nods, raising one eyebrow at me. It might be the first time I've ever asked one of my friends that question. I usually listen and observe, only responding when prompted. The home I grew up in wasn't exactly the best place to learn how to express feelings or talk about any issues—at all.

"I, uh, I made a mistake." A lot of mistakes actually, one right after the other.

He nods, indicating that I continue. I force out a sigh, drumming up the courage to come clean. I know it'll make me feel better.

"I've been emailing Kenna."

The words hang between us for a few seconds. He seems to be expecting me to elaborate.

"And she doesn't know it's me," I quickly add.

His eyes widen this time, and he places his laptop on the table between us. "Uh, okay. How does she not know it's you?"

I look around, making sure no one is near enough to be eavesdropping.

"She signed up for tutoring, and my name online is just...Mr. Taylor. I really don't want to talk about why." I swallow after admitting the truth.

He doesn't react like I expected, but he scrunches up his brows.

"So...what's the big deal? You're just tutoring her?"

I look away, suddenly wishing I hadn't brought it up. *How can I admit the next part?*

"She...it's kind of gotten...flirtatious." I shift in my seat, placing my elbow on the table.

He throws his head back in a laugh, drawing attention from a couple of girls across the café. They smile at Silas, but his attention is on me.

"That all sounds like a good thing. When are you going to tell her it's you?" He smirks at me.

My mouth drops open.

"I...aren't you mad at me?"

Is he as disloyal of a friend to Dan as I've been?

I never thought a girl would become more important to me than loyalty to one of my friends.

That was before I met Kenna.

"Why would I be mad at you?" He seems as confused as I am.

"Be-because she's dating Dan. I'm a horrible person, and I have to tell him about it. I don't know if he'll ever forgive—"

Silas shakes his head now, holding a hand up to stop me from continuing. "Whoa, whoa, whoa. Why do you think she's dating Dan?"

I stare at him, my mind scrambling to fill in the gaps.

"They went to the dance together and...on a date. They clearly like each other. I don't know how serious it is." I lean back, crossing my arms over my chest as a group of girls walks by our table. Once they pass, I go on. "Either way, I'm overstepping the boundaries of our friendship by secretly talking to her."

He stares at me blankly for a few seconds before leaning back to match my stance. "Kenna and Dan aren't dating."

His calm words settle over me, seeping into my skin. I stare at him, waiting for some elaboration.

He chuckles. "Man, you gotta start paying attention. He liked her, and they went out, yeah, but she told him she just wanted to be friends. That was before the camping trip. Of course, you basically hide in your room all the time, so I'm not surprised you didn't know."

Silas always tries to push me out of my comfort zone, but I generally resist his efforts. I know his heart is in the right place. He doesn't want to see me end up as a lonely hermit, which is a viable outcome for the path I'm on.

"So, she...she and Dan never really dated?"

He shakes his head.

I feel a weight lift from my shoulders. I'm actually not a terrible friend. She never even liked him.

Does she genuinely want to meet up with Mr. Taylor, or does she want me, like it seemed like she did last night in the kitchen?

Why are women so damn hard to read?

"And by the way, I know you've had a thing for her since the day you met, but you can barely admit it to yourself, much less to her." He knows me too well. Silas is the closest thing I'll ever have to a brother. "I gotta say, I don't know how you're going to pull off admitting to her that you're her tutor. Girls don't like when you keep shit from them."

I take a slow sip from my coffee mug. I guess I never really considered that she'd be mad to find out I kept it from her. My social anxiety, the incident in my bedroom when she surprisingly climbed on top of me, and believing that she liked Dan all left me thinking I didn't have a shred of a chance with her anyway. So what would be the point of telling her that I was Mr. Taylor?

Am I really considering it now?

Silas is studying his notes, and I realize we need to get to work on his tutoring if we're going to finish before we have class.

"Okay, well, I don't know if I'll even tell her. She's not my type."

He squints up at me. "Yeah, okay."

He clearly doesn't believe me, but I'm being completely serious.

I meant what I told her as Mr. Taylor. Guys like me don't end up with girls like her.

Pulling up my notes on my computer, I'm relieved to see that I have a new email.

From: McKenna Mae

To: Mr. Taylor

Mr. T,

Wow, I'm so embarrassed. I did drink a bit too much last night, but yes, I'm okay. I'm sorry for coming on to you so strong like that. You like someone else, and honestly, I do too. He just won't give me the time of day...and for some reason, you remind me of him.

I'm so sorry for pulling you into my drama! Please don't drop me as a student. You've helped me so much. I promise I can keep it professional from now on.

—Kenna

Silas is right. *How can I ever tell her who I really am?*

From: Mr. Taylor

To: McKenna Mae

Kenna,

I'm glad you're okay. You don't deserve to be disregarded that way.

I'm not upset about the message at all. I understand that you were under the influence. I hope you aren't feeling ill or have a headache.

I've enjoyed getting to know you better and tutoring you. I would never drop you as a student.

What is it about me that reminds you of him?

—Mr. T

I nearly don't hit Send, but I finally manage to press the button. I have to know the answer.

"Okay, I'm emailing you my updated notes for your quiz. You need to work on the formulas. If you'd had those down better, you wouldn't have had a problem on your quiz," I tell Silas, and he nods.

I add the attachment to the email and hit the button again just as my inbox lights up, sending a spark through me.

From: McKenna Mae

To: Mr. Taylor

Mr. T,

You seem a little too good to be true, honestly. Are you sure you're a man? Ha-ha. I have a headache, but thankfully, I only have one afternoon class on

Fridays. I think I'm just dehydrated.

Well, you're both super smart. You're inexperienced, and I know he is too. You're thoughtful, and even though he's super hot and cold with me, when he's being nice, it's like he's... hmm...I don't know, but I want to just lick him all over. A little extra in some places.

I kind of want to do that with you, too, so it's confusing as hell.

Consider it some kind of weird kink for science guys. I need to test a theory I have.

—Kenna

P.S. How's that for breaching protocol? You already said you'd never drop me, so you can't take it back!

;)

My face is as red as my T-shirt. I can't mistake this for anything other than flirting. Kenna is hitting on me.

"Are you talking to her right now?" Silas interrupts my slowly degrading train of thought.

I don't answer, and he smiles.

"What's she saying?"

I read the message again. I absolutely will never show him this, but I could fish for ideas of how to respond.

Yes, this is my first time to flirt, but my outgoing friend has done it plenty.

"I think she's...kind of hitting on me." I look up to see his reaction.

"Let me see."

I shake my head, pulling the laptop closer to my side of the table. I lower my voice. "She just said she...wants to lick me." Saying it out loud makes it sound stupid, but Silas grins at me.

"Yeah, I'd say she's one hundred percent hitting on you. What are you saying back?"

I stare at my blinking cursor in the blank reply box.

"I want to do it to her too? To the seventh zone." I feel pretty confident about my answer, starting to type it out.

He looks at me blankly. "Uh, what's the seventh zone? If that's some kind of science thing—"

I shake my head, in awe that I know something about sex that he doesn't. He's still a virgin—barely. He went pretty far with a girl back home before she moved away.

I pull up the chart I saved into my Favorites and email it to him.

"She told me about it. Apparently, a lot of guys don't know it exists, but it's some kind of vital secret chart of the female anatomy."

His eyes drift back up to me after he studies it for a few seconds. "She told you about this?"

I nod, looking back down to type out my reply.

"Okay, so you two have been talking about sex?"

My eyes jump back up, looking around the coffee shop for nearby patrons as I lower my voice. The S-word makes me uncomfortable.

"A little bit."

I begin typing again, fueled with confidence by the fact that someone else has confirmed that she is hitting on me.

From: Mr. Taylor

To: McKenna Mae

Kenna,

I am definitely a man.

Drink something with electrolytes, like broth or pickle juice, for your recovery.

I think I'd like to return the favor, but I'll need a long time to cover the seven zones. I'd prefer to start at number one and work my way down... slowly.

If you agree to be a willing participant, we could make some much-needed discoveries.

For science, of course.

—Mr. T

Kenna

My theory is this: the silent, invisible nerd guy is actually better in bed than the confident jock who's nailed a million girls.

I have yet to test it out, but it is a hypothetical idea based on these facts:

Smart guys know how to study and learn. Meaning they know how to concentrate and focus.

They love a challenge just as much as a jock—maybe more.

They don't think they're God's precious gift to women, ultimately only in it for their own satisfaction and a notch in their belt.

They know how to appreciate a woman and would *never* let their eyes stray to someone else.

Since Levi isn't an option, I'm determined to start testing my theory on Mr. T.

His last email was surprisingly bold, and I have a feeling if I keep it up, he'll come more out of his shell and be willing to meet me in person. It doesn't have to be anything serious.

I bite my lip in anticipation as I type out a response.

From: McKenna Mae

To: Mr. Taylor

Mr. T,

You can take as much time as you need. I'm partial to numbers 1, 3, and 6 getting the most focus.

Also, do you wear glasses? I have a thing for that too.

Actually, I want to wear them, so...can you see at all, like up close, without them?

Do you have any preference for what you would want me to wear?

I have a test on Monday, and I'm super nervous! Is this study guide the TA gave out okay to use?

(Attachment)

—K

I force myself to close out the email and focus on the paper I need to write for my other class. Papers don't challenge me. If I buckle down and crank them out in a few hours, I can usually make a B-plus or an A-minus.

Harley texts me a few times to check in on how the party went, and I type out a brief response, complaining about the migraine-inducing paper-writing dilemma.

A knock sounds on my door right as I hit Submit on my paper.

Ugh, it'd better not be Maya.

I reluctantly roll out of bed to answer it. A guy dressed in a food-delivery uniform with a fork logo is standing there with a brown takeout bag.

"Davis?" he says, chewing on a piece of gum with his mouth open.

I nod dumbly, and he hands over the bag. I shut the door and set it on my desk.

After digging in, I find the contents to be a bowl of steaming chicken tortilla soup and all the toppings to go with it. An enormous smile stretches across my face at the uplifting gift.

The receipt doesn't reveal the sender, but my name is printed across the top in big block letters.

Was it Harley...or possibly Mr. T? If so, how did he get my dorm number?

My inked friend is a nice girl, but somehow, this seems over the top for her. She's more likely to drop by with a six-pack of Mountain Dew and the offer to smoke a joint, which can supposedly cure a headache.

After slurping up half of the delicious contents of the bowl, I excitedly check my email for a new message.

Nothing. My inbox is empty. I know he's a student, so maybe he's in class. My stomach rolls with unexpected nausea from my night out. I should stay home and rest, but I've already made plans to be out tonight with Maya and the girls. Harley and Adam have a date night, which is fine with me. I want to get wasted and forget what day it is.

My little sister, Lia, should be turning eighteen today. I won't be driving tonight. I never get behind the wheel on this day. I'm also never sober.

We were less than a year apart in age. I was the older sister, the one who was supposed to protect her. She was driving us to school that day because I had stayed up late talking to my boyfriend instead of studying, and I was cramming for a biology exam. She braked for a deer in the middle of the road, swerving to the right to careen head-on into a tree. The scars on my side are the only visible marks I have from the accident.

They told me that Lia died instantly on impact.

My phone pings with a text, interrupting my downward spiral of memories.

> Maya: hey, biotch! are you ready to get shit-faced tonight? I think the Lambda Alphas will be there for Jake's birthday. I told them we'd make it a special night for him. you in?

> Kenna: as long as there is whiskey involved, I'm game. what are you wearing?

Maya is a horrible person, but I'm glad I have her as a distraction tonight. She's a shitty enough friend that she won't ask or care why I'm getting wasted.

> Maya: something short. I need some action tonight. I'll come over to get ready with you.

> Kenna: sounds good.

I refresh my email to see a response from Mr. T that lights up my insides.

From: Mr. Taylor

To: McKenna Mae

Kenna,

I would think numbers four and five would be more stimulating than one and three.

I take a minute to consult my chart before continuing his message. Number four is breasts, and number five is butt. I prefer the neck and inner thighs, but seven deserves some attention. I keep reading his email.

I'm intrigued to be hearing this.

I do wear glasses. I can see up close with them, yes. I am nearsighted. I think you would look ravishing in anything or nothing at all. I would ultimately prefer to see you in a damp white T-shirt, if I was allowed a preference.

I can't believe I'm having this conversation with a student of mine, but I find myself unable to resist.

The study guide from your teaching assistant is grossly lacking. I have altered it to be more sufficient.

(Attachment)

—Mr. T

I can't help but snicker at his disgust with the TA's study guide. The mechanical way in which he is addressing sexual preferences is both odd and endearing. I'm about to type out my response when I see the green light next to his name is lit up.

It must be a new feature because I've never noticed it before. I click on his name, and a chat box opens up on the bottom of the screen.

McKenna Mae: Mr. T, are you there?

For a moment, I think the green dot must not mean he's online because after two whole minutes, he still hasn't responded. I play on my phone, scrolling through my social media while I wait. Finally, I see three little gray dots popping up under his name.

Mr. Taylor: Yes. Hi, Kenna. How are you feeling? Did the soup help?

I bite my lip, excitement zipping through my stomach. I quickly send a message back.

McKenna Mae: Thank you! It was delicious. I'm okay. Just lying in bed, thinking about you. I'm wearing a white T-shirt. What are you wearing?

I know he's as inexperienced as they come—well, almost— but I still find myself pushing the boundaries with what I should be saying to my tutor.

Okay, I saw the line, and I leaped over it. So what? It's the worst day of the year, and I want to feel something besides misery. Talking to Mr. T is a distraction I desperately need. My mom has already called three times because she knows how hard today is for me.

> Mr. Taylor: I'm wearing a shirt with a pi symbol on it and a pair of jeans. Are you only wearing a shirt?

> McKenna Mae: I'm wearing lacy purple underwear. Can you solve a Rubik's Cube?

> Mr. Taylor: I can only imagine how beautiful you look. Yes, I can. Can you?

Well, if that's not a hint, I don't know what is. After pulling my shirt up around my waist, I lift my phone to snap a photo from the side. The lower half of my face is in it, and you can see the outline of my breasts under my thin shirt and the side of my hips and butt in my cheeky underwear. I AirDrop it to my computer and send it in my chat.

> McKenna Mae: No, I can't. Your turn, Mr. T.

I don't hear back for a few minutes, which doesn't surprise me. If he's really as innocent as he seems, that photo might be the first he's ever received like it. Finally, the dots appear, and I watch them in anticipation, drumming my fingers along the keyboard.

A photo pops up on the screen. It's of a very broad, fit chest of a man.

I thought this guy was twenty years old?!

The chest and trim waist of Mr. T belong to someone who knows how to lift some weights and apparently does it on a regular basis. I stare at my computer after enlarging the photo, not failing to notice the veins of his bicep on the very edge of the screen. My mouth is open, eyes glued to the first glimpse of my crush I've gotten. He didn't include any of his face, but I know he's shy.

Mr. Taylor: I hope you don't mind me noting that you are the loveliest creature I have ever beheld.

McKenna Mae: I don't mind at all. Note away. You're sexy as hell. I can't imagine why you're so shy! I want to take a nap on that chest. After other vigorous activities, of course.

Mr. Taylor: You can use me as a pillow anytime. As for the other activities, I would relish any opportunity to touch your skin.

McKenna Mae: Any chance you want to meet up tonight? My friends and I are going out.

He doesn't reply for another ten minutes. I watch the screen, alternating between scrolling on my phone and sipping the tortilla soup. Finally, I decide he must have needed to go.

I force myself to put him out of my mind and get the rest of my homework done.

I lost count of how many shots I took last night. That scenario is both good and bad. Good because I blacked out like I'd intended, but bad because now I can't stop throwing up. My memory is hazy at best. I know there was a bar, and I know the fraternity boys made sure to keep my drink full. Maya left with one of them, so I don't remember how I got back to my dorm.

My stomach turns over again, and I dry-heave into a plastic bowl. I have nothing left to throw up. I catch sight of blonde hair on the bed Harley rarely sleeps in anymore.

Raelynn—that's how I got back.

My phone starts to ring, reminding me that I have a splitting headache. I see *Bad Barbie* on the screen as I swipe to answer.

"Hello?"

Harley's scratchy voice comes through the speaker. "Hey, what are you doing?"

"Wishing I were dead."

"Why?"

"Hangover."

"Ahh, yeah, you were drunk-texting me. I'm sorry. Drink Gatorade."

The thought of consuming anything sweet right now makes my stomach churn.

"Gross. How was your date?"

"Well, I'd say it went pretty well."

I stand up to walk to the sink for a glass of water. My entire body protests.

"That's good. Where did he take you?"

"Um, he took me to a vineyard."

Harley's boyfriend, Adam, treats her like an absolute queen. It's a healthy reminder for me to not settle for some half-committed boy. I want a man.

"A vineyard? You're not twenty-one."

"He proposed."

"What?!" I stop in my tracks, my jaw dropping open. I knew it was going to happen, but it still feel surreal.

She laughs, and I hear Adam chuckle in the background.

"You're getting married?! Oh my gosh, that's amazing! I'm so excited for you!"

My shouting wakes up Raelynn, whose head slowly turns toward me. Her eyes barely squint open.

"Sorry." I walk up to the sink to get some water. As I glance in the mirror, my eye catches on a massive bruise at the top of my thigh. *Party foul.*

"Yeah, apparently, the guys have been planning a Vegas trip for the bachelor party this summer."

I laugh. "Yeah, I was a little shocked by that too, but I thought it could be fun to see those boys in Sin City. They want us to meet them there."

I grab two pain pills for my headache before I walk back to my bed to lie down.

"I heard. My birthday is next weekend, so...Adam and I don't want to wait."

My body stills. We're both quiet for a few seconds.

"Are you saying you want to...get married *next* weekend?"

She laughs. "Yes, that's exactly what I'm saying. We want to do it in Vegas. I should be asking you this in person, but I'm going with Adam now to tell his parents, which could mean I won't make it out alive. So...will you be my maid of honor?"

My feelings are a jumble of shock, disbelief, and excitement.

"Oh my gosh, yes! Of course I will!" From the corner of my eye, I see Raelynn moving, so I lower my voice. "Harley, I'm beyond thrilled for you, babe. Are you...sure you want to get married *this* weekend?"

"I am so in love with him, Kenna, but it's more than that. He's the guy I want to spend forever with. He's the guy who will always protect me, always be there at my back. I am one hundred percent, without a doubt, ready to marry him."

I hear rustling over the phone and the distinct sound of smooching.

"Well, in that case, I would love to be there by your side. Let's go to Vegas, baby!"

16

Levi

Eight Years Earlier

"Sarah is...gone, Levi." My mother's voice cracks at the word *gone.*

I want to comfort her.

What does she mean, she's gone? Gone where?

"Why?" I grip the edges of the kitchen chair until the tips of my fingers ache.

I thought I was being called in here for dinner. The college-level chemistry I was studying was fascinating, and all I wanted five seconds ago was to go finish the article I found on MIT's blog. Now, my world has been thrown into a free fall.

She isn't trying to hide the tears now, blotting them with the kitchen towel before slowly folding it into a neat square. "She, um, she was talking to a young man over the internet." She looks up at me, blinking away the moisture. "Did you...did you know about that, Levi?"

My eyes widen as I slowly shake my head. Sarah and I get along, but with our five-year age difference, we rarely speak. She resents our parents to an extreme extent, and even if I don't fully comprehend why, I wish they could all just get along. She pushes their boundaries more than she should, but I know it's wrong of my father to punish her the way he does.

I've learned to keep my head down and stay in my room most of the time to study and learn. Sometimes I'm allowed to go work on the farm with Adam, Dan, and Silas, and I enjoy the company of my friends. But most of my life is still here, usually in my room with my books. There's nothing more peaceful to me than being buried in a textbook...when the house is quiet.

My mother turns away from me, mechanically stirring the pot on the stove. "Sarah isn't coming back, Levi. I don't know if...I don't know if we will ever see her again." Her voice is weak.

My heart is thundering in my chest, but words won't reach my lips. I have so many questions and no courage to voice them.

Silence is safety.

I hear her choked voice again. "I'm just telling you this, so you don't ask about her. Your father won't want to hear her name, okay?" She pauses, and the only sound is the ticking of the old clock hanging in the wallpapered kitchen. "Don't speak her name ever again."

Present Day

There has only been a handful of times in my life that I've truly wished I'd been raised by different people in another place. There's no sense in dwelling on the past and the things I can't change about my upbringing, but it's times like this when I want nothing more than to be normal. I want to be the guy who can say yes to a social-gathering invite, get up and style my hair, wear a nice shirt, and walk out with a smile to go pick up the gorgeous, flirty girl who invited me.

But instead, I ignored her message and sat in bed in my dark room, staring at the photo she'd sent me of herself in her white shirt and lacy panties. Instead of being a man and growing a pair, I was a coward.

I wouldn't know how to even begin socializing at a party. I wouldn't know where to stand, what to say, or how to interact with any of the strangers there. Even as I think about it now, my palms are sweating.

Every time I see Kenna, she is somehow the center of attention. She doesn't ask for it, but she's just that girl who draws the eye with her big, curly blonde hair and wide green eyes. I don't know why God gives some people the prettiest smile and the ability to be everyone's best friend, but he gave her a double portion of those gifts.

I've been kidding myself, even pretending I have a shot with her. The party invite last night was a bright-red flag that reminded me there was no way in hell we would ever work out.

I roll over in bed to reach for my phone. The screen lights up to reveal something unusual. Last night, I got ten new emails. They must have come in late because I stayed up until past midnight, working on tutoring plans for my students.

When I open the email app, my heart rate sputters as I see that the messages are all from Kenna, starting at one a.m.

To: Mr. Taylor

From: McKenna Mae

Mr. T! I wish you had decided to come out with me tonight. I'm wearing a white bodycon dress just

for you. ;) If you change your mind, we're at the
dance hall on Fifth Street.
—Kenna

The next one was sent two hours later.

To: Mr. Taylor
From: McKenna Mae
Mr. T!
I'M SO HOT FOR YOU.
Oops, sorry. All caps was an accident, ha-ha-ha.
Please tell me you're on your way?!
—Kennzz

The next one was sent only five minutes later.

To: Mr. Taylor
From: McKenna Mae
I'm so glad you're a nice guy and you talk to me!!!
You've made me realize not all smart guys think
they're better than people like me who need
tutoring. There's this asshat brainiac named Levi
who pretends like I don't even exist. Like, sorry not
all of us can be Isaac Newton.
I HATE guys like that! You're so nice and fun to

talk to, and I'm just soo glad I've moved on and found you. I hope we can meet soooooon!

—Kennzz <3

The steady rhythm of my heart beats faster with each word I read.

She hates me. She thinks I dislike her. She thinks I'm an asshat brainiac?

The messages get less legible as they go on until there's a video attachment. I almost don't open it, but in the end, curiosity wins me over.

It's a video of Kenna dancing with the phone held in front of her face. She's smiling at the camera. The music is loud in the background, and the entire scene looks chaotic with people bumping into her and loud laughter.

I would rather walk over hot coals than experience something like that.

Her beautiful face is smiling at me as she says something inaudible over the music.

Then an arm snakes around her waist. It's clearly a man's, and he jerks her body toward his. I barely catch a glimpse of him whispering something in her ear before the video cuts off.

The room is spinning. I have to sit down, leaning over to rest my forehead in my palms, elbows on my knees. *What a complete and utter moron I am.*

Kenna Davis is so far out of my league that it's laughable, and here I am, pretending to be someone else just to have an excuse to flirt with her. She was out, partying and dancing with guys, and I was at home in bed, preparing a study guide for her next test.

I'm a pathetic cliché. The unpopular nerd in love with a cheerleader—only it's college and I'm not only unpopular, but I'm also completely invisible.

And she hates me. She *hates* the real me. Learning that she thinks I've been pretending she doesn't exist makes my stomach churn.

Is it too late now? If I told her who I was and how I really felt, would it fix things?

Now that I've seen a glimpse of her lifestyle, I'm realizing there's not a chance in hell I could be with her. No then, not now, not ever.

I have to put a stop to what I've been doing. She needs my help with tutoring, so how can I shut down the flirtatious emailing without making her feel rejected?

I sit up straighter, pulling out my laptop. After bringing up my email, I drum my fingers over the keys without a clue as to what to say.

I finally draft something up and hit Send before I even reread it.

To: McKenna Mae

From: Mr. Taylor

Kenna,

It sounds like you had a fun time last night. I hope you were able to make it home safely.

Under the current circumstances of my being your tutor, I really feel responsible for how out of hand this relationship has gotten. It was completely unprofessional of me to engage you in flirtatious and borderline-salacious emails. I have no intention of dropping you as a student, but I'd like to formally apologize for my behavior.

Please understand that I think you are a wonderful girl, but I cannot continue to send messages and photographs with such unethical content.

From now on, I will not allow this relationship to be derailed from the original intent of tutoring you in biology.

I have attached a new study guide for your upcoming quiz. Let me know if you need clarification.

Sincerely,

Mr. Taylor

"If everyone is cool with missing classes Friday, we'll leave Thursday night and come back Sunday afternoon."

Harley and Adam called a wedding-party meeting in our apartment. Adam is sitting in a kitchen, taking the lead with relaying the plans, while Harley stands behind him, massaging his shoulders. I don't know if I'm the only one slightly uncomfortable with their constant need to touch each other, but I feel like I can't look directly at them without interrupting something.

Kenna and Dan are sitting closer than necessary on the sofa while Silas and I stand near our bedroom door.

"I might have to take a quiz online when we get there, but I'm fine to miss," Silas says. During baseball season, he's only supposed to workout with his team.

Dan smiles at Kenna. "Don't have to twist my arm to miss class. What about you, Kens?"

I hold my breath as she smiles back at him.

"Dumb blondes like me usually struggle if we miss class." She looks directly at me for a split second before turning to Harley and Adam. "But I guess for your *wedding*, I can make an exception."

I force myself to keep breathing. *There's no way she knows. Does she know?*

Kenna hasn't replied to my email, and I've felt like shit since I sent it two days ago.

I clear my throat as all eyes in the room turn to me. "Yeah, I can miss."

Dan laughs. "You're probably the only one of us who should miss." He stands up to walk into the kitchen. "You want a Claw, Kenna?"

Silas follows Dan into the kitchen, and my eyes naturally trail back to Kenna. She's shooting me a death glare from the sofa. Her blonde hair is piled high on her head as she sits cross-legged. She's wearing tiny pink shorts and a white shirt that doesn't cover her stomach. I need fresh air.

"Yes, thanks," she calls back to Dan, eyes never leaving mine.

Her pink lips are pursed, and a cute little crease in her forehead gives her face an adorable, angry expression. I shift on my feet, ready to hide back in my room.

But I miss her. We haven't talked in two days, and I had no idea it would affect me like this.

She hates you, idiot.

Harley and Adam get up to join the others in the kitchen, and I hear them discussing whether they should order a pizza or cook something. Kenna and I are somewhat alone now in the living room space.

She shifts her body, bringing her knees together and stretching her feet over to where Dan was just sitting on the sofa. My eyes travel over her skin as I fantasize about what it would be like to touch her long, tan legs. I feel myself getting warm before I notice an enormous bruise on the upper part of her thigh.

I step closer, the skin on the back of my neck pricking. She looks up at me, eyes growing wider. I sit down on the edge of the sofa, my body closer than it's ever been to hers—besides the incident in my bedroom. I reach out toward her, stopping right before my fingers connect with her silky-smooth leg.

"How did this happen?"

She's motionless, except for her lips parting as she gapes at me.

"Kenna, what happened? How did you get this bruise?" I lean a little closer to inspect the injury, trying to decipher what could have caused it.

She seems to partially recover, finally glancing down at the purple part of her upper thigh. "I don't remember. I blacked out."

My senses are starting to fill with her sweet cherry-vanilla scent. *Does it ooze from her pores?*

I'm getting overwhelmed with her nearness, but my concern outweighs the social anxiety and intimidation she normally ignites in me.

"When?" I look back up into her luminous eyes.

"Uh, two nights ago. I went out for my sister's birthday."

I swallow over the lump in my throat. "Your sister who passed away? Who were you with?"

She blinks, looking down at my hand suspended in the air next to her leg. I withdraw it. She nods before speaking.

"I was with Maya and the guys from Lambda Alpha." Her knee suddenly brushes against my side.

I can't tell if it's an accident or intentional, but the contact sends shivers over my body. She feels like a live wire loose on my skin.

"The fraternity?"

She nods. I feel the increase in my heart rate as I think about the Greek letters for the fraternity on the guys around campus.

Did one of them do this to her?

Based on her emails, I know she was highly intoxicated. She said she blacked out, so how much of the night does she remember?

The thought of some lowlife taking advantage of her gives me a surge of adrenaline. *How often does she go out? How often does something like this happen?*

"It's fine. I bruise pretty easily. I probably fell." She shrugs like it's no big deal.

I'm about to offer to go with her as a bodyguard next time, but I freeze up. The video she sent me with the arm snaking around her waist and the loud music showed where I would have to go. That's her life. That's what she does.

She's not yours to want. She's not yours to protect.

I desperately need to be near her, but I'm at war within myself over wanting her and knowing she can't be mine.

She can never be mine.

I stand abruptly from the sofa. Her leg falls to the side from where it was resting against me. She peers up at me, hurt etched into her expression.

"Please be careful," is all I can think to say before I walk away to hide from her yet again.

17

Kenna

On the flight to Vegas, I finally find the will to respond to Mr. T's email. I know he's probably confused by my silence, but to say I'm hurt would be an understatement. I finally bared my feelings for him, and all he had to say was, *I stepped over the line.*

How *dare* he take the blame like that. I was clearly the one to pull him down to the level of suggestive emails, and even though he didn't resist in the slightest, it irritates me that he thinks he was the one to start our student-tutor affair.

Of course I'm upset that he wants to cut things off with me, but I get it. He's a buttoned-up nice boy, and I went and got wasted and spammed his inbox. I'm a little embarrassed, but if he can't handle the fact that I'm a bit of a hot mess, then we wouldn't have worked out anyway.

It strikes me as odd that Mr. T had asked if I made it home safely, but he never messaged me back to be sure.

Maybe he was able to see my status as active online?

Good. I hope he knows I'm ignoring him.

Dan is sitting next to me, so I tilt my body away slightly so he can't see what I'm typing.

To: Mr. Taylor
From: McKenna Mae
Mr. Taylor,
Does that mean I have to stop sending you salacious emails?
Thanks for the study guide.
—Kenna

I smile to myself after I hit Send. He might not respond since it's the weekend, but—

My inbox lights up with a new message almost instantly. I quickly open it.

To: McKenna Mae
From: Mr. Taylor
Kenna,
You have free will, so I can't stop you if you choose to do so. I just want you to understand that I won't allow myself to cross that line by continuing to respond to any content that is not strictly related to biology.
—Mr. Taylor

He won't allow himself?
Hello, line. Meet Kenna.

To: Mr. Taylor

From: McKenna Mae

Mr. T,

I have a biology question. What is the female equivalent of a morning erection? Otherwise known as

Before I can keep going, I hear a cough from the row of seats behind me. I turn around to see Levi shifting in his seat, eyes on me. His neck is flushed pink.

Is he spying on me?!

Great. Now he thinks I'm sexting a professor or something. If his opinion of me could drop any lower, it just nosedived a mile. I wish things were different between us, but it is what it is. I was being dramatic when I told Mr. T that I hated Levi, but he's definitely wounded my ego...several times. Part of me still thinks he could be gay.

I turn to Dan. "Psst. Hey."

He looks up from the textbook he was studying. "What's up?"

I lean a little closer to him. "Are y'all absolutely *positive* that Levi isn't into guys?"

He laughs. "Kenna, why do you keep asking about that? Why do you care so much?"

Oh my gosh, evasive answer much?

I shrug, frowning. "I don't care. I just feel like it's weird that he never talks to girls. Silas went on a date the other night. You date."

Dan looks ahead for a moment, pondering my words.

I continue, "Think back to growing up. Did you ever see him with a girl? Did he ever talk about having a crush on any?"

Get over it. You are so pathetic.

I have to know. I have to.

He finally responds, "I mean, now that I think about it, no. But he's got major social anxiety. You can't comprehend what a dick his dad is. He was grounded for a month one time for failing a test. He told us he did it on purpose just to see what would happen. And by grounded, I mean, he was literally locked inside of his house with no contact with the outside world. We didn't see him. So, he's never really been social. Even in our group, he's the listener. He doesn't talk to me. How would he talk to a girl he doesn't know?"

I feel a pang of guilt over my assumption that Levi doesn't like me. *Is he intimidated by females in general?*

Dan and I chat the rest of the plane ride, and I don't realize until we touch down in Las Vegas that I never sent my email to Mr. T.

I quickly bring it up, finish it off with *otherwise known as morning wood* before I hit Enter. *Let's see him stick to biology-related topics now.*

I'm attempting to retrieve my Louis Vuitton bag from the overhead compartment when it comes crashing down on me. Levi's corded forearm reaches out to catch it, saving my face from the impact. My eyes jump to his as he effortlessly lowers it down to the ground. I know how much it weighs; he shouldn't have been capable of doing that.

"Thanks," I mumble.

He nods, his chest rising steadily with his breath. We're trapped behind a line of shady passengers itching to embark on their vacation of gambling and prostitutes.

These strangely intimate moments keep finding us. We can't really move, but neither of us wants to.

In front of me, someone wearing a backpack tries to stand, causing me to lose my balance and stumble back. My body collides with whoever is behind me.

Levi. He reacts instantly, holding me upright. I slowly twist around to face him, still leaning in his direction. His hand reaches up to grip my upper arm, and his pure male scent reaches my nostrils. My palms are pressed against the hard planes of his abdominal muscles.

Oh, how I want him. I wish it weren't so palpable, but I can taste my desire for this quiet, mysterious man.

His blue eyes are glued to my lips. I'm under his spell, unable to resist the obvious opportunity we're presented with to simply *look*. Everyone else around us is irritated that the runway is crowded with aircrafts already landed and waiting to unload, but I couldn't be more content with the situation. I can't help but notice that he doesn't seem to be in any rush, either.

My body is latched on to his. His pectorals are in the vicinity of my chin, meaning my eyes are level with his jawline. Technically, there's enough room for me to take a small step back, but I don't want to. His hand slowly releases my arm, but he doesn't step away.

"You spying on me?" I murmur.

His ears turn slightly pink at my inquiry, and I can barely make out his nod of confirmation. His lips part to allow more oxygen to travel into his lungs.

"Did you like what you saw?" I don't know what spirit is possessing me, but I can't stop talking.

My head is tilted back just enough so I can see his throat bob as he swallows. His eyes dart down to my lips before shifting back up to my gaze a few beats later. I jolt as I feel his fingertips begin to trail up my forearm. The tension between us is as active as a wire from an electric pole collapsed in a thunderstorm.

I guess that's his answer.

My nipples harden against him, and I wonder if he can feel them. We're both struggling to catch our breath, and I'm desperate for him to kiss me. More than anything, I want to finally feel him on my mouth.

His fingers graze over the tender skin inside my forearm, and I'm glad female arousal isn't as obvious as a male's. I can feel his want for me right above my hip, but mine is a secret. My tongue darts out to wet my lips, and he quietly hisses at the sight.

If ever I wanted him, it's never been as strong as it is now.

What about Mr. T?

I'm waging war internally, simpering over two brainiacs who are strangely similar. One is in my life but won't talk to me. The other talks to me but won't meet me.

What a perfectly irritating conundrum.

The line of passengers finally starts to move, and I stand upright, smirking at him before turning round and walking down the aisle.

The strip in Vegas is lit up like a Christmas tree. The driver of the UberXL we're taking is jabbering away, asking us about our weekend plans. We finally arrive at the casino, but my mind is still trapped in the middle of the commercial jet with Levi pressed up against me.

The casino my parents frequent is one of the best in Nevada. We have a complimentary room and steak-dinner vouchers, thanks to my dad's numerous visits. Our bags are deposited on the sidewalk, and Harley and I walk in to check in while the boys get the luggage.

"What was that?" she asks.

"What was what?"

"Um, you and Levi on the airplane? We were right behind you."

My head turns sharply toward her. Her bright-blue eyes are twinkling at me as she smiles.

"I—he helped me with my bag." My stupid, starstruck brain was so focused on him that I nearly forgot there were other people around.

"Okay...and all the *touching* was your thank-you?"

"There was no touching!" I nearly shout, and the echo sounds around us in the lobby.

She snickers, shaking her head. My inked friend thinks I still have a crush on him because I did the entire last semester of college, but I am completely over it.

"I am totally over him. I like someone else now."

We step up to the check-in counter.

"Reservation for Davis."

"Hmm, really. Who?"

I can tell by her tone that she doesn't believe me.

"My tutor, actually. He's very sweet and definitely sexy and super smart, and he actually pays me some attention instead of acting like I blend in with the crown molding."

The front-desk woman hands us two key cards.

"Could we have two more?" I ask.

"I thought you were getting tutoring online?" Harley leans her elbows on the counter.

"I am. We haven't met in person yet, but I think once we do..." I give her a meaningful look.

The woman hands us the keys, eyeing the four strapping males who have walked in behind us.

"They're all virgins," I inform her for no apparent reason.

Her eyes widen, and Harley bursts out laughing.

"All except one," she clarifies as we walk back to our group of Southern gentlemen.

They look like they could start stripping at any moment as part of a Vegas show.

"Why do they have to wear plaid all the time?" I mumble, forcing myself to exhale. I've never been good at window shopping.

Levi's eyes are on me again, always following my movement. If he would just stop being so damn good-looking, I wouldn't have to struggle to focus on putting one foot in front of the other.

This weekend is going to suck if the things I want keep staring back at me, begging to be purchased, taken home, and enjoyed. My parents have never denied me anything, and I'm accustomed to getting things I want.

This is like the lesson in self-denial I've always needed, but it couldn't have come at a worse time.

Our group goes up the elevator to the suite with two bedrooms and a pull-out couch. We have a view of Vegas that my dad must have requested when he booked the room.

"Tell Mr. Davis we appreciate the accommodations, Kenna. Are you sure we can't pay him back?" Adam says as he observes the blinking lights below.

"The casino never charges him for the rooms. He brings hordes of businessmen here, and they spend plenty downstairs to make up for it."

My grandfather started an oil company in West Texas in the '90s, which my father bought into after he got his engineering degree. He offered to let us take his private jet here, but Adam wouldn't accept it. Public airports are not where I usually fly out of, but I would've felt guilty taking it on my own while they flew commercial.

I toss my bag on the bed Harley and I will share until after the wedding tomorrow.

"Who else is hungry? I'm starving." Harley already looks ready to go, dressed in a little black dress she must've slipped on while my back was turned. She always looks flawless.

"Can I change first? I smell like a public restroom."

She nods, leaving me alone, probably to go make out with Adam. I zip open my suitcase, pulling out the outfit I bought specifically for this occasion. It's a backless minidress with silver sparkles and a deep scoop-neck front. It does justice to my form everywhere, and if Levi is going to start ignoring me again, then I'll find someone around here who won't be capable of it. I dab on some fresh peachy-pink lipstick and spritz myself with perfume before slipping into a pair of heels to match my lips.

When I walk out to join the others, Levi looks up from his phone. His jaw effectively drops, just as I hoped.

Game on, Smallville.

18

Levi

How is that dress even attached to her body?

At any moment, it could fly off in the wind, and everyone would see her. I'm walking close behind Kenna in case I need to step in and shield her from the prying eyes of the travelers around us on the street.

She's laughing with Harley as if nothing is wrong, but I can't catch my breath.

"Whoa," Dan says from beside me.

In the corner of my eye, I glimpse a woman in a skimpy outfit, but my gaze doesn't stray far from the girl I'm walking behind.

We finally arrive at the restaurant, and miraculously, there is no wait. Before we go inside, Kenna hands me, Dan, and Silas each a card. I look down to see my face from my student ID on an official-looking driver's license. *How did she do this?*

We're ushered back to a corner booth.

I can't determine if they do it on purpose, but somehow, Dan and Silas end up on Adam's side of the horseshoe-shaped booth while Harley sits by him in the middle, leaving Kenna and me on the other side. I inadvertently brush her thigh as I squeeze in.

"Sorry."

She doesn't hear me, or she ignores me altogether. The waitress asks us what we want to drink as we settle in.

"Yes, these two are getting hitched tomorrow, so we will take six of your best wedding-themed shots and an appetizer of calamari." Kenna smiles at the woman, who nods.

"IDs?"

We all hand the woman our IDs. I'm only twenty, and Silas and Dan are both underaged too. The woman muses on six cards, and to my surprise, she hands them back before bustling off.

"Y'all are welcome." Kenna smirks.

I open the menu to have something to do with my hands. All I want to eat is a burger—at least, that's what I keep telling myself. All I really want is actually sitting next to me in a skintight dress.

"Where are we going later?" Silas leans forward to address the group. He and Dan are the most outgoing of us guys, always looking for excitement.

"I would love to take y'all to a Cirque du Soleil show." Kenna smiles at him, and I feel my jaw clenching.

I never responded to her email. I was attempting to type up a reply when she emerged from the room, practically naked.

Silas smiles back. "That sounds fun. Will these IDs get us into the casinos?"

"I'm perfectly content hanging out with my fiancée and my best friends wherever y'all want to go." Adam leans in to nuzzle Harley's neck.

"I'm perfectly content to take some shots!" Kenna shouts as the waitress returns with six shots.

After she leaves, Kenna leans in toward the center of the table. "Your IDs should get you in anywhere."

I glance around the table at my friends. Everyone is holding their shot glass, raised in the air.

"To Adam and Harley and a lifetime of PDA that makes us all slightly uncomfortable." Dan beams.

A round of chuckles passes around the table before all eyes land on me. I pick up the glass of clear liquid, lifting it slightly toward the others.

"Cheers!" Kenna tilts her glass back, and everyone else follows suit.

I have a split second to decide if I'm doing this or not.

It's Adam and Harley's wedding eve, and I truly am happy for my friend. The bitter liquor touches my tongue before burning down my throat. It's my first taste of such strong alcohol, and I try to conceal my wince. When the waitress returns with the calamari, Dan requests another round of wedding shots.

We have two more rounds, all except Adam. Kenna somehow ends up closer to me as the night goes on. I don't know if it's me or her increasing our proximity, but by the time our plates are cleared, my arm has wound itself behind her, resting on the back of the booth. Our thighs are touching, and I can smell the vanilla of her blonde hair. It's either her or the alcohol—maybe a combination of both—but my brain is swimming with desire.

I've never in my life craved *anything* like I do her in this moment. Dan tells a joke, and the table erupts in laughter. Kenna leans back, her bare skin connecting with my forearm. I'm wearing a plain blue button-down shirt with the sleeves rolled up, and her skin is surprisingly cool. Normally, I would pull away, but I somehow find the courage to lean in.

"Are you cold?" I whisper in her ear.

She turns to me, bright-green eyes lit up, even as her smile fades. She shakes her head, gaze dipping over me. This restaurant must have the AC turned off because I'm suddenly overheating.

With uncharacteristic boldness, I reach out my knuckles to trace over the skin of her shoulder blade, down and around to the middle of her back. I'm holding my breath because I can't think about this moment and breathing at the same time.

She's perfectly still, allowing me to touch her even though I have no right to. My body, aside from my hand, is incapable of moving. The indulgence I'm being permitted feels like getting high for the first time—at least, this is how I imagine it would feel. Euphoric beyond words.

"I like your skin," I say, which is the dumbest thing a man has ever uttered to a gorgeous woman, but she doesn't turn away.

Her pink lips part as her eyes dip down to my mouth. I could kiss her. I should kiss her—right here in this booth. She might not slap me away.

Even if she did, it would be worth it.

I try to remind myself that to her I'm only Levi. The conversations she's been having with Mr. T have been with someone else in her mind.

I lean forward the slightest bit, my fingers now trailing over her lower back. I can't stop touching her. Her head is turned to face me, and as I dip down toward her, raucous laughter interrupts us.

"Levi! Remember old man Gerald?" Silas's loud voice reaches my ears.

I turn to see a smile on his face as he and Dan laugh about our hometown, Bonnet Valley.

Kenna's breath brushes against my cheek as she turns to face the table.

"Yeah, I remember him. Asshole hated me."

Adam and Harley are cuddled up in the curve of the booth, but they both look at me as I speak. The alcohol swimming through my bloodstream is giving me a loose tongue. The usual pang of nerves I feel when speaking in a group is taking the night off.

"Let's go somewhere with music."

They all look at me strangely, but after the waitress comes with the check, we file out of the booth. As we walk out onto the dark street, I let the others go ahead. When Kenna passes by me, I capture her hand. My fingers tingle at the contact.

She doesn't object, and our steps fall in line with each other.

"You look beautiful tonight." I've never felt capable of sharing my thoughts out loud like this, and it's like the lid I've kept on tight for so many years has busted open.

Kenna jerks her hand away from me. I turn back to look at her. She's motionless in the stream of tourists. Her arms are crossed as she gapes at me.

"What?"

She cocks her head to the side. "Are you gay?"

I stare at her face for a moment, my feet glued to the sidewalk. "Why...why would you ask me that?"

Her lips purse before she scoffs. "I've had a thing for you since, like, forever. This is one of the first times you've acknowledged my existence. I thought...maybe you weren't into girls."

I stay silent, unsure of how to respond. *She thinks I'm gay?*

"I—I like girls. I mean, I like you." My mind rejects the idea of opening up to her, but something is making me spew my feelings—probably vodka.

Her eyes somehow grow wider. "Then why have you been pretending like I'm *invisible* for the past eight months?!"

I attempt a smile, but she doesn't return it, so mine fades.

"I'm...sorry I've acted that way. You're the opposite of invisible. Whenever we are in the same room, my eyes won't stop looking at you."

A few beats of silence pass by us. The tourists continue on, weaving around us.

Her lips finally turn up slowly. I smile wider at her, and she lets out a laugh. I reach my hand out. She looks at it, and I hold my breath, releasing it right as she grips my fingers tightly.

"In that case, I'm glad to learn you're not actually gay." Her electric smile could power an entire village.

We trail behind the group, and I try to mentally steady my thudding heart rate.

What comes next? She apparently doesn't hate me.

We arrive at the next venue, and everyone else in our group has already given their IDs to the bouncer. Kenna and I hand ours in before walking through the door. It's a dimly lit lounge of sorts with a band up onstage. I can't think about much of anything besides the bare skin of her exposed back and her pretty pink lips. I want to do so many things, but I don't know where to even begin. My pent-up desire is ready to skyrocket out of me.

Dan motions to a waitress, speaking low in her ear. I hope he asked for more alcohol. I'm going to need it.

Harley and Adam are swaying on the dance floor under the neon lights. Dan reaches toward Kenna, gripping her forearms before leaning in to whisper in her ear. My pulse jumps up. I'm ready to shove him back, even as I realize that thought is irrational. She lets go of my fingers, sliding away from me as he pulls her to the dance floor.

I watch them, unable to avert my eyes. He wraps his arms around her waist, daring to rest his hands on the bare skin of her lower back. His chin is in the vicinity of her shoulder.

My skin lights up, fire igniting inside my veins. *Mine.*

Someone claps me on the shoulder, and I turn to see Silas handing me the shot the waitress brought us.

"Now's the time, man. You either gotta go for it or she's gone."

I take the tiny cup from him, tilting it back to let the liquid burn down my throat. I'm bound to become an alcoholic after experiencing the freedom of what it's like to not be afraid to speak.

"I told her I like her. She still wanted to dance with him." My skin pricks with the confession.

Silas laughs—actually laughs—at me. "You're by far the dumbest smart guy I know. You've been effectively ignoring her for how long now? You give her one iota of attention, and you expect her to fall on her face in adoration?" He shakes his head, drinking his shot.

I stare at him, my eyes drifting from him to Kenna, wrapped in Dan's embrace. I reach for the tray with four shots left, all intended for my friends. I take two, downing them one right after the other.

Silas tries to intervene. "Levi, you've never—ah, shit. Good luck with that headache tomorrow."

Liquid courage, don't fail me now.

I approach the couples on the dance floor, barreling toward Dan and Kenna. I reach out to grip his shoulder, pulling him back. He turns to look at me, a spark of irritation in his gaze.

"I'm cutting in."

He blinks, staring at me for a second before slowly releasing her, a grin spreading across his face. He leans in to me. "About time."

Kenna's green eyes are shining in the lights above. I step closer, unfamiliar boldness fueling my steps. She tilts her head back, and I dip my head down to the space between her neck and jawline, where her pulse is throbbing.

"Dance with me?" My fingers are greedy, wrapping around her waist and tugging her close.

I feel her nod, her hair tickling my cheek.

My mind is a blurry, old photograph with black-and-white shapes, but she's in bold color.

19

Kenna

After what seems like forever but also only a few seconds, I push back from the cage of Levi's arms. His gaze is intense, and I'm having trouble processing these new emotions with him so close to me.

I lean close to his ear. "Let's get a drink."

He nods, letting go of my waist to pull my hand toward the nearest bar.

"I'll take another." He pulls out a credit card.

His body is swaying slightly, voice slurred. We've both had a lot of alcohol tonight, but we've reached the point of not caring about the consequences.

If he's going to keep paying attention to me, I don't want to think about the reality of how he's ignored me for the past eight months. I want him, and he finally wants me. It's pathetic, but I've drunk just enough tonight to not really care.

"Two double shots of Patrón with lime." Levi orders for us, and I can't find the will to protest.

The bartender nods as he starts to prepare the drinks. Levi stands at my back, pressed up close to me. Each point of contact he makes with my skin sends another surge of excitement through to my belly. We get our drinks, and I turn to face him.

"What are we drinking to?" I smile up at him, clinking my glass against his.

He doesn't hesitate to mention a worthy cause. "To our first kiss." He tips the shot back, taking my heart with it.

The Patrón burns down my throat, but Levi's lips are my chaser. His head dips down, lips pressing to mine. He's drinking me up, softly caressing my lips. I see stars when his strong arms pull me in. The rough calluses on his fingers scrape against the tender skin of my arched back. I can feel his desire, and I need him to be closer.

I reach my arms up around his neck, still holding my cup. He brings our bodies closer, sealing us together in all the right places. My breasts are crushed against his muscular chest.

The intimate moment grows more intense, the crowd around us fading away. I'm wrapped up in his strong arms, safe and cherished. Our tongues brush together, trying to learn what the other likes. I nip at his bottom lip, suctioning it through my teeth. I feel the vibration of his moan. His grip on me tightens, his fingers digging into my lower back. One hand trails down over my butt, and as he squeezes it in his big hand, I hitch my leg up slightly.

He leans farther down, gaining better access to me. His lips abandon mine, pressing kisses over my cheek, jawline, and down my neck.

"Kenna..." His gruff, deep voice sends shivers over my exposed neck and shoulders. He sounds completely out of control, his tone unlike anything I've ever heard pass through his lips.

"Levi," I whisper back.

The Patrón seems to infuse my bloodstream at that moment.

The craziest, most illogical thought pops into my head. *He's going to hate me again tomorrow. Once the alcohol wears off, he won't want anything to do with me.*

That's the variable here. He's a twenty-year-old virgin, drinking heavily for the first time. I'm the only single girl around he knows.

What can I do to make him not revert back to ignoring me tomorrow?

"Let's take another shot." I turn back to the bartender, signaling for a round. My hands are shaking, anxiety beginning to surge through me.

My skin tingles as I feel him tracing a circle on my shoulder.

"How does this dress not fall off?"

I laugh at his question, turning back around with our drinks. "Magic. I get to pick the toast this time."

His eyes laser in on my lips, and I can hear his thoughts.

"To this new adventure we're embarking on together." I clink his glass with mine, throwing back the shot that I know is flavored with bad decisions I might regret tomorrow, but tonight, I can't make myself care.

I want him, and I have a crazy idea for how I'm going to keep him.

I can't stop laughing. *Who knew Levi could be so funny when he's brave enough to speak?*

"No, Kenna, I'm serious. I wanted to die. You'd barely touched me. I've never been mortified like that in my entire life."

Tears are streaming down my cheeks as I try to control the laughter causing my stomach to cramp. "Okay, but of course, I was flattered. You shouldn't have been so embarrassed! I was ready to keep going."

He scoffs, shaking his head, his hand curved around my waist. We separated from the others, subconsciously needing to be by ourselves. We're swaying down the busy sidewalk, the lights and people around us a blur in the corner of my eye. I'm looking around for a film crew because this entire night feels like a movie script. He's perfect, all muscly and delicious. His glasses are so sexy. I'm about to ask if I can wear them, but I'd rather wait until we're back at the hotel room.

"I'm sorry. I'm so drunk right now. I could tell you anything. I should tell you everything." His face suddenly turns somber as he looks down at me.

"Nothing serious! I'm having so much fun. You're finally talking to me, and it's the best night of my life." I'm practically shouting, but the colorful Vegas crowd doesn't even acknowledge me.

A wide grin spreads across his face. "You're right. Tonight is the best night of my entire life."

I stop right there on the sidewalk, pushing up on my tiptoes to give him a kiss right on his lips. "You know what would make this night even better?"

"What?" His eyes are on my mouth, his hands on my body.

"If we did something crazy...something insane that no one would ever guess we did."

He laughs, leaning farther down to nuzzle my neck while his fingers start threading through my hair. "I'm listening. You smell so good."

I need more than this night with him. This isn't enough.

"Okay, first, can you tell me...how much you like me?" My brain is swimming with wedding shots. I don't even know how much of this I'll remember in the morning, but I need to hear him say it.

Levi's head lifts up just enough so that he can look into my eyes. "More than I can express." He leans down, pressing a soft kiss to my lips. "More than I even understand myself."

I blow out a sigh, tugging on his hand to keep walking. We're still wrapped up in each other, moving as one down the sidewalk.

"Do you think you're going to wake up tomorrow and want to talk to me like this again?"

He doesn't respond, and my heart sinks down into my belly.

"But why? You have nothing to be nervous about anymore. It's all out in the open now."

"You are so far out of my league, Kenna. We're not even in the same galaxy. Our worlds don't work together. I would give anything to change that. I would do anything to be with you, but..."

"No buts! We both want it to work, so why can't we make it happen? You give up some; I give up some. A compromise. I can't take you walking away from me after a magical night like this, experiencing what it's like to...be together." I start to get choked up, thanks to the increase of the alcohol percentage in my bloodstream.

He smiles, halting right beside a big fountain. He sits, pulling me into his lap. He blinks his big blue eyes slowly as his hands continue to trace over my skin. "I want to keep you forever, Kenna Davis...but would a guy like me even know where to begin with a girl like you?"

"I feel like you're already saying good-bye, and we've barely even started anything." My voice cracks as I look away from him.

The water from the fountain is misting us. I believe at any second, the clock will strike midnight, breaking this spell.

He puts a finger under my chin, gently turning my face back to his. "I'm not saying good-bye. I'm saying, let's make the most of tonight and see where we end up tomorrow."

I peer up into his eyes, his face a little blurry. I nod, holding my breath for a moment before finally releasing it and spewing out a horrible, ridiculous idea. It's the only thing I can think of that would force him to keep paying attention to me after he's back to sober Levi.

I drop my voice into a whisper, leaning into his ear because I can't look in his eyes while I say this. "We should get married."

20

Levi

"We should get married."

Did Kenna Davis just propose to me?

She must be joking. I know people do crazy, stupid things when they drink, but that seems to be quite extreme.

Her face is buried in my shoulder.

"You must be thinking I'm someone else."

She pulls back, looking down at my chest while she fiddles with my shirt collar.

I want to kiss her again. I never want to stop kissing her.

Maybe it's not that crazy.

"I'm just kidding! I only wish there was some way to make you remember me after this."

I stare at her for a moment, completely bewildered as to why she thinks *forgetting* her is even an option in my brain—with or without alcohol.

"I have a photographic memory. I couldn't forget you if I tried." I laugh, hoping to cheer her up.

She smiles, but it doesn't quite reach her eyes. "Let's go somewhere. I want another drink."

I nod, brushing her hair back from her face. "Anything for you, beautiful."

We stumble to the closest bar. The theme is clearly Elvis, and we're the youngest people there by at least thirty years. Every bartender looks the same with black wigs and dramatic sideburns. We get the house-special drinks, and I hold her close while the horrible karaoke singers take the stage, one by one. The group dominating the scene looks like an old biker gang. Men and women with leather pants, studded vests, and faded tattoos decorating their wrinkled skin are only singing songs by the King, of course.

The night only gets better as it goes, but my brain function drops lower than it's ever been. I can't stop touching Kenna, and lucky for me, she doesn't seem to mind. We escape for a while to make out in a dark corner, but I can't take much more of it without going further. I want her in every way imaginable, and I want it to take a very long time. All the time I've silently craved her is building up inside of me, and I'm about to explode.

She's sitting in my lap, laughing at the latest singer belting out the lyrics to "Can't Help Falling in Love." The moment is nothing but comical, but every time she moves, I feel it.

As the song ends, I lean in close to her ear. "Your turn."

She hops up, and I immediately regret my suggestion at her absence. She tries to pull me up with her, but I'd rather observe her from here.

"You got this, baby."

She smiles at me before bouncing up onto the stage. My chest squeezes, and I realize I can't possibly survive this night without falling completely in love with her.

"Who is this gorgeous, little missy? What's your name, sweetheart?" The MC of sorts is a short, heavyset version of

Elvis, whose costume is two sizes too small, giving us all a view of his hairy belly. Sweat pours down the side of his face from the effort he's putting forth to show the crowd a good time.

"Hello! My name is Kenna, and I want to sing…" She leans in toward MC Elvis to whisper in his ear.

He grins, nodding at her words. "Oh, that is my favorite too. Jimmy, let's hear the music to my favorite Elvis hit!"

Piano Elvis begins to play as the MC steps off the stage. Kenna was made for the spotlight. She bobs her head to the tune, swaying side to side as her sparkling silver dress reflects the light of the disco ball. The crowd isn't accustomed to such a beautiful young singer on their stage, and I can hear the whispers around me about how she should be performing every night.

She lifts the mic up, belting the words to "Hound Dog." I smile wider at the sound of her out-of-tune voice. No one around us even seems to notice. She walks across the stage, singing to each side of the room and making eye contact with individuals who sing with her. She captures and controls the spectators, each one vying for her attention.

I laugh as a bald elderly man actually stands up and asks her to marry him. She shakes her finger at him, singing directly to his face that he's simply a hound dog.

Someone beside me grips my arm, pulling me toward them. "Is that your honey?"

I feel myself nod, suddenly overcome with the fact that she might sort of be mine right now. *What about tomorrow?* I shift in my chair.

"You shouldn't let that one go, young man. She's a doll. They don't come around often."

"I won't. I won't let her go." My voice sounds strange in my ears, but I had to say it out loud.

She has to stay mine.

I will do anything *to keep her.*

My head is pounding, and I feel worse than I did the Christmas when the turkey gave my whole family food poisoning when I was eleven.

I crack open my eyes to see an unfamiliar ceiling. The fan is spinning slowly, only increasing my nausea. The room is lit by a slim beam of sunlight. I feel a foreign object wrapped around my torso, and something heavy is resting in the crease of my elbow.

I groan, rolling to the side before I freeze.

Why am I in bed with Kenna Davis?

I stare at her perfect face. Her full pink lips are parted as she sleeps soundly. Her tangled strawberry-blonde hair is splayed out around her, giving her an angelic appearance. She's the heavy thing weighing down my elbow.

My mind scrambles to find an explanation. My memory from last night is a jumble of fragmented scenes that feel like some kind of fantasy. I have no idea what was real and what was a figment of my imagination.

I'm back in my dorm room all over again, Kenna straddling my lap unexpectedly. I look down over her form to notice that her shoulders are completely bare. I can see the tops of her full breasts. She's barely covered by the white hotel sheet, but it appears that's all she has on. In a moment of pure panic, I lift the covers over me to see that I am completely naked.

How did we get into this position?

I remember almost none of the events of last night, but based on the throbbing headache and nausea I'm feeling, I must have drunk an extreme amount of alcohol.

What about the beautiful woman who's potentially naked in your bed? How did that happen?

I close my eyes, forcing my mind to recall the events of last night. I'm not used to not remembering things. I'm the one who always remembers.

There's a scene in a restaurant. I was sitting beside Kenna, and she was stunning as always. I was worried her dress would fall off. I remember touching her back and being overwhelmed with her cherry-vanilla scent.

After that, there's not much at all. It seems like I had a dream about dancing with her, and maybe she sang to me at some point.

That must have all been in my head. I drank too much. Adam and Harley probably ended up in the same bed, and I somehow stumbled in here with Kenna after she was already asleep. I hope I didn't do anything else stupid or embarrassing, although this is bad enough.

How mortifying. I have to get out before she sees me.

I open my eyes again. My body goes stiff as her green eyes stare back at me. She blinks slowly, but other than that, there is no reaction. I expected a screech of surprise, or at least a quizzical brow.

I open my mouth to explain that I don't remember anything, but the words are trapped in my throat.

"Morning," she murmurs. Her morning voice is scratchy and incredibly sexy.

My throat is constricted. I can't speak.

"How did you sleep?" She tugs on the sheet, readjusting her grip. My cheeks heat at the movement.

Naked, naked. Exposed skin.

I have to speak to her. I know I do.

"Good," I finally croak. My lower half is responding to her nearness, the rush of blood pooling between my legs.

She smiles, the tiny curve of her lips far more attractive than it should be.

"You promised you'd keep talking to me today."

She reaches a finger out to trace the side of my face. The contact is heavenly, but I have no idea what she's talking about.

"You can take a few minutes to wake up, though. Are you a morning person?" She smiles wider, leaning closer to me. Her lips suddenly meet mine as she presses a kiss to my mouth.

My body has no idea how to react. My mind is a pan of scrambled eggs. I'm completely at a loss for what to do. Her breasts are pushing into my chest, only separated by a thin white sheet. She pulls away a moment later.

"Did you have fun last night?" She bats her eyelashes, and I get the distinct feeling that I had quite a bit of fun last night.

I nod. "Did you?"

She bites into her lip, nodding.

Of all the times my memory could have failed me...why now?

Women are not my most predominant area of knowledge, and I'm unsure of how she will react if I tell her last night is a complete blur for me.

"I honestly don't remember what happened after singing Elvis. Do you?"

Singing Elvis?

I breathe out a sigh of relief at her admission, shaking my head. "I don't."

She slowly sits up, her bare back exposed to me. She's still holding the sheet to her front. I swallow, rising up beside her in bed.

"I wonder how we got back...and where everyone else is. I don't usually black out this bad." She turns to me with a smirk. "You sure do come out of your shell when you drink."

I don't have a clue what she means, and the feeling of not remembering anything but waking up in bed with her is making my skin itch.

"What did I do?" I finally ask.

I'm already drumming up an apology before she speaks. My stomach bottoms out as I realize I might have told her about being Mr. T. *Surely, that wouldn't have gone so well...*

"You kicked an old lady while she was trying to cross the street. Stole candy from a baby. Um..." She trails off with a laugh. "I really don't remember much either, but up until the fuzzy part of the night, I know we had fun. You were dancing with me. We talked about things."

I swallow. "What kinds of things?"

She narrows her eyes, stretching out her arm and leaving one hand to hold the sheet up. My eyes laser in on her torso, and I try not to make it obvious that I'm breathing heavier.

"How much do you remember?" she asks.

I rearrange myself under the covers, hoping she can't see how affected I am by her and the possibility that I lost my virginity, but don't even have the luxury of remembering it.

"I recall drinking...and dancing. You sang, I think..."

She laughs, shaking her head. "Wow, okay. What about kissing?"

I stare at her before slowly shaking my head. Then the fog clears slightly, and for a moment, I have a vague recollection of holding her close with my mouth pressed to hers.

"We made out—a lot. You were all over me."

My cheeks burn, heat crawling up my neck. She's watching me, her expression unreadable. I can't tell if she's angry or indifferent.

"I made you promise not to go back to ignoring me...so don't do that, please."

I'm still hung up on the mental image of us making out and me being "all over" Kenna, who doesn't seem put off by the idea at all.

And you don't remember it. I'm trying to shake off the anxious prick of my skin at not being able to remember what I did for the first time in my life.

As my eyes dip down again to the sheet she's clutching to her front, I notice a ring on her hand that I've never seen before. Her eyes follow my line of vision, sticking to the simple piece of jewelry with a crescent moon shape on the gold band. She holds out her hand, observing her left ring finger.

The sheet drops, and my eyes widen at the unexpected reveal of pink nipples and full, round breasts. She pulls the cover back up, smirking at me like it was no big deal.

Is she messing with me?

My pulse is pumping wildly, and I feel the urge to yank the sheet away from her and take a closer look. It's an irrational, uncivilized thought that I shouldn't be having, but it's there in my mind, nonetheless. I grip the sheets harder.

"Um, so...do you remember where this ring came from?" Kenna moves on from the *flashing of skin* moment seamlessly.

I swallow down over the lump in my throat, adjusting the bulge between my legs yet again. "No, I don't."

She looks over, almost like she doesn't believe me. Her eyes narrow on my face before turning back to look at the ring.

I drop my eyes down, needing a moment to stop staring at her beautiful, unguarded face so I can catch my breath. I suck in a lungful of oxygen before slowly expelling it. My left hand has a death grip on the hotel comforter, and I notice another strange ring, but it's on my finger. It has a sun symbol engraved into the gold band.

I lift my hand up, studying the foreign object.

Kenna gasps, and I jerk my eyes up to her face.

"What?"

She's gaping at my hand while still holding hers up. She claps it over her mouth, emerald eyes widening as she slowly brings her gaze to meet mine.

"Kenna, what is it?" I reach out to her, pausing right before our skin touches.

She lowers her hand, pursing her lips as she looks around the room. I do the same, my mind searching for an explanation to her shock.

"Um, I think we...we might have..."

I finally find the courage to touch her, my fingers indulgently brushing over her skin before I grip her arm in my hand.

"Please tell me." I'm desperate for some answers about this bizarre morning.

She struggles to get the words out. "I think we...it looks like maybe we...got married."

My stomach drops.

Married?!

21

Kenna

Levi's face says it all. He's devastated, distressed beyond belief. His eyes keep flitting from my face to the moon ring on my finger and then back to the sun-shaped one on his.

This is every little girl's dream. Marry the guy you're in love with on a drunken night in Vegas—the first time he ever really pays any attention to you—only for him to wake up and act like it's the worst day of his life.

I know it's partially the alcohol's effects, but I'm ready to be sick.

"Yeah, well, we can get it taken care of. I'm sure an annulment won't take long." My voice nearly breaks, but I manage to keep it controlled.

"Are you sure that we actually...got married?" He looks at me skeptically, blue eyes trailing greedily over my exposed back and shoulders.

I have a flashback of his eyes doing that same thing repeatedly last night, and I shiver.

"I think so."

A fuzzy recollection appears in my brain of the MC at the Elvis bar announcing that he doubled as an ordained marriage officiant and he was offering a free ceremony that night along with a round of half-priced pints.

My mother is going to fillet my flesh and feed it to the birds.

Levi looks like he wants to reach out and touch my skin, but after five long seconds of nothing but his motionless stare, I slide off the bed.

I'm still clutching the sheet to my chest. As far as my brain can recall, nothing physical happened aside from the intense make-out sessions. All I can recall is, once we got back to the hotel, we fell into bed, both needing to pass out. We definitely kissed more, but he never tried to take it further.

Did he see my scars?

The scars on my side from the car accident are jagged and ugly from the emergency surgery to save my life. I no longer have fallopian tubes or the ability to conceive children naturally. I never even got the chance to tell him that, and now he's potentially married to someone infertile against his will.

I notice something out of the corner of my eye, and as I turn, I see a document on the side table that looks official...like *marriage license* official. I pick it up to see my and Levi's signatures scribbled across the bottom. It should be a dream come true, but instead, it's my own personal hellish nightmare.

The ring on my finger feels like a lead weight. I look back over at him, his eyes studying his left hand.

I want to die. This is the worst possible outcome. Last night could have been a turning point for us, but now it's a giant roadblock.

"So...what do you want to do now?"

Say, let's worry about it later, and we should talk about how we feel about each other.

As my brain continues to clear up, I remember more of the night.

Getting married was my idea. I wanted to keep him, even after the alcohol left his system. Obviously, it was a terrible plan, but from the look on his face, you'd think someone ran over his dog.

He finally stirs, glancing up at me as he reaches toward the nightstand, grabbing his black-framed glasses and putting them on. "I guess...we should see a lawyer."

After the glasses are on, he picks up the document. As he studies it, shirtless, I study him.

His male form is flawless. He's got a dusting of dark hair across his chest, and I want more than anything to run my fingers through it. I love when guys let their hair grow, like a real man. His focused eyes with the glasses on is my ultimate kink. The shoulder and chest muscles I've seen him working on at the campus gym are begging to be touched and massaged, so I tuck my hands around my waist to keep them to myself.

He can't make me divorce him. I just won't sign. He's mine now!

If I could keep him married to me forever—my reluctant, silent husband—he might eventually grow to love me. I'm inherently lovable. No one has resisted me up until this point in my life, and the stubborn part of me wants to plant my feet and insist that we start a real relationship to see where it goes.

But he should initiate it. You've already tried.

I don't want to have to force him to be with me. I'm on the verge of tears, so I turn away from him.

The emails from Mr. T are also in the back of my mind. Even if I'm on the road to an annulment with Levi, I would feel guilty, still flirting with my tutor. I have a crush on them both, really, unable to decide between the two men who seem so similar.

And now, I'm married to the one who *doesn't* want me.

I walk into the bathroom, shutting the door behind me. I look into the mirror, trying to decide what Lia would do. My sister wouldn't be in this mess in the first place, but I know she'd help me get out of it. My grandmother's smiling face pops into my head, and I nearly trip on the sheet as I tear out of the bathroom in search of my phone. She's the person I can always talk to when life is overwhelming.

Levi is still in the bed, and he looks up from his phone as I enter.

"Kenna, I'm really sorry I—are you okay?"

I shake my head, a tear slipping down my cheek. "I don't want to talk about it." I swipe away the moisture with the back of my hand.

He leaps out of the bed, holding the comforter up to cover himself. I grab my phone from the side table, turning to walk back to the bathroom as more tears stream down my cheeks.

"Kenna." He meets me around the bottom of the bed, holding up the blanket to his front, the ridges of his stomach muscles taunting me with the fact that they'll never be mine.

His opposite hand reaches out to steady me, and I look up at his face, brows pinched in desperation.

"I—" he cuts off, staring down at me with a pained expression.

He hesitates, and I start to walk away again.

He stops me with a strong arm gripping my waist and hauls me back toward him with the brute strength I knew he possessed but had yet to be subjected to.

Holy shit...

He leans close to my ear, his deep voice low and desperate. "I want to keep talking to you today. I want to talk to you every day. I think about you...constantly. Most of my days are spent wishing I were with you, wherever that is." His breath is on my ear, lips brushing against the skin of my nape.

I was completely unprepared for the show of masculinity and uncharacteristic sharing of his true feelings. I breathe deeply, relishing his hands on me. The sheet I was clothed in has slipped down, only held to my stomach by his strong arms.

"I want to hear more. More Levi thoughts." My voice is hoarse.

He chuckles, the deep tone spreading through me, caressing my skin all the way down to my toes. His fingers tighten around me, pulling my back flush with his front. The thick comforter must have dropped because the only thing separating our bodies once again is a thin sheet, and he is all man back there.

"I want to tell you all the thoughts that go through my head, believe me. You probably aren't ready for that yet."

The fact that I can't see his face must be emboldening him to say these things to me when he's usually so silent and guarded.

"I'm ready. I want to know." I need to know now more than ever before. I'm still feeling a bit emotional about his coldness earlier.

What does he want?

"I think you are the most exotic, irresistible woman I've ever laid eyes on."

I hold my breath, basking in the glory of the internal dialogue of a man who is typically so closed off. He's gently swaying us side to side, like a dance.

"I ache to touch your skin. Every time I see you, I fantasize about it. I wanted to strangle my best friend for dating you. I watched you with him and wished I could injure him for it. Mostly because he's a better match for you. He can talk to you, flirt with you, take you places—all the things I want to do and can't. You deserve someone like him, and I detested him for it. I've never felt so irrationally jealous and angry as I did when he took you out."

"We...we were just friends, really. I wanted you. The whole time."

I reach my hand around to caress his neck, and he leans in closer to me at the contact. His lips dip down to press a kiss to my bare shoulder. My breasts are exposed to the cool air. Electric currents shoot through me, powered by the confessions being whispered in my ear.

"I desire you more than anything else I've ever wanted in my entire existence."

It's time for me to turn around and face him. I do it, and he very respectfully averts his eyes from my uncovered breasts.

"Levi." I cup his cheek, directing his face down to mine.

His blue eyes focus on my gaze, his chest rising with each intake of oxygen.

"I want you too. I've literally had a thing for you since...the first day we met. You're the one who's always ignored me. I thought you hated me, honestly." I drop my hand.

He looks away at my words, clenching his jaw. I reach back up to direct his eyes back down to mine.

"Hey. I'm not finished. You're reserved and quiet, and I realize that I'm...basically the exact opposite. But I *want* you. I think you are so damn sexy. I fantasize about you holding me close like you do that big, thick textbook you're always staring at. If you feel the same, then why aren't we doing this thing?"

I should write romantic greeting cards.

His lips part, eyes dropping down a few inches to examine my mouth. He visibly swallows, his hands now grazing over the tender skin of my back.

"I won't be able to take you to the parties you like."

The vulnerable expression he's wearing tugs on the strings of my heart, and I give him a reassuring smile.

"I'd rather stay home with you...if you promise to keep touching me and holding me like this. And talking."

He finally allows himself to see me, looking down over my body. "Can we start practicing now?"

I laugh, nodding as I stand up on my tiptoes to kiss his jawline. He lets me do it once before dipping his head down. He pauses right before our mouths meet.

"I want to remember every second I get to spend with you from now on. No more drinking so much."

I nod, ready for him to kiss me again. He does, lips greedy from the start. He's hungry, and he wants me. I'm his life source, and he needs me to survive. In this moment, it's only us and our newly discovered mutual desire. We're the only ones who can fulfill each other's fantasies.

His lips nibble at mine, not as aggressive as he was last night.

I clearly need to loosen him up. His bulky arms cage me in, but I gently push him back until he has to sit on the edge of the hotel bed. Repeating the scene from his dorm room, I crawl into his lap, straddling his hips. He inhales, hands clutching my legs right at the crease of my knees.

"I'm all yours," I tell him, feeling like he might need the reassurance.

He nods, apparently not in the mood to talk anymore.

His mouth is on mine again. I can feel him directly between my spread legs. I wonder if he's ready to take me all the way. I will definitely wait for him to initiate it, even though I'm craving that level of intimacy. His hands are clawing at my body, burning to take us further.

I'm giving him the lead, enjoying the high we're on with each stroke of his hands and swipe of his tongue. He's so big and sexy. I relish in the feel of being his little plaything.

When I reach down and grip his length, his usual composure shatters into a million pieces. I'm lifted up, spun around, and tossed back onto the bed.

I look up to see a foreign expression on his face. Pure, unbridled desire.

Aimed right at me.

22

Levi

I've found the pot at the end of the rainbow, the fountain of youth, the forbidden fruit of all desire.

Kenna Davis's thighs hold it captive, and I'm the lucky bastard who gets to quench my thirst with her.

I lift my head to see her mouth forming an O. She moans out my name, apparently in agreement with the actions of my tongue. I would feel self-conscious about what I'm doing, considering I have no clue how to please a woman this way, but her lack of coherency reassures me that I'm not *completely* failing at it.

"Levi. Levi. Levi."

Her body tenses for several long seconds, and I hold her down until she relaxes against the bed again.

I look up again to see her wide green eyes on me as she sits up, gorgeous breasts on display, begging for my attention.

I lavish her with more of it, unable to resist the urge. Her fingers grasp my hair, nails scraping along my scalp. I finally become overwhelmed by my own desire to be nearer to her. I sit up, her fingers falling from me as she pants for breath.

"I don't—"

My words are interrupted by a sharp knock on the door. We both jump, startled by the sound.

"Kenna, can I come in?" Dan's voice trails through the closed door.

Her eyes widen at me, and I reach over for the sheet we abandoned on the floor to cover her.

"We're worried about Levi. He disappeared last ni—"

The door creaks open, and Dan's voice halts. I'm still lying between her legs, my torso halfway covering hers, as my face is in line with her breasts. My bare ass is in full view of the door.

"She found me." I look up at Dan, whose jaw has dropped to the floor.

I can't say I don't love the smug feeling of my current position of power. Dan has paled, eyes seeming to doubt the sight clearly in front of him.

A few very awkward beats pass by before he recovers, bursting out laughing.

"Shit. I thought it would never happen. Silas, get in here!" He grins, twisting his body back to allow Silas to poke his head in.

Kenna shifts underneath me. I check to make sure the sheet is covering her fully, winking at her. She giggles, covering her face with her hands.

"Oh hell. I don't believe this," Silas says.

Kenna laughs out loud, attempting to wiggle away from me again, but I hold her down.

"If you two are done with your perverted stares, we'd like to continue."

"Oh, hell no. You can *continue* after you tell us how this happened," Silas says. "Last time we talked, you were worried because you—"

Oh no, no, no.

"Hadn't told her that—"

I shift on the bed, standing up so that my back faces them when I interrupt Silas. "I mean it. Get out, so we can at least get dressed."

I reach down for a pair of boxers, stepping into them as I hear the door click shut behind me. I release a sigh, turning to face her.

She's studying me with an approving gaze, still lying in bed. "That was such a *boy* thing to do."

I can't disagree, but sometimes, marking your territory needs to happen. If I could, I would do it all over again with any man who's ever even glanced in her direction. I know it's irrational. I don't care that I'm not going to be her first, but it's a basic instinct to want everyone to know she's *mine* now.

"Ugh, you're always going to make me beg to hear what you're thinking, aren't you?" She stands up from the bed, abandoning the sheet to walk into the bathroom, completely naked.

My eyes refuse to look anywhere other than her body. Her curves are flawless, just enough to drive me completely wild. Her hips sway with each step, the nip of her waist accenting her flawless Coke-bottle frame. On her side are jagged scars, the slightly darker flesh appearing to have had stitches at some point.

She leaves the bathroom door wide open as she turns on the shower. I'm still standing here in my tented underwear, unsure of my next move.

Technically, we're husband and wife. I could walk into the bathroom and shower with her. That's what I really *want* to do.

On the other hand, as Silas reminded me, I haven't told her about being her tutor. I'm praying she doesn't send me—as Mr.

T—another flirtatious email. If she did, how would I react? We're married, but we've never been on a date or even had actual sex.

You could just come clean and tell her who you are.

As soon as she's talking to me and letting me touch her? How would I even phrase it? It's been so long now that she'll no doubt be angry. If I can make her fall in love with me first, maybe she'll forgive me for the lie of omission. Maybe she'll understand why I kept it a secret.

The guilt overwhelms me, and I decide to practice the scenario in my mind.

Hey, you know how you've had this tutor for months now, helping you with biology? Well, it's been me this whole time. So, when you told me—Mr. T—you hated Levi, that really sucked...

Who says I have to tell her soon? I could save it until we've been together so long that she'll think it's funny...or romantic even. My stomach cramps with uncertainty. I should've confessed it in the very beginning when I figured out who she was.

You mean, back when you didn't have the balls to even talk to her?

I slowly get dressed, the fear of her sending Mr. T a suggestive message causing my skin to go clammy. Surely not. Surely, she wouldn't do it.

I send back a very businesslike reply to her flirtatious question about morning wood for females.

To: McKenna Mae
From: Mr. Taylor
Kenna,

I'm not exactly sure if, biologically, there is a female equivalent to morning wood or if there is simply the fact that women might wake up in a state of arousal due to a dream or other various factors. Science truly knows very little about this subject.

—Mr. T

I hit Send, unsure of what I want her response to be, but praying she somehow chooses me, the real Levi. It's a complicated desire because I am both Mr. T and Levi, but I don't know what they both might mean to Kenna.

She's with me now, and she wants to be. For the first time since I met her almost a year ago, she's talking to me and willingly allowing me to put my hands on her body. If I screw it up too early, she might not give me a real chance.

It turns out, being with Kenna is like living on the greener side of life. Not only is she stunning one hundred percent of the time, but she's also sweet and funny, and when her attention is focused on me, I nearly lose my mind.

We spend the day acting like typical tourists around Vegas. The High Roller gives us the ultimate view of the city. My favorite activity is The Mirage's Volcano. When I was seven, I went through a serious obsession with volcanoes.

Dan and Silas are itching to know how Kenna and I went from not speaking to each other yesterday morning to being unable to stop touching. Every time I reach for her hand or she kisses me, they either laugh out loud or shake their heads in disbelief.

Kenna and I have kept the whole marriage thing a secret. We silently agreed to omit it from our stories of the night before, focusing instead on how we ended up in the Elvis bar and Kenna's showstopping performance. She fills the group in with a brief overview, leaving out the part with make-out sessions and the marriage ceremony.

Harley and Adam don't seem as convinced. They've been studying us while sharing meaningful looks with each other. I'm sure they would push for more details if Dan and Silas weren't here. It's also their wedding day, so by default, we spend our time doing things to prepare for that.

Harley is an orphan with no family, and even though Adam loves his parents and ten siblings, he wanted their wedding to be focused completely on them. His family is adjusting to him pairing with a girl covered from top to bottom with ink, but to relieve her stress, she and Adam decided a Vegas wedding with friends would be the best choice for them.

"We're going to get ready at the hotel while you guys go to the venue early to wait for us. We can only have it for two hours total, but the ceremony shouldn't be longer than twenty minutes max," Harley instructs us as we gather in the lobby of the casino hotel.

The guys got dressed in simple jeans and white button-down shirts.

Kenna's hand is interlaced with mine. We're about to part ways, and I feel a strange sense of dread at having to be away from her.

I need to get ahold of myself. I can't be so addicted to her.

She smiles up at me. "I miss you already."

She pecks a kiss on my lips, turning away to follow Harley. I jerk her back to me, maybe a little too hard. I catch her smile in the corner of my eye as I drag her to the back wall of the lobby near a big plant. We're partially hidden from most of the room, but more importantly, we're out of the speculating eyes of my friends.

She giggles when I draw her to me, wrapping my arms around her lower back and lifting her up close to my lips, our bodies sealed together. The height difference gives me the perfect excuse to hold her like this.

"I need a better kiss than that," I murmur in her ear.

She doesn't hesitate to oblige me, her arms circling my neck. I dip my head in to kiss her. She's sweet, like vanilla, and I taste the milkshake she shared with Harley on her tongue. She's letting me set the pace, and I'm trying to keep it appropriate for the public place we're in. I nip at her lips before sucking her bottom lip into my mouth. She gasps, hands tightening their grip.

I'm getting the hang of this whole kissing thing. She's got me in another world, unable to concentrate on anything aside from her reactions and how to please her. Her lips are the perfect size, plump and soft, clearly made to be worshipped by me. Her tongue suddenly enters my mouth, and I suck on it eagerly. Her feet are already off the ground, but she wraps her legs around my waist. The closeness and the feeling in my groin bring me to another level. I moan into her mouth, hands on her butt. I dip my tongue in to join with hers. Her face is slightly higher than mine in our new position.

She's pliable, moving her mouth with mine. She pulls back slightly to nibble on my bottom lip. "You're, like, catching on to this, aren't you?" She's breathless.

I take advantage of her pause, leaning toward her to nuzzle her ear and let my thundering heart slow down. The heat between her legs is bringing me to another level, and I have to think about something—*anything*—else before I can return to the open lobby.

Kenna shifts her weight, and I reluctantly lower her down to the floor. She keeps her hips pressed into me, leaning back to look up at my face. Her lips look like they've been thoroughly kissed, all pink and swollen. I reach my thumb up to trace her mouth, memorizing her face like this. This moment is forever etched into my mind. Even if she leaves me, I'll never be able to banish her from my memory bank.

"I want an X-ray machine, so I can read your innermost thoughts when you look at me like that."

She smiles, and I lock it away into the back of my head, inside my catalog of Kenna.

"We should probably go back out there now, hubby."

"I need...a minute," I grunt out.

She snickers, taking a step back. "I guess I'm not helping the situation by grinding up on you."

I feel her absence, my gaze darkening on her face. "I wasn't complaining."

"Levi, you ready, bro?" Adam's voice is close by.

"I just need another...thirty seconds."

"We need to let the girls get ready."

Kenna reaches out to rub her hand over my arm.

"Maybe if you...stopped touching me, it wouldn't take as long." I don't want to hurt her feelings, but I can't calm down with her hands on me.

She drops it, eyes sparkling like she knows exactly what she's doing.

We stand in the little shadowed corner, eyes roaming over each other and wishing we could spend the entire day in the room. I'm ready to be with her, and I know she wants it too, if I've gotten as good at reading her expressions as I think I have.

I finally close my eyes, inhaling a deep breath before adjusting the bulge in my jeans. We turn back to make our way over to the group.

I nod at Kenna before walking out with Adam and the guys to wait at the chapel. I want to give her a goodbye kiss, but I doubt my ability to stop at one.

"It's about ten blocks. I say we walk," Adam says.

We take off in the hot Las Vegas sunshine. I'm surprised when they wait over thirty seconds before the questions start.

"So, what the hell?" Dan laughs.

"Yeah, I'm gonna need a full story time," Silas adds.

I look down at the sidewalk, unsure of how much to share. "I like her."

"Okay, um, that's not news to anyone. How did y'all go from not talking to her being all over you?" Dan says.

I can't help but feel like they think I cracked some kind of female code and can share with them the big secret of how to do it.

"I guess she...she likes me too, and she has for a while." Even as I say the words, disbelief crowds my mind, but I continue. "Y'all saw most of it. I stepped out of my comfort zone—drank my way out, really. She thought I was gay." I notice Dan shooting Adam a look. "I honestly don't remember the last part of the night."

The ring I woke up with is still on my left hand. No one has noticed it yet, but I still stick my hand in my pocket.

"She asked me if you were gay," Adam says.

I turn sharply to face him.

"Me too." Dan tries to cover his laugh up with a cough.

"So...what did y'all tell her?"

Dan shrugs. "Well, at first, I said no. Then, I started thinking. You've never really even talked about girls."

Silas cuts in, "Wow, Dan, really? Levi doesn't talk about much of anything."

"Did you think I was gay?" I look over at Dan as we approach the little chapel, and he shrugs.

Adam pipes up, "I never did."

"Well, just to set the record straight, I'm not."

Dan laughs. "Yeah, clearly not." He opens the door.

I feel irritation spring up inside my chest. My social issues and inability to be charming have always been my cross to bear, but I thought my friends were the few people who understood that about me. Dan admitting he all but told Kenna I wasn't into women lights a fire inside my veins, especially since he dated and liked her.

"You could have asked me if you weren't sure." I cross my arms while Adam talks to the clerk at the desk.

Silas claps me on the shoulder. "Does it matter now? You have her, and she's into you—big time."

I need to confide in Silas about the Mr. T thing since he's the only one who knows. We follow Adam back toward the groom's room.

"I don't know what to do about the tutoring thing." I try to keep my voice casual as we walk.

Silas clears his throat. "She doesn't know?"

I shake my head.

"Damn."

My palms start to sweat. His reaction isn't helping my anxiety.

"So, how do I tell her? When do I tell her?"

We walk through the narrow doorway. It's a small space, but it's plenty big enough for the four of us. The walls are plain white, and it holds a few chairs and a basic plastic table. A bottle of champagne and four glasses are in the center.

"Ahh, man, I don't know anything about women at all. Ask Adam."

I would, but it's his wedding day. It feels selfish to ask the groom about my own relationship problems.

I turn to Silas as Dan and Adam approach the table and start to have a brotherly moment.

"What do you mean? What about Scarlett?"

Silas's eyes widen as he stares at me. "What about her?"

I pause for a few beats, trying to analyze his strange reaction. "You and she were, like...together. Up until she moved."

He shakes his blonde head. "We were friends...sort of."

Why is he blatantly lying to me?

"Um, okay. But you had a thing for her."

I literally saw them making out behind a hay bale before she and her mom moved out of town. Also, it was always clear as day to me that he was in love with her.

He smiles, shaking his head. His eyes are a bit too wide for the smile to be real. "I think everyone had a little crush on her. She was gorgeous."

I decide to let it go, considering he doesn't want to open up and be honest. I understand the feeling.

Adam and Dan walk over to us with the champagne.

Dan is smiling. "A toast to my big brother. I don't want to get emotional or anything, but I love you, man. I'm so glad you and

Harley found each other."

Adam smiles, and we clink our glasses together.

"You will all get it one day. I'm sure of it."

23

Kenna

He is sex on a stick. A tall, muscular, dark-haired, blue-eyed Clark Kent stick.

I can't keep my eyes off of Levi as I walk down the aisle. I'm wearing Harley's choice for a bridesmaid gown. It's a sleek, short white dress with ruching on the side. It has off-the-shoulder sleeves draping around me. I protested wearing white to her wedding, but she insisted.

Levi's eyes aren't going to stray from me, and I can feel his gaze like a physical cloak around me. I stand in the appropriate place across from him and the rest of the guys. His eyes trail over my body before he finally meets my gaze.

Hi, he mouths silently.

Hi, I mouth back to him.

The minister steps out to complete the service. I look up at him, and my heart ceases to pump blood through my veins.

It's the very same one who wedded Levi and me at the Elvis bar. He's dressed as a real minister now instead of chubby Elvis, but it's definitely the same guy. I gape at him, trying not to panic.

It's okay if they find out. It's really okay. None of them will tell your mother.

The minister doesn't seem to recognize us, smiling out at the back of the chapel as Harley starts to walk down.

Levi studies the guy, confusion creasing his brow. He looks back at me, and I realize that he doesn't remember as much as I do from last night.

It's no big deal. I was just startled by the sight of him. I give Levi a reassuring smile before facing the back, where Harley is walking down.

The smile on my face grows at how gorgeous she is in her black dress. It's lace with a nude slip underneath, a slit up the leg, making it the perfect balance of elegant and sexy. I tear up as she and Adam say their vows, and he adds on that no matter where life takes them, she will always be his home.

"...my guiding north star, my consistency in a world of chaos."

I can see his expression of pure adoration from here, and a tear trails down my cheek. The minister asks for the rings, and Adam produces them from his pocket. They exchange the rings before the anticipated moment of the big kiss.

We all feel the need to look away when these two lock lips. It's no exception at their wedding, but we smile and applaud while they share their intimate kiss.

"I pronounce you Mr. and Mrs...as husband and wife."

The words ring in my ears—*familiar*. I grip my long-stemmed lilies harder.

I'm literally married...

***

I read Mr. T's email thread while in the restroom of the bar. Levi is out there, waiting for me. I hate the complicated feelings

I have for both of them even if I know my heart truly wants Levi.

Why do I still feel this strange pull for my tutor?

It's inexplicable, and I wish I could ignore it. He's helped me cope with the cold, silent rejection from Levi all this time, so I feel like dropping him like a hot potato would be cruel.

I won't do that, but I also really feel the urge to tell him about me and Levi.

My fingers tap absently on the glass of my phone screen for a few minutes before I finally type out a message.

To: Mr. Taylor

From: McKenna Mae

Mr. T,

I've definitely had dreams like that. Thank you for answering me and being honest.

I just wanted to let you know that guy I've had a thing for seems to finally want to start something with me. You are incredibly sweet, and I like you so much. But I've decided to give this relationship a shot, and I would like for you to continue tutoring me if you are willing to.

Thanks,

Kenna

I pocket my phone after I send it, my stomach cramping with unease.

What if Levi changes his mind and Mr. T was the one for me all along?

It won't do any good to dwell on it now, so I shove the uncertainty aside and walk out to join the wedding party.

Adam and Harley are smooching in the corner of the bar, and I'm ready for Levi to either pull me onto the dance floor or take me back to the hotel room. I've only had one drink, but with him, I don't need any more than that.

He's leaning back against the bar, an empty cup in his hand.

"Do you want another?" I ask him.

He shakes his head. The band is playing, and I want to dance. I reach out my hand to Levi. He looks at it for a moment, and for a split second, I think he might not take it. Then he does, and we walk out to the dance floor.

The music is low and sensual, a crappy remix of a popular hit. I turn away from him, grinding my back to his front. His hands are on my hips, hugging me close. We're in an imaginary dome of privacy. It's just us and the slow thrum of the bass. The sexual tension is palpable and real. I reach my arms back and around his neck, and he dips down to kiss the top of my shoulder.

We stay like this for several songs, getting to explore the feel of each other's bodies before he finally whispers in my ear, "Let's go back to the hotel."

I face him, slowly nodding. I'm ready to get out of this white dress.

He leads me out of the crowded bar. I make eye contact with Harley, and she smiles at me. I'm sure she and Adam will leave soon too, for their honeymoon suite.

We walk hand in hand the twelve blocks to the hotel. Neither of us speaks. We've moved beyond words. Actions are the only logical conclusion for where we're at.

Once we're in the elevator, I'm hoping he'll at least make out with me, but he doesn't. He plants himself on one side of the metal box, leaning back against the railing. His eyes are as dark as I've ever seen, trailing over me for the journey up five floors. I rest against the railing, returning his salacious stare with one of my own, licking my lips for good measure.

"You ready for this, baby?" My sultry voice is low and suggestive.

He doesn't respond, licking his own lips as the door opens up. His big, muscular body moves out after me, walking behind me to the door of the hotel room. I want him all over me—now.

Hold me close like that genetics textbook, baby.

He slides the key card in, and the green light ushers us inside. The door clicks behind him, the sound finalizing our decision to take this relationship to the next level.

24

Levi

I trail behind Kenna toward the room we woke up in together this morning. The testosterone I've battled my entire adult life is flaring up, ready to be satisfied by the wiles of this woman and *only* this woman.

"Dress off," I hear myself say.

She doesn't hesitate to obey, and the instincts I wasn't aware that I possessed are roaring inside of me with pleasure. In the shadows created by the light pouring in from the window, she reaches down, tugging on the hem of her white dress. She pulls it up over her head, revealing the tantalizing, curvaceous, yet slim body underneath. She's wearing a strapless bra and small, lacy pink panties that don't cover much of anything, but it's still too much for my liking.

I reach over toward her. A bold desire that I was unaware of has overcome me. She doesn't speak as I rip down her underwear, baring her to me. She waits patiently as my hands trail up the smooth skin of her waist until they reach her bra. I work for several long seconds at the hooks, but I've never undone one before.

Right before I'm ready to tear it down the center, she reaches up to unhook it herself. Her breasts spring forward, erasing the sense of frustration that was building inside me, replaced with a whole new feeling of desire.

"You're stunning," is all I can manage.

Her hands reach around to encase my neck in an embrace, tugging me closer. My breath comes in shorter bursts as I become slightly overwhelmed by her figure and her skin.

This is Kenna.

The same Kenna I've been obsessed with and secretly emailing for months now.

What if she knew? What would change if she knew it was me?

She begins to unbutton my shirt. It's slow and meticulous, but I'm just happy to be here. Her delicate fingers push the little buttons through the holes, her eyes dipping down at each one.

"You know, I kind of like that we're secretly married and no one knows but us." She smirks at me as her hands undo the last one.

I swallow over the lump in my throat, attempting to speak. "I like it too...my secret wife."

She smiles wider, biting down on her lip. "Am I your dirty little secret?"

I'm on the verge of telling her who I really am, unable to hold in the truth for any longer. *I'm Mr. T, so yes, you quite literally are my dirty little secret, considering you're my student.*

The fear of her complete rejection and mortification is the only thing holding me back. I'm about to have sex for the very first time—with my unexpected *wife*, no less. She's the girl I've been in love with for almost an entire year. I can't mess this up now.

I choose instead to shove down the guilty feelings by lifting her up under the knees and tossing her back on the bed. She laughs, her golden hair spreading around her like a halo. I've never been so thankful for my photographic memory as I am now, adding the image to my collection of Kenna moments for all of eternity. She's immortalized now, etched into my mind exactly like this.

I crawl on top of her, itching to be as near to her as I possibly can. She spreads her legs to make way for me.

"You're perfect...everywhere. Did you know that?" I lean closer, my head dipping toward her lips to press a kiss to hers.

She welcomes me eagerly. Her hand curls around my neck, tugging me down until I feel her body under mine. I'm dying to be closer. I won't survive much more of this without taking the final step of intimacy.

Her tongue grazes over my sealed lips, and I open them up to finally let her in. She's warm and wet, deliciously ready for me. She dips inside, savoring me like I'm capable of satisfying all of her cravings.

I suck on her tongue, needing her *now*. My legs are trembling with desire. Her hands graze up over my sides, reaching to scratch over the skin of my back and causing me to shudder.

"Kenna..." I sigh, my voice breaking.

She presses her softness up against me, the motion cutting through the last barrier inhibiting me from taking her. I reach down to pull my jeans and underwear off. I start to direct myself to her entrance, and she goes silent at the last moment.

"I have a condom."

My movements halt. *Of course, idiot!*

The protection aspect didn't even cross my mind. She probably thinks I'm a selfish bastard, completely unconcerned for her.

"Okay, where is it?"

She directs me to her cosmetics bag on the countertop in the bathroom, and I finally find the tiny box of little foils.

"My mom makes me carry them around...just in case."

She doesn't need to explain herself.

"I'm glad you remembered." I slide it on over myself before crawling back over her.

It's a long pause before I find the courage to continue. She caresses my shoulder, her fingers trailing up around my ear.

Before going all the way, I reach down with my hands to touch her. She hitches a breath as I make contact, and I spend the next few minutes exploring her female anatomy. I know the mechanics of it from a textbook, but the real thing is infinitely more enjoyable to study. Eventually, I find the courage to use my tongue, and she directs me with little gasps of approval. It becomes too much for me to handle, so I rise up, panting for breath.

I don't wait for her approval or for my anxiety to hinder me again. I get closer, positioning myself to push through.

It's heaven, pure ecstasy, and better than any drug I could've ever imagined taking. She's the softness I never knew existed on this planet. I would've talked to her *months* ago if I'd known this was where we would end up.

"Levi..." she moans my name, and my movements speed up. She's holding on to me, her grip slipping as sweat beads on my skin.

"You're mine now. Forever." It's possessive and irrational, but she needs to know it.

She audibly agrees as we come to a climax together. I try to support my own weight, so I don't crush her.

She's the light to my entire world now, and I won't be able to forget her now or ever. I'm terrified of this newfound realization.

I'm panting for breath. My Kenna obsession is in full swing. I collapse to the side, wrapping my arms around her. She's breathing hard, too, and I can only hope she enjoyed it just as much as I did. There's no way she's as into me as I am into her, even if we're married and we just had sex.

"Wow," she says.

Wow?

I have no idea if it's a good wow or a bad one, but I'm hoping for the former. I wait for her to elaborate, but she doesn't. Instead, she rolls toward me, wrapping an arm around my waist.

"Can you see without your glasses?"

I blink at the unexpected inquiry. Surely such a quick subject change wouldn't be possible if that experience had been enjoyable. I want to blow her mind next time.

Next time, I will.

"Up close I can."

She smiles. "Can I wear your glasses in the future?"

I simply nod, words not forming in my mouth. She seems completely serious.

She said this to Mr. T too...

"Why?" I brush my thumb over her exposed nipple, feeling the urge to lean over and taste it.

"I just...I've had this fantasy about it for a while now."

My eyes cut to hers. "Fantasy?"

She looks down between us, running her fingers through my chest hair. "You know, imagined it happening a certain way—"

"I know what a fantasy is," I cut her off.

Surely she doesn't mean...

"You've had a fantasy about me?"

She looks up at me, green eyes illuminated in the moonlight. "Of course. Lots of them. I pretend you let me wear the glasses. Then I read you a textbook, but it's all about...dirty things instead of real school stuff."

My mouth hangs open. I'm completely at a loss to hear that she's been fantasizing about me, just like I have about her.

"What? Don't you have fantasies?"

I attempt to speak, but again, I'm unable to. She's not ready to hear the salacious, inappropriate things I've envisioned involving her.

"Come on. Tell me. Maybe I'll do it." She giggles, leaning closer to me.

My hands trace over her skin, and goose bumps pebble her shoulders. I sit up to pull the blanket over us.

"I like...I like it when it feels like we're...from two different worlds." I'm not brave enough to really share the full scope of my fantasy with her.

She smiles, staring at me for another few moments. "Okay, like how?"

I have to look away from her face. I stare up at the ceiling, debating how to say it without sounding completely ridiculous or going way too far.

"I...I guess you lying here with me is like it's already happening. You could be with any guy. I can't form a sentence around strangers, but you...you're always the center of attention. You got up onto a stage and sang in front of a hundred people, but you were looking at me. So...what I'm saying is that you...you are my fantasy."

I hold my breath, not looking at her. She's quiet, and the only sound is my galloping heartbeat. Once I finally gain the courage to face her again, I'm surprised to see moisture in her eyes. She blinks, causing a tear to trail out of the corner of her eye, wetting the sheet under her face.

I reach out, curling my fingers into her blonde hair. She closes her eyes, hand covering mine tenderly.

"I thought you hated me. I don't...I don't understand."

I lick my lips, willing my pulse to slow. "You have to understand how hard it is for me to...speak to people, how much my mind rejects the idea. I want to be like you. I want to be like Dan. Even talking to you now is...stressful. Not because of you, but because of the screwed-up part of my brain telling me that every word out of my mouth is..." I swallow, needing a moment to breathe. If I keep going, I'll end up telling her why I struggle with this so much.

She laces her fingers through mine, pulling my hand to hug it against the silky skin of her chest. "It's okay if you can't explain it. I have issues too. Going out all the time isn't what I constantly want to be doing. I can't stay home and watch TV when there's so much life out there to live. It's so short, and it can vanish in an instant. But still, sometimes, I get exhausted with the sorority events and party hosting. I wish I could let myself be a hermit occasionally."

I can't envision Kenna not living it up the way she does now. I'm envious of her ability to make friends and socialize, but I have no desire to be at any of the parties she frequents.

Part of me wonders if we can really make this work long-term. Surely, two people so vastly different from each other have never succeeded at it before.

As I stare into her emerald eyes, rimmed with dark lashes, I know one thing without a doubt. The strength of this feeling is too much for me to deny.

I'll do anything and everything in my power to keep her.

Six Years Earlier

"You should snag a slice of Mrs. Haines's apple crumb cake. It's to die for. When Mr. Haines dies, I'm marrying her." Dan is inhaling the cinnamon dessert while we sit on the picnic table under the tabernacle.

Silas looks over at his plate, licking his lips. "How much was left?"

Dan responds with a shrug.

Adam nudges my arm, leaning in close to speak quietly. "Have you heard anything about Sarah?"

I slowly shake my head, glancing over my shoulder.

Silas and Adam exchange looks.

I shift in my seat, feeling my face heat. *It's my fault. I should have done something.*

Silas opens his mouth to speak, but he barely begins when a fifth person with mousy-brown hair joins our table, cutting his words short.

"Who's up for a game of kickball? Only room for three." Scarlett Cohen is smacking a piece of gum as she looks at the four of us boys. Well, she looks at the three of us, excluding Silas.

Dan begins to stand up. "I'll play, but I wanna pitch."

"No way." She pulls the ball closer. "I'm team captain."

My gaze drops down to Silas. His complexion has turned ruddy as he refuses to look up at Scarlett.

"Then I'll be the other team captain," Dan says.

She rolls her eyes. "Anyone else? Last chance."

Adam shakes his head. "Not feeling it today, Scar."

"No, thanks," I mumble.

Silas is quiet, and she only lingers another few seconds before she and Dan walk off to join the group of young teens to play the game.

"Dad told me the Cohens are moving out of state," Adam says.

Silas's head whips around from watching the circle split up into teams. "What? When?" His eyes are wide.

"I overheard him and my mom talking about it. He said Mrs. Cohen is pregnant."

We both gape at him.

"But...she's not married," Silas chokes out.

Adam slowly nods, like that's exactly why she's moving.

Silas's face pales. He falls silent, continuing to watch Scarlett and Dan bicker about the kickball teams.

Adam turns back to me. "Do you want me to ask my parents if they've heard anything about Sarah? They might tell me if they know something." He's older than us, almost sixteen.

I debate his offer for a moment before answering, "I think maybe it would be better not to. If he decides to ask my dad, it will just upset him." I choose my words carefully. "I mean, because they miss her so much."

Adam gives me a curt nod. "Well, if I overhear anything, I'll let you know."

I nod in appreciation.

I don't know how, but I know he won't. Sarah is gone.

25

Kenna

"I don't know how else to explain it. I only drink apple juice when I eat movie popcorn. It's the ultimate combo."

"Baby, that's adorable. I love learning little things about you."

I grin so hard that my cheeks hurt. "Did you just call me baby?"

Levi opens the door to the theater for me, and I barely catch the little smile on his face. "Can I not call you baby?"

"Of course you can. You're, like, my real-life husband." I reach for his hand, and he squeezes it like he never wants to let go.

"I picked a scary one," he whispers.

"Is that why there's blood on the cover? I was hoping for vampires. Why would you do that to me? You'll have to let me sleep over, or I'll be terrified."

"That's exactly why."

I smile in the dark. I basically live with him now, anyway. Adam and Harley moved into their own apartment off-campus the week after we got home from Vegas. In the three weeks since then, Silas has basically taken Adam's place in Dan's room since

I'm always snuggling with Levi in his. Okay, we do a lot of pre-snuggling activities too.

"I've never seen a horror movie," he confesses as we find our seats.

"What?! Oh my gosh, I always forget your parents are psychos. We need to make you a bucket list to start checking off all the things." I toss a piece of buttery popcorn into my mouth.

We're early to the movie, and the previews haven't started yet.

He nods, adjusting his glasses. He runs a hand through his dark waves, and I nearly need an oxygen tank.

"I want to tour the *USS Arizona* in Hawaii."

I pull out my phone, starting a new note and writing, *See a horror movie*, with a check mark beside it before adding, *Tour the USS Arizona*, to the list.

"What else? Have you ever left the country?"

He shakes his head. "I went to California for my aunt's funeral."

I gape at him. "Didn't your family take vacations in the US?"

"No, my dad didn't see vacations as a good use of money." He stretches out his long legs, looking around us as a few more people file into the theater.

Guilt folds over me, and I feel like the spoiled rich kid, thinking everyone can afford to go places.

"I'm sorry. I didn't mean to sound like—"

He cuts me off gently. "Kenna, it's okay. Where did you guys take trips to?"

He really doesn't look offended, and I relax a little into the leather seat.

"We went to a lot of places. For Saint Patrick's Day, my dad loves to watch the parade in Dublin, so we've been for that.

Almost all the fifty states and Canada. My grandmother took me to Australia, Russia, China, and a few other countries. My favorite was the city of Rome."

He reaches over for my hand, sending tiny butterflies through my fingers as he interlocks them. His eyes focus on me. "Why was it your favorite? I'd love to see the Colosseum."

I love it because it was the last trip Lia and I went on with just our grandmother, and the memories are precious to me. I don't want to dampen the mood, so I don't tell him the full story.

"It's so beautiful, and the food is immaculate. The entire city is so rich in culture and history, and I loved every second of it. The art is unreal everywhere, but all the cathedrals and everything just make you feel like you're tasting a little bit of the past."

He listens carefully. The lights in the theater dim as the screen brightens.

"Maybe we can go back someday," he whispers, leaning closer to me.

We don't talk anymore as we watch the movie. It's scary in a cheesy kind of way.

I decide halfway through that Levi's mouth is much better entertainment, and he seems to agree. I've worked myself into a hot and bothered state as the credits roll, and I can feel his mutual excitement through his jeans.

He leads me through the crowd of other moviegoers out to the parking lot. Once we get to my red Jeep, he opens the passenger door. I get in, and he walks around to the driver's side. I've never asked why he doesn't have a car, but now I know it's because I've picked up on the fact that his family is poor. It doesn't matter to me, and I hope I can express that to him without making him feel bad.

"I had more stuff planned, but—"

"Uh, absolutely not. Straight back to the apartment."

He chuckles, gripping my hand tighter. "Whatever you say, baby."

"We're all stuck here together, taking summer classes. We might as well try to enjoy ourselves while we're at it." Maya inserted herself without an invitation at our table in the cafeteria. Silas, Levi, and I were having a pleasant conversation until she plopped down next to Silas.

Dan went to his family farm at the end of the semester to work for the summer. Adam and Harley have been renovating the old house they bought a few hours north. Most of the students are on summer vacations or moved back home. Originally, I planned to live at home and see my friends, go to the beach, and maybe get a job until the fall semester began, but Levi's plans to stay here and take classes altered my summer schedule.

"What did you have in mind?" I'm trying to be polite.

Maya grins. "You're going to throw a party with me. The best party of the summer. I think we could use Lambda Alphas' house because hardly any of them are living there, and it has a pool."

Levi is silent beside me, but Silas nods. "I'll come. I could grill burgers."

Maya turns to face him with a sweet smile. "What a gentlemanly offer! That would be perfect. I'm thinking this Saturday. What should the theme be? Bikinis and burgers?" She wiggles her eyebrows.

I shrug. "Sure. I might have to get a spray tan. I'm so pale."

She looks me over. "Yeah, you should. I've been laying out because I have nothing better to do."

Levi hasn't said a word.

I look up at him. "What do you think? Are you tutoring Saturday?"

He shakes his head.

I found out he was a tutor last week. I laughed about it, considering my former crush on Mr. Taylor. I didn't want to tell him about it since it was the same time we started dating.

"Do you want to go to a *bikinis and burgers* party?"

This is at least the fifth party I've invited him to, but since we're now secretly married and publicly dating, I'm really hoping he'll finally say yes.

"If you're there, I'll go." He squeezes my hand under the table.

"I could invite some guys from the team. About half of them live close enough, or they're staying over the summer," Silas says.

Maya perks up at the mention of the OTU baseball players. "Oh, hell yes. I one hundred percent approve." She leans her elbow on the table, tilting her body toward Silas. "What position do you play?"

"Pitcher," he answers her right before taking an enormous bite of his double cheeseburger. Silas has the classic athletic build with sun-kissed dirty-blonde hair and green eyes.

"Oh, wow. You're, like, the MVP then, right?"

I roll my eyes. She's probably hit on every guy on this campus —twice. I would rescue Silas, but she's a dog with a bone when she sets her sights on someone.

Instead, I lean in closer to Levi to whisper in his ear. "Are you okay with this?"

He reaches a hand up to brush my hair back over my shoulder. "Yes. I'm fine with it."

I'm not sure if I believe him, but I don't have much of a choice.

26

Levi

My stomach feels like it's clamped on both ends and being stretched with a thousand pounds of pressure. The pool party is already filled with students in swimwear, holding blue plastic cups in their hands. I don't know a single one besides Silas, Kenna, and Maya.

Kenna bought me a pair of white swim trunks with little pink flamingos on them. She's wearing a matching bikini top with tiny denim shorts.

"I hope you know that when you signed up to marry me, you signed up for endless matching outfits." She reaches her arms up to wrap her hands around my neck, planting a kiss on my lips.

I can't help but feel a swell of pride in my chest that she's mine, and now everyone here knows it. "I'll match you whenever you want. The flamingos are cute."

She tosses her head back in a laugh. Her blonde hair is piled high on her head.

"Hey, I was wondering if you would like to tutor me for my chemistry class next semester?"

My heart stops at her request.

"I like the one I have, but then we could have more excuses to study together."

She presses her body closer to me, and I can smell her cherry-vanilla scent.

You have to tell her. It's been way too long already.

I've come up with a million excuses not to confess the truth. At first, I thought I could just not ever tell her, and it would be fine. Then I reasoned that I would have to tell her, but I would wait until school ended and she was ready to go home because if she wanted to break up, then I wouldn't be tortured by seeing her.

Basically, I'm a coward, and I'm too afraid of losing her because of my stupidity and selfishness. She's been all business with her emails to Mr. T, which I'm thankful for, but it makes me feel even worse.

"I think we should talk about it a little later. Maybe after the party?"

Her face falls a bit, her smile dimming.

"Kenna! Lemon drop shots are up!" one of the girls who came with Maya calls out to her.

She pulls away. "You want a shot?"

"Not right now." I tuck my hands in my shorts pockets.

"Okay." She walks away, her steps noticeably less peppy.

If this is how she reacts to me telling her we should talk about it later, how will she respond when I break the Mr. T news? The thought of losing Kenna—the only positive thing in my life—makes me want to vomit.

The party goes on around me. I'm socially stunted. Talking to strangers gives me crippling anxiety. My hands start to get clammy as I watch a group of guys join the girls at the makeshift bar as they take lemon drop shots. They're laughing and chatting like it's the easiest thing in the world to meet strangers and make small talk.

Kenna is always the center of the group, and today is no exception. She's glamorous when she smiles. Not a single male in attendance can take his eyes off of her flawless body. I'm hopelessly in love with her, and even though she says she feels the same...how can I make this work? This isn't my life. I'll never fit in here.

Get over yourself. Go talk to her. You're not locked in your room anymore. Silence isn't your safety place here.

Just because I've physically escaped my childhood doesn't mean I've moved on mentally. I talk to my mother to check in on her. I don't know if I'll ever be able to go into that house again, but somehow, I still feel the walls around me.

I jump as a hand clamps over my shoulder, cutting into my thoughts.

"Sorry, man." Silas chuckles.

"It's fine."

He watches the group with me for a few seconds. Kenna looks up, waving us over. Silas and I start to walk toward them.

"What's your deal?"

I shrug, and he halts his steps.

"Come on, man. You're with Kenna now. What's eating you if it's not your hopeless crush?" He folds his arms over his bare chest.

I adjust my glasses. "I just don't see it working out. Look at her." I gesture toward my drop-dead gorgeous wife, clearly eons out of my league.

He shakes his head. "You're pathetic."

"Thanks."

"I mean it. Grow a pair, damn it. She's yours now. You grew up with shit, but we all did. I bet even Kenna did."

He doesn't know the full story, but I know he's right. I turn to keep walking up to her, wrapping my arms around her from behind. I'm determined to fit into her world.

"Hey," I say to her. My heart is beating out of my chest as the group of at least ten people stare at us.

"Kens, introduce us to your man," one of the shirtless guys says.

I stretch up to my full height, knowing I'm the tallest of the group at six foot four.

Kenna makes the introductions. "This is Levi. Levi, this is Chase, John, Peter, Sam, and Preston. I went to high school with Chase and Preston."

The one who asked looks over at me before stretching out a hand. "Chase Colson."

I clench my jaw. So he's known her for a long time.

Were they always just friends?

Chase is a good-looking guy, and he hasn't stopped looking at my wife since he got here.

I shake his hand, keeping my other arm wrapped protectively around Kenna's waist. "Levi Taylor."

Kenna's body immediately stiffens. I look over at her to see her bright-green eyes narrowed at me.

"Did you just say Taylor?"

My heart plummets. *No...*

Chase keeps talking. "Oh yeah, are you related to...was it Marcy Taylor? Wasn't she a year above you, Kens? I think y'all were in cheer together."

I'm still looking down at Kenna, attempting to form a response.

She blinks at me, her brows furrowed. "I thought your last name was Wright?"

I stutter, the words escaping my lips in a jumble, "It—it was. It was before. Well, it still is."

"Then why did you just say it was Taylor?" She stares up at me, along with ten other people.

My heart is pumping faster with each breath I take.

"It's both. I—I mostly go by Taylor now." I can't explain to her right now, in front of all these people, why I don't want to share my father's last name anymore.

She pulls back from me, and I drop my arm like it's too heavy. *Not now, not here.*

"My tutor's last name is Taylor."

I look up at the people around us. Most of them are at least pretending not to listen, even if their ears are trained toward us. My skin pricks with nerves at the tension between us and the listening ears. Chase is openly observing us, a smirk on his lips. I feel an irrational urge to wipe it away with my fist.

"I know it is." I look back at Kenna as I say it, realizing that there's no way around it anymore.

She recoils from me. Her eyes are wide as she presses her hands to her side. "What the hell?" She seems oblivious to the people surrounding us, who are all clearly enjoying the show. "You're...Mr. T?"

My throat feels like it's swelling up. It's getting harder for me to breathe. Everyone is watching. Kenna isn't just angry. I can see in her eyes that she's *pissed*. My skin feels like it could catch fire.

"I wanted to tell you."

Her eyes widen. "Why didn't you?"

Chase moves closer to her, and even though my limbs are tingling, I feel completely prepared to physically remove him from the premises if he touches her. She's still *my* wife.

"I wanted to. I'm...I'm sorry."

Her jaw drops. "What do you mean, you're sorry? Sorry for what? Lying to me? Sorry for making me feel stupid for not knowing? For making me think that—"

"Kenna." Chase reaches his hand out, daring to touch her skin.

My chest flares up, and I grab his wrist. My steel grip is locked around him, removing his hand from her arm and shoving it down and away from her.

"Don't touch her." It's not a warning; it's a threat.

He stares at me, completely motionless. "Did you just fucking touch me?"

My pulse hasn't slowed since I entered this stupid party. It's nearly blowing a hole in my skin at this point. "You'll get another chance to experience it if you ever lay a finger on my wife again."

"Ha!" He throws his head back. "Your wife? Kenna, who is this psychotic loser?"

Kenna's face has turned pink. "Why would you say that? Do you think that's how you're going to fix this? Play the husband card?" She flips around, starting to walk away.

Chase smirks, following her. He lays his arm around her shoulders. I take one long step in the same direction, jerking him back by grabbing for his wrist again and swinging his body around.

"I told you not to *touch* her." I don't know whose voice that is, but it sounds strangely like mine. I have no idea if the rush of adrenaline is because we're having our first big fight, the increase of proximity to strangers, or the fact that this guy is laying his hands on my woman. Whatever it is, I feel completely out of control.

He visibly rises up, eyes wide. He presses his hands to my chest, shoving me back. I barely move, planting my feet firmly into the ground.

"Whoa, Levi." I hear Silas at my back.

I see Kenna's blurry frame turning back to face us, but my gaze is focused on the prick who touched my woman.

"I made a very simple statement, but just in case you're hard of hearing, I'll repeat it. Don't touch *my wife* again." I clench my fists by my sides.

The prick smiles like it's the best day of his life. "You're fucking with the wrong guy, Taylor, Wright, whoever the fuck you are." He lunges for me, his fist connecting with the side of my face as I jerk away a second too late from the unexpected attack.

The world tilts before righting itself a moment later. The edges of my vision blur, and I'm swinging back. I hear a crack as my fist makes contact with his jaw.

A scream tears through the air, high-pitched and female. I don't process who it came from before Chase lunges back at me, eyes blazing.

"You're going to die today, bitch."

He swings at me, but I'm ready for it now. I duck to the side, jabbing my fist out toward his face. This time, it makes contact with his nose. I feel the break under my fist immediately. Blood begins to pour down his face a few seconds later.

"Levi! What the hell?!" Kenna runs up, pushing me out of the way to stand in front of Chase.

He's wincing in pain, clutching his bloodied face.

"You really are a psycho, man."

Kenna turns to gape at me. Someone hands her a white shirt, and she faces Chase again to stop the bleeding.

"Let's take you to the ER, so they can reset the bone," she coos to him, her voice soft and comforting.

Ice cold seeps into my bloodstream.

It's over. Kenna and I are over.

Three Years Earlier

"I wanna know what happened to her. Have you even heard from her in all this time? Don't you care?" My mother's voice is shrill, and I can hear it through the closed bedroom door.

It's nearly midnight. I'm not supposed to leave my room after eight p.m., but I snuck out to get a drink of water and something to eat. I'm hungry all the time. If my father sees me, he'll start dead-bolting my door from the outside again, but my rumbling stomach won't let me sleep.

"I'm sick of you asking me that over and over like it's my fault she left. She ran away, Judy. She made a whore out of herself with a random stranger on the internet. You're the one who was too lazy to keep teaching the kids and insisted that we let them do online classes. Doesn't that make this all your fault?" My father's voice is calm, but his words still cut.

I grip the refrigerator door tightly. My quickly growing body lets me see the top of it, and I stare at the collection of teapots my mother saved for Sarah.

Her voice is quiet for a moment, and I can't make out her words. Then the sound of soft whimpering overshadows a tearful request.

"I want to find her! I want my daughter back! Wherever she is, I'm leaving tomorrow to search for her."

"She made her choice," his voice commands, growing louder. "She won't live under this roof again. Even if you do find her, she can never come back."

The crying continues, and I hear footsteps. It's too late for me to get back to my room without being seen, and my big body won't fit in any of the places I used to hide, like under the table or inside the sink cabinet.

I decide to stay still, puffing my chest out a bit in preparation for the inevitable confrontation. The bedroom door opens, and I stop inhaling and exhaling as my father appears. He's a big man, too, and I'm only seventeen. I've started working out with my friends, but I know I'm no physical match for him.

I don't know how long he'll lock me in my room for this offense, but my skin starts to tingle with the anxiety I'm already experiencing over it.

He doesn't see me. He shuts the door, walking right past the kitchen, down the hall, and into the small mudroom. He opens the exterior door, slamming it shut behind him. I continue to hold my breath until it's forced out of me. I gulp in the air I was subconsciously denying myself as I start to quietly walk back to my room.

Then I stop. *I didn't hear a car.* Meaning he didn't leave.

I turn back around, tiptoeing back into the kitchen, right up to the sink. The window above has little white curtains with cherries on them, and I tentatively brush them to the side to peer out. I see my father leaning back against the side of the house. A glowing brown stick in his hand. It's too thick to be a cigarette, so I'm guessing it must be a cigar.

He smokes?

All the times he's told me how it's horrible for you and sinful and wrong to indulge in unhealthy things like smoking flits through my mind. I watch him for another moment, standing there in the dark with his cigar. I'm about to retreat to the safety of my room when I see him raise up a glass bottle to his lips. He tips it back, gulping down the amber liquid.

Liquor?!

This surprises me more than the smoking.

My father secretly drinks and smokes.

What else is he hiding from us?

27

Kenna

I'm next in line at Crumble, the best bakery in town. They specialize in enormous *mouthwatering* cookies. The woman in front of me finishes paying, and I step up to place my order.

"I need four chocolate chip, two double dark chocolates, and one red velvet."

"If you get an even dozen, the last one is free," the teenage kid working the counter tells me as he begins to bag the cookies.

My aching heart jumps at the suggestion, and I surrender to the sugar therapy, adding in more flavors I haven't tried.

I don't even wait until I'm out the door before biting into one of the warm delicacies. It melts in my mouth immediately, and I moan like I'm alone. I've lost all ability to care about what people think.

Cookies will never lie to me. Cookies don't have secret identities. They're just sweet, perfect cookies.

I finish the first one, and I'm sticking my hand in the bag for number two when my phone starts to ring. I pull it out, answering when I see my mom's caller ID.

"Hey, Mom."

"Hey, sweetie. How is summer school? I miss you." I find myself emotional at the sound of her voice. She sounds strange, different than usual.

"It's fine. I'm thinking about coming home this weekend." I wasn't until just now, but her voice suddenly makes me homesick. I open the door to my car before climbing in. I start the engine to ward off the Texas summer heat.

"Well, that's good to hear. Your grandmother is...not doing so well."

My stomach plummets to the floor of my Jeep. The uncertainty in her voice is immediately evident to me, and I realize why she sounds that way.

"What's...what's wrong with her?"

"Well, honey, she's eighty-four. Her mind isn't what it once was. She was asking about Lia last night. I had to explain the car accident to her, and it was like she was hearing about it for the first time. She cried for...hours."

My heart lurches inside my chest. Grandma and I bonded over Lia's death. We were all three best friends, so when she passed, it felt like I was suctioned even closer to my grandmother in my sister's absence. I'm eternally trying to fill the void that Lia left.

"I...I'll drive home tonight." Tears are already forming in my eyes, and the only two people I wish I could talk to about it are either dead or losing their mind.

"Okay, baby. Do you want me to book you a flight?"

"No, I'd rather drive." As I say the words, my vision blurs, and I nearly miss the looming Stop sign.

I slam on the brakes, the rubber screeching to a halt. I'm panting for breath, the accident flashing to the forefront of my mind. Lia was driving then.

"Honey, are you sure? You sound really upset. Let me book a flight." My mother sounds desperate.

The thought of standing with a hundred strangers in a cold airport at a time like this fills me with misery.

"Mom, please don't. Maybe I can ask a friend to drive me."

A sexy smile pops into my brain. I've never seen Levi drive. I shove the image of him behind the wheel out of my head. *Asshole.*

"Okay, please do. You don't need to be behind the wheel when you're upset like this. Please, promise me you won't drive yourself." She's remembering the accident now too.

"Okay, I promise."

I take a deep breath before knocking on the apartment door. He's probably in there, sending flirtatious emails to his students. I wonder if he teaches anyone else biology the *explicit* way he taught me.

The door swings open, and I'm face-to-face with the tall, broad-shouldered man of my dreams. His black hair is disheveled, like he's been running his hand through it in frustration. His eyes widen at the sight of me, and I lift my chin as I push through the opening. He steps aside, closing the door with a confused crease in his forehead.

"Is Silas here?" I set my stuffed Louis Vuitton bag on the kitchen counter. When I turn to face him, I notice the bruise on the side of his jaw where Chase punched him. *Good.*

Although I know Chase looks much worse with a shattered nasal bone and black eye.

Levi nods. His eyes sweep over me in that way that used to send chills all over my skin, but now it only angers me. Okay, it does both.

"Well, where is he?"

"Hey, Kenna. What are you doing here?"

I didn't even hear the bedroom door open, but I turn to face Silas. "Silas! I'm here to ask you a favor." I walk up to him, needing to put some space between me and Levi, my lying asshole husband.

Silas looks at me suspiciously, eyes jumping from me to Levi. "Sure. What's up?"

I flash him my prettiest smile. "My grandmother is sick. I need to drive to West Texas to visit her. My mother is worried about me driving myself for reasons I don't want to disclose at the moment. I would like for you to drive me, and I will buy you a plane ticket back here."

He blinks at me, and I wonder if he heard it all.

"I'll pay you for your time, of course. You can be the DJ. I also have a lovely collection of audiobooks, so you can—"

He raises his hands up, cutting off my words. "Kenna, I'm sorry. I wish I could." He looks behind me at Levi before continuing, "I have an off-season practice today and work later." He places his hands in his jean pockets. "Maybe Levi can take you." He gives me a half-smile before turning back to walk into his room and closing the door.

I don't turn around. *Maybe I can call Dan. Maybe Maya would...*

"Kenna." His voice is deep, and he sounds like he's right at my back, as close as he can be without touching me. "Please let me take you to see your grandmother."

I breathe in, needing more oxygen. "I don't like you right now." My voice is shaky, and I hate it.

"I know. I won't talk if you don't want me to. I'm good at that."

I bark out a laugh, finally pivoting around to face him. "You can't—" He's *so* close to me. "You can't kiss me either."

He swallows visibly, slowly nodding. He's so tall that my eyes are level with his pectorals. "I won't."

"My aunt is a lawyer," I blurt out.

He blinks, waiting for me to continue.

"We should...get an annulment." I can't believe I just said it as soon as the thought popped into my mind.

He looks like I shot him with a bow and arrow. The wounded expression in his eyes could rival a little puppy. I almost take it back right then, but then I remember the confusion I felt when I wanted Mr. T and him and feeling shitty about it. I grit my teeth.

"Okay," is all he says. A mask of indifference drifts over his face, hiding the obvious pain he felt moments ago.

He now looks unaffected. This will make both of our lives easier. Who wants to be married at nineteen, anyway?

I'm starting to think he truly might feel neutral about the idea until I see the veins in his forearms popping out as he clenches his fists by his sides.

28

Levi

She wants an annulment. She wants to be cut off from me, our brief relationship severed before it even had a chance to become something real. My hands feel cold, my body tense.

"I didn't know you could drive." She's breaking the silence rule less than thirty minutes into the trip.

I shift my grip on the steering wheel.

"I got a license and a car last week."

It's only been a week since we broke up, but I couldn't just sit around thinking about her. I'd been planning it for a while, and not spending every second with her gave me the motivation I needed to go do it.

In the corner of my eye, I see her strawberry-blonde mass of curls turn.

"Really? What kind of car?"

I keep my eyes on the road, worried I'll be distracted if I look at her. "An old Ford Focus." It's nothing to look at, but it gets me from one place to the next.

I had no trouble with the driving test, but the thought comes to me that she might not feel safe with a newer driver behind the wheel.

"Do you...want me to take you back? I passed the test with a perfect score." I finally chance a glimpse at her, and just as I suspected, the light on her skin is addictive.

She shrugs. "If you don't drive me, I'll have to fly."

"Why is that?"

"My mom is worried."

I understand that. My mother never ceases to worry, even though the only one of us in danger is her.

"Why is she worried about you?"

Kenna lets out a sigh. "Because I was upset about my grandmother and my sister died in a car accident."

A brief memory of her talking about it with Silas flashes across my mind. My heart squeezes with concern. I should've asked her for more details about it sooner.

"How old was she?"

"Fifteen."

I turn toward her. "I'm sorry." My voice is low, and she looks into my eyes briefly before I turn back to watch the highway.

"I was sixteen, but she had a permit and was driving us to school. I don't know how it happened. I blacked out."

She seems to need to talk about it, so I let her talk.

"We were less than a year apart, so it felt like we were almost twins. She was...my best friend." She looks over at me. "I don't know why I'm telling you this."

I wish I could express my sorrow and deep desire to be her listening ear. She needs someone with all the right things to say.

"I had a sister too." I'm not sure I'm ready to talk about Sarah, but it feels like it might be the right move.

"Really? Is she...gone?"

The answer to that question is complicated. *Tell her, you pathetic, socially stunted moron.*

"I haven't seen her since I was twelve. She ran away when she was seventeen, and...I've been looking for her." I hold my breath after sharing the confession. Kenna is the first person I've told about my search.

"Oh my gosh, Levi...I'm so sorry. That's awful." Her voice sounds sincere.

The tension in my muscles dissipates slightly.

"I just wanted to say, I sort of understand how you feel, losing someone."

I feel her fingers brush against my forearm unexpectedly. The contact is everything I've been missing, and a weight seems to lift off of my chest.

"Maybe she's still out there. What's her name?"

"Sarah."

"How old would she be now?"

"Twenty-five." I think about what the private investigator told me about her maybe being in San Francisco. "I might have a lead, but I don't know for sure yet."

"If it were Lia, I can't fathom how that would feel. If you hear anything, will you tell me?"

I look over at her and see sincerity in her gaze. I can only manage a nod before facing the windshield.

"We should get some tunes going. What do you want to listen to?"

"Elvis." I know it's a long shot, but she obliges me anyway.

She starts with "Hound Dog," the one she sang karaoke to at the bar in Vegas.

Halfway through, I turn to her. "I like it better when you sing it."

"I thought you didn't remember anything?"

She's leaning back in the seat, her breasts looking round and perfect. I want her now and always.

"I remember some. Enough." A lie. I'll never have enough Kenna-flavored memories.

"Do you remember what you said to me after the vows?" There's a challenging glint in her eyes, and I know she thinks I don't.

The thing I've recently discovered about having a photographic memory is that after you get blackout drunk, you wake up and think you don't remember things, but as you dwell on it, the mind actually recalls much more than you were originally aware of. I've been suffering from flashbacks from our wedding night ever since we left Sin City.

"I said meeting you was like waking up from a nightmare I hadn't realized I was trapped in." I pause for a moment, the revealing words on the tip of my tongue. "I fought against falling for you because I knew I'd never come back from it once I gave in to loving you."

She's silent, and I wait for what feels like hours before looking at her.

She's blinking back tears. My stomach tightens. I feel powerless. I don't know how to fix it. She's the only person I've ever been this close to, the only girl I've ever cared about besides my sister and mom, but that love was nothing like this.

Talking it out is an idea I have no concept of. Emotions are something you clamp down until they become a permanent part of your insides.

I don't know what to say, so I stay silent.

Silence has always been my safety.

We arrive at their modern, enormous home right around dinnertime. We're ushered in to the smell of baked potatoes and grilled steak. My stomach rumbles, and I realize I haven't had a home-cooked meal in almost a year now.

"Well, hello there. You're just about as handsome as they come." A warm hand grips mine. "Kenna, who is *this*?" Her mother smiles, clearly the depiction of Kenna in the next twenty years. She's naturally beautiful with blonde hair and green eyes, like her daughter.

She doesn't give Kenna the chance to answer. "I am so pleased to meet you! Kenna hasn't told me anything, and we will certainly be having words about that. What's your name?"

If being homeschooled and locked away my entire life, except for church visits and farming, taught me anything, it's how to talk to adults with respect.

"Levi Taylor. I'm pleased to meet you. Kenna and I have been friends for a while, and"—I look over at her, almost stopping there—"I was her tutor for biology."

Her mother's brows shoot up in surprise, eyes widening. "Oh!" She looks over at her daughter. "I guess you did tell me. I just didn't realize he was so good-looking."

"Mom, please stop," Kenna whines. "Where is Grandma?"

"She's in her little house out back. Why don't you go say hi, and Levi can help me with the salad." It wasn't a question.

Kenna nods before heading to the back door. After it closes, I make my way to the kitchen sink to wash my hands.

"Well, you certainly were raised right," Mrs. Davis remarks.

"Yes, ma'am." I dry my hands with the dish towel, awaiting instructions.

"Call me Sherry. You can cut the tomatoes." She hands me a knife, directing me to a wood cutting board with tomatoes already on it.

I begin the task, glad to have something to do with my hands.

"Well, Levi, tell me about yourself. Are you a tutor full-time? You must be smart to teach Kenna biology. She's never gotten an A in any science class."

I feel a small swell of pride. "Yes, ma'am. I tutored about twenty students during the school year. The summer classes aren't as full, so I only have ten right now."

"Oh my! That's quite a load. Did you also graduate from OT?"

"No, ma'am. I'm a student. Tutoring online is through an affiliate company. OT does not employ me. I took several intensive courses to become certified."

Mrs. Davis has taken her place, leaning against the counter several feet from me and sipping on a long-stemmed glass of red wine. "So, you must be intelligent. How old are you?"

I look up at her. "I'm twenty."

Her face shows surprise. "Your parents must be very proud."

I simply nod. My mother is proud. I haven't spoken to my father since I left. I finish with the tomatoes, moving to the sink to rinse my hands.

"Well, we certainly are thankful Kenna was able to find such a dedicated tutor."

Our conversation is interrupted by the door opening. I turn, expecting to see Kenna but instead see a tall older man who must be her father. His eyes narrow in on me. I don't break eye contact until I see a younger boy running up behind him.

"Is Kenna home yet? I saw her red Jeep out front!" A boy with dark hair, who looks around ten years old, runs up to his mother.

"She's visiting with Grandma. Wait until they come inside."
She smiles up at her husband as the boy runs right past me into
the next room. "Honey, this is Levi, Kenna's tutor. He drove her
here." There's no fear in her eyes, and my muscles relax.

The dark-haired man turns to smile at me. "Nice to meet you,
son. My name is Joseph Davis. Glad to have you here. Thanks
for bringing our girl home safely."

He reaches out to shake my hand with a firm grip. If there's
one thing my father did teach me right, it was how to shake a
man's hand.

He seems genuine, and my throat feels a little tight. At first, I
only nod, and then I force my voice to work. "Yes, sir."

I don't know if he can sense my nerves, but he claps me on
the shoulder. "Do you want a beer?"

"I'm not twenty-one."

He looks over at his wife. "Well, you're staying the night,
aren't you?"

Kenna's mom pipes up, "Oh, yes, absolutely. I will not take no
for an answer. We have more than enough room."

I swallow over the lump in my throat. *Why are they being so
welcoming to me?*

Mr. Davis walks over to the oversize stainless steel fridge. He
extracts two beers, pops both tops, and wraps them in koozies
before handing me one. It's a blue bottle, and the label on the
side says *Michelob Ultra*. I've never had this one, but I lift it to
my lips, and I like the crisp, cool taste.

"Thank you."

"It's nice to have another beer drinker in the house. The
ladies always outnumber me with their wine."

Even though I struggle to socialize with anyone, talking to
adults is infinitely easier for me than to my peers. Always

responding politely and respectfully was deeply ingrained in me.

The back door opens, and Kenna walks in with her arm hooked with an older woman's.

"This is actually my first beer, but I like it." I've only had White Claw and the liquor we drank in Vegas. Maybe I should stick to beer.

"Kenna, honey, do you want some wine?" Mrs. Davis offers.

Kenna nods.

Her father walks up to her, engulfing her in an intimate embrace. I observe them from my place near the cutting board in the large kitchen, in awe of the intimate moment between a father and his daughter.

"I'm glad you're home, sweet pea."

"It's about damn time." Her grandmother smiles.

Everyone's eyes are a little misty. Now that I know about her sister passing, I think I understand why.

"Kens!" Her brother runs in from the hallway he disappeared into, nearly tackling her to the ground with a bear hug.

"Ha-ha. Hey, bud. I missed you so much." She grins as he seems to crush her with the force of his hug.

Our eyes meet from across the room, and her smile fades.

"Please tell me you aren't leaving again. Mom and Dad keep watching documentaries."

Their parents laugh, saying he always gets to watch his own show on his iPad, anyway. He protests that he wants someone to enjoy the cartoons with him, like Kenna always did. As I observe silently, a strange sense of peace overcomes me. Kenna's family is acting like I'm their long-lost son.

I realize this is the type of healthy family dynamic that I want, if I ever get to have one.

29

Kenna

Three Years Earlier

"I can't believe you don't want to be in a sorority. Lexi says they are the ultimate way to get connected on a college campus. You will miss out on *all the things* if you don't rush." Lia is applying a nude-pink lipstick in our bathroom mirror.

Lexi is our older cousin who will be starting college next year.

"I just don't like the cliquish mentality. I also can't fathom being forced to go to every event of the year." I lean forward, opening my eyes wider as I brush my lashes with black mascara.

She turns to me. "Okay, I get that, but think about the alternative. You basically can't make friends with sorority members if you aren't in one. All the fun people join them because they know it's the place to be. We'll be in it together. Will you at least try it for one semester? For me?" She smiles at me pleadingly, big blue eyes staring into my soul.

"Ugh, fine. I'll try it for *one* semester." I roll my eyes at her dramatics.

She claps excitedly. "I can't wait for college. I feel like it's the last enjoyable part of life before the mundane years of adulthood." She makes a frowny face into the mirror.

"That's not true. Mom and Dad are happy with their lives."

"They might be happy, but do they ever have fun?"

I tilt my head, debating her question. "I think they have fun, but not in the same way that we have fun."

In truth, Lia and I don't have fun the same way either. She wants to be at every social event ever created, and while I enjoy them, deep down, I'm a homebody.

"I guess. I'm just not ready for that part of life. There's so much more fun left to have, and I don't want to miss a single thing."

I hug her from behind, wrapping my arms around her small frame as we look into the mirror. We get mistaken for twins all the time with our almost-identical looks.

"I think college will feel like high school once we're there. We'll have fun, but the closer it gets to the end, the more we'll be ready for the next step up." I give her shoulders a squeeze, and she smiles at me in the mirror.

"You're right, sis. Where would I be without you?"

I pretend to think about it, humming my lips. "Alcohol poisoning, possibly an unplanned pregnancy."

She swats my arm, shaking her head. "Yeah, okay, but you wouldn't have a lick of fun without me!"

It's true. I probably wouldn't.

We walk out of the house. I jiggle the keys to my blue Jeep.

"Hey, can I drive? I need more practice." She reaches a hand out for the keys.

I toss them to her. "Sure."

Present Day

It's not that I don't want my parents to be welcoming to Levi, but it is slightly annoying that they seem so enraptured by him. He's charming them like a snake. Where is the shy, silent man I've known for the past ten months?

He's laughing at my father's jokes, complimenting my mother, even chatting about LEGOs with my younger brother. I've been standing on the sidelines, wondering what has possessed him to become so…outgoing and friendly.

"I'll take a look at it tomorrow if you'd like. Maybe you missed a step along the way. Sometimes another set of eyes is all you need." Levi smiles at my brother, Brooks, who grins back like he just won the Powerball.

My mom stands up with a sleepy smile on her face. "Okay, kiddo, it's late. Let's get you off to bed. Kenna, honey, can you show Levi to the guest room? The sheets are fresh." She smiles at him before turning away.

My dad stands up next, bending over to kiss me on the cheek. "Love you, sweetie. Glad you're home." He nods at Levi as he follows my mom out of the room.

My grandma didn't say much at dinner, other than a brief introduction to Levi. She was taken back to her little mother-in-law suite in the backyard after dinner. My stomach feels hollow at the realization that she's much worse than my mother let on over the phone. She recognized me, but at the same time, the spark in her eyes that I'm usually greeted with was gone.

I'm lounging on the plush white sofa while the credits roll on the Tom Cruise movie we all watched together. Levi is in the oversize chair to my left. I feel him turn to look at me, but I don't get up.

I'm beyond sad right now. I'm…melancholy. Almost like I'm too sad to really feel it. Coming home is like walking into a gray cloud. It's a confusing sensation because I love my family so much, but this house is jam-packed full of Lia memories. At OT, I've essentially become some twisted hybrid version of me and my sister. Here, I just want to curl up into a tiny little ball.

And then there's Levi. The guy I'm mad at for pretending to be someone else when I do it every day of my life.

The effort I've been exerting to maintain a coldness toward him is wearing me thin. I'm depressed about my grandmother's change and the obvious absence of Lia here. Reality settles over me like a wet blanket.

I need to feel something other than...all this.

I sit up from the sofa, making eye contact with him. He's watching me behind his glasses, steely blue eyes burning into me. I stand up, slowly turn, and begin to make my way toward the stairs.

At first, I don't hear anything, but I force myself not to glance back to see if he's following me. Once I'm halfway up the staircase, I hear a slight intake of breath from below me. I make it to the top and continue on to one of the guest rooms. I lead him through the door to the room with the comfiest bed. Everything is sleek and modern without sacrificing comfort and functionality.

"Bathroom is across the hall." I indicate the door.

He stands at the threshold, hands tucked into his jeans. He's absolutely stunning, a dream to look at. I'm about to just toss myself onto the bed and call a truce for the night. He steps fully into the room, filling it with his muscular, tall frame. One thick black wave is flopped over his forehead, just like Superman.

After taking a deep breath, I manage to put one foot in front of the other, stepping out into the safety of the hall. I exhale the sexual tension, feeling the change immediately.

What does he do to me?

He has some kind of aura that I find irresistible, and I absolutely despise my inability to put myself on defense. Even through our emails, when he was posing as my tutor, I felt it.

I walk to the end of the hall, two doors down. Right as I turn the knob, I glance back and see him going into the bathroom. He looks up at me for a brief moment before I go in and shut the door.

I can't sleep. The digital clock by my bedside seems unusually bright. I get up, cover it with a T-shirt, and lie back down. Then my night shorts seem to keep getting twisted up, so I take them off and throw them on the floor. I turn up the white noise machine by my bed, hoping to drown out my own thoughts.

I finally realize the problem is that I forgot to take off my bra. With a grunt of frustration, I sit up, unhook the back, and fling it toward the wall. Once I lie back down, I stare at the ceiling, thinking about...the guest room.

Okay, fine, the *occupant* of the guest room.

Is he sleeping? Does he dream? What does he dream about?
Not you.

Okay, I have to stop. I'll think about biology. That's always a surefire way to bore me to sleep.

But my tutor made it oh-so not boring at all. I reach for my phone on the nightstand to reread my favorite emails from him. It's a whole new experience for me now that I know who they were really from. My body feels warm as I pore over message threads from the very beginning. He was so polite from the start, but he slowly began to loosen up and flirt with me. I wonder if he knew who I was the entire time. I guess there's a chance he didn't figure it out until I told him to call me Kenna, but why didn't he come clean right away?

I'm finally drifting off to sleep, my mind floating into a world where Levi is my biology professor. He asks me to stay after class to go over my test, but I already know I failed. *Is he mad at me? Am I going to be punished?*

My heart rate starts to increase, my pulse jumping higher every few seconds.

I've floated into that odd state of dreaming where it feels like I'm still half-awake and in control of my decisions. I sigh indulgently as Professor Taylor's face grows stern, his brows pinched together.

I failed the test, and he's unhappy with me. I can do better than this, and we both know it. He adjusts his glasses as he leans over his desk. Our fingers brush against each other, but he doesn't jerk back quickly enough.

He wants me, and it's clear as day. I'm about to reach for his hand when I feel his warmth all over me. He must have come around the desk and pulled me into an embrace. I don't have time to doubt the unusual jump in the timeline, and I reach up to wrap my arms around his neck. He smells delicious and familiar, something like pine cones. Professor Taylor must be outdoorsy. Surely, I can cure him of that.

He starts to nuzzle my neck, and I can feel the stubble on his jaw, like it's as real as my own skin. Fantasy-themed dreaming is grossly underrated.

I wrap my legs around him so that I can squeeze him even closer to me. His body is hard and perfect. I know he's tall and all man, but feeling him against my soft, small, feminine frame makes me ache with want. He pulls his head back slightly, and I can feel his warm breath on my cheek.

I want to say something to him, but I'm afraid I'll wake up. It's too good of a dream to ruin *now*. Instead, I start to touch his face with my fingers in the dark. I have it all memorized, but feeling it this way is like seeing him in another way. I hardly ever get to touch him.

This dream is unbelievably real. His stubble scratches my fingertips, and I trace the shape of his lips. I will dream Levi to kiss me.

He doesn't.

I push my breasts into his chest and squeeze his lower half closer to mine. The enticement does nothing. He's still holding me, but there's no kissing.

I decide I'll have to take matters into my own hands, leaning forward slightly just as his deep voice jerks me out of my sleep.

"You seem so sad."

Holy shit.

He's right here.

My eyes shoot open, and the dim lighting allows me to barely make out the outline of his face. He's not wearing his glasses, and I didn't even notice during my creepy inspection. I cringe at my own weirdness.

"Kenna." His voice is a gruff whisper, warm on my cheek.

"Levi." I'm breathless, my body tingling with his proximity.

"What's wrong?"

I want to tell him. It might help...but at the same time, I need this moment to keep going the direction it was headed in first. My body needs it too.

"I need you to be...Professor Taylor first."

I can't make out his expression, but he doesn't seem to be breathing. A few long seconds tick by before he starts to move over me. I'm at his mercy, and it's everything I've ever wanted.

He starts to kiss me. His lips are soft and smooth, slowly moving over mine. He's bracing himself over me, pressing down just enough. I open my legs to bring him closer.

It instantly affects him. He increases the pace, his tongue finally getting involved. He's being a little less gentle, a little rougher. He wraps his hand around the base of my neck, his thumb caressing the skin of my collarbone.

The room is heating up, my skin on fire under the covers. He must feel the same way because he throws them off. I can't stand the interruption, wrapping my arm around his neck and pulling him back down to me.

We resume, but this time, he's not gentle *at all*. We're both a little aggressive, and in my head, the bed is a desk, and the bedroom is his classroom.

He stops, pulling back again.

"What?" I'm not okay with this interruption.

"If I'm Professor Taylor, who are you?"

I can't believe he just asked me that. *Is he getting into the fantasy with me?*

"Your student, of course."

That must not be who he wants me to be, because he doesn't keep going. He sits up, and for a moment, I feel a burst of fear that he might leave. I slowly come to a sitting position.

"Or...whoever you want?" *If he says some other girl's name, I swear...*

"I want you to be Mrs. Taylor."

I freeze. *He wants me to play...his wife?*

You literally are his wife.

I did say I would be whoever he wants me to be, and after I swallow over the lump in my throat, I nod. I forgot we are in the dark and he isn't wearing his glasses.

"Okay," is all I can manage.

I reach out for him, climbing into his lap. His hands move around to my backside, his lips crashing back to mine.

We don't stop again. He lets me maul him while sitting in his lap, and he kneads and caresses my legs and butt like he can't stop touching me.

He finally pushes me back against the ~~mattress~~ desk again. He pulls my top off like it offends him, followed by the boy-shorts underwear. I do the same to him, tugging down his gym shorts and removing the soft T-shirt he has on. I'm guessing by feel that it has the pi symbol on it.

We only stop to get the little foil packet from my nightstand that I'm praying isn't expired. My mother is the type to teach abstinence and supply condoms "just in case."

He takes a moment to put it on, and I wish I could see better. He slowly moves over me again, and right before he begins, I realize the pressure to feel perfect and perform has never been so far from my mind.

Deep down inside my heart, I want this man. And I know that whoever I am with him—even the real Kenna—will always be enough.

I feel a mass of emotion rise in my throat as he pushes in, and I force it back down. I can feel the love and desire he has for me as we come together as one.

Our skin is heated and slightly damp, but he whispers my name, "*Mrs. Taylor*," into my ear.

Near the end, I'm scratching my hands through his hair, and I finally find the courage to tell him how I feel.

"You make me feel like being me is...enough."

He stills, his hand finding mine in the dark to interlace our fingers. "You are more than I could've ever dreamed of."

He keeps going, and he takes me over the edge. I guess sappy, sweet words are my kink. He slows after he finishes.

He doesn't pause to hold me. Our breath mingles as he pulls away, standing up from the bed. I get up to show him the en suite bathroom, and we clean up in the dark.

I feel a pinch of nerves when we walk back into the bedroom, and I'm hoping he isn't going to return to the guest room. I find myself reaching for his hand and pulling him to the bed.

He doesn't resist. I slide under the covers, still in the nude. He follows me in. His strong arms wrap me up, his chin resting on the top of my head. My cheek is pressed to his bare chest. This skin-on-skin cuddling is almost as intimate as sex. I release a slow exhale, closing my eyes. I feel safe and protected, away from all the worries and sadness.

In Levi's arms is the first sense of peace I've felt in far too long.

30

Levi

I wake up to the blissful joy of holding Kenna in my arms. She's angelic as she sleeps, the epitome of pure, natural beauty. I brush a blonde curl out of her eyes, trying not to wake her.

I can't help but wonder how she'll respond to me this morning. She's been angry—with good reason. I couldn't resist finding her last night, unable to sleep. My mind kept swirling with images of her, and I finally went down the hall to seek her out.

Her response shocked and thrilled me. It's so much more than physical pleasure with her. I'm desperately in love with this woman. How can I ever express enough remorse for what I did with keeping my identity a secret?

Telling the truth felt like admitting to something far worse than being her tutor. It felt like I'd have to go into detail about how my father had kept me locked in a room for most of my life and banished my sister from our home. I know Kenna would be kind and understanding, but she would also have no choice but to feel pity.

Pity for the poor, lonely, abused smart boy. Pity for my social awkwardness and my inability to party like all the fraternity brothers and guys she knew in high school. I want to appear strong and independent—worthy of her love. Not some damaged victim of childhood trauma.

Her pink lips move slightly with a barely audible whisper. She must be dreaming. I brush my fingers lightly over her temple, wondering what images are passing through her brain right now. I want to consume everything about her, down to her dreams and most secret desires. My intense need to know all that encompasses her being frightens me, and I have to close my eyes and inhale a deep breath.

When I open them back up, her emerald gaze is on mine. She blinks in the morning light streaming through the blinds, wiggling her body beside me. I remember with a start that she's still unclothed. My body responds instantly, and she smiles as my erection presses up against her thigh.

"Damn, didn't your mama teach you to buy a girl breakfast first?" She bites her lip. She seems to intentionally lean into me, so her statement must have been a joke.

"I'd rather cook you something. Do you like omelets?" I wish I knew her preference.

"Don't bother. Rosie probably already has it going." She pulls away from me, and my skin cools with the absence of her warmth.

"Who?" My eyes are incapable of looking away from her as she stretches her pale arms above her head, the sheet barely containing her breasts. My mouth is dry as I drink her in. *Am I still dreaming?*

She seems to be in full color and definition, but I'm still having trouble believing the reality of her existence in this bed with me.

"My mother's chef. Her entire family was slaughtered in a civil war in Ukraine. She was my and Lia's nanny."

Her arms finally reach back down. I breathe out the lungful of air I held captive.

"Oh." I don't know if the story surprises me more or the chef/nanny situation. I look around the room we're in.

My parents had a pull-out couch in the living room that out-of-town family would sleep in on important holidays. I realized last night that Kenna's family was wealthy—judging by the size of their home—but having actual employees brings them into a whole new perspective.

She rolls out of the bed, tugging a fuzzy white blanket around herself as she gets up, so all I see is a flash of pale skin on her side before she wraps herself up.

"I'm going to shower." She walks into the bathroom, the door clicking shut behind her.

I'm uncertain of my next move. It would probably be best to go back to my room to shower and get dressed. *What if someone sees me?*

I debate my options for a moment before crawling out of the cloud-like bed. I find the clothes I shed last night in a haze of lust and pull them on before sneaking out into the hall. I'm nearly to the door of the guest room when I hear a yawn.

"Hey...Levi, what were you doing in my sister's room?" The voice of Brooks reaches me.

I freeze on the threshold before slowly pivoting to face his sleepy expression. "Hey, man. We were talking." I give him a reassuring smile.

His brown eyes narrow. "Are you in love with her?" He crosses his skinny arms, widening his stance.

I take a step closer to him, glancing in both directions to ensure we're still alone. "Can you keep a big secret for me?"

He thinks for a few seconds before nodding. I take one more step closer.

"This is a man-to-man talk, all right?"

He nods.

"I'm in love with Kenna, but I need to prove it to her."

His eyes light up, brows rising. "Oh my gosh, *yes*! I knew it!" He claps his hands excitedly, reaching for me to pull me into a tight hug.

I chuckle, something in my chest feeling weird and fuzzy. "You're smart, so I'm not surprised you knew."

Brooks and I hug for a few more seconds before he pulls back, a grin splitting his face. "I've always wanted a big brother. You're the best I could've ever wanted. Please don't leave like Lia did."

My heart thumps loudly as I shake my head. "I'll stay as long as Kenna lets me, okay? I want to stay." A tinge of guilt settles in my gut as I basically enlist her younger brother in a plan to win her back, but it seems like it would be worse to let him go with this information than to use it for my advantage and wooing.

Brooks rubs his hands together. "Kenna likes expensive stuff. You should buy her a diamond."

At first, I have my doubts about the plan, but as I look around the elaborate home she was raised in, I realize he might be right. Would a flashy wedding ring be the missing piece to our tumultuous relationship? I know my hidden identity was the main issue. Would she forgive me for that screwup if I had a ring to prove my commitment?

I'm ready to nod in agreement when I hear Kenna's door squeak open. She's in a short white sundress. Her hair is tied up high on her head, and her face is fresh and beautiful. She blinks at me and Brooks, huddled closely in the hall. Her expression is blank for a moment before she turns her eyes on her brother.

"What are we going to do today?"

"I want to go to the LEGO store." Brooks turns to me. "Will you come with us?"

I nod. "Sure. Let me shower and get dressed first." I turn and walk into the guest room, shutting the door behind me. I start to dig through my overnight bag when I see my phone light up on the nightstand where I plugged it in.

Samuel Rogers flashes on the screen and a chill runs over me. I swipe the Answer button.

"Hello?"

"Taylor? This is Rogers. I have some news."

"Go ahead." I almost want to hang up the phone and tell him not to call me again. I don't know if I can emotionally handle the news I've been dying to hear. I grip the device harder, knowing I have to hear whatever he has to say.

"Sarah Taylor is in downtown San Francisco lockup. She was brought in last night for prostitution and possession of an illegal substance."

I'm downstairs with my bag by the door. I jiggle the keys in my left hand while I listen to Kenna and Brooks laughing with a woman's voice I don't recognize, probably Rosie.

I walk slowly into the room. Kenna's smile drops when she sees me with my bag in my hand.

"I—I have to go."

Brooks is looking now too. "What about the LEGO store? You said you would stay if Kenna let you."

Her eyes sharpen in on her brother before cutting back to me.

"What did he say?" She's still staring at me as she addresses Brooks.

I start to try to explain, but he cuts me off.

"He said he loves you, but you don't believe him."

My face drains of color. He has no idea that he just dropped a bomb in the middle of our tense relationship. He doesn't know we're married and that she wants an annulment.

I find the courage to look up at Kenna's face. Her eyes are wide, cheeks pink. Her lips have parted slightly, and her chest rises and falls steadily with her breath.

"Why are you leaving?"

I can barely hear her, so I take a step closer.

"I found out that my sister...needs my help—immediately. I have an Uber coming to take me to the airport." I hold out her keys to her. She doesn't take them, so I set them down on the counter.

I feel like it's a cop-out to not address what Brooks just revealed, but I don't know what to say other than, *he's right. I'm in love with you.*

She sets her coffee mug on the countertop. "Can you wait five minutes while I pack a bag?"

I stare at her. My feet shuffle over the wood flooring. "Pack for what?"

My phone dings, and I look to see that the driver is seven minutes out.

"I'll come with you."

I don't have a response. I stare at her, and the world seems to stop spinning.

"Think about it while I throw some clothes in a bag." She runs upstairs, leaving me alone with Brooks and Rosie.

Kenna doesn't even know the situation. I just found out that my long-lost sister is in jail in California—which is a far cry from anything Kenna has ever had to deal with, I'm sure.

Do I want to introduce her to the messy, unkept part of my life?

I check my phone, wondering if I should buy another red-eye plane ticket.

Brooks hops off of the countertop, trotting over to me. "You gonna come back to go to the LEGO store?"

I nod. "Yes. I'll come back, and we can go, I promise."

He smiles, closing in on me for another hug. I pat his back, wishing I could have experienced having a loving family with siblings. He pulls back, telling me about his friend Pierre, who he does Zoom chats with to discuss LEGOs. I try to listen, but my mind is preoccupied with Sarah and whatever mess she's wrapped up in.

Kenna's steps come pounding down the staircase. "I'm here! Let's go."

The phone dings at the same time, telling me our ride is here.

"See you soon, bro." I high-five Brooks.

Kenna is still in her white sundress with the side cutouts. She put on nude platforms, and she's clutching her leather bag. I take it from her as we exit the house.

"Bye, Rosie! Bye, Bubba." She hugs her brother. "I'll come back soon, I promise."

Rosie waves and tells us to be safe. Brooks is noticeably upset, his eyes rimmed red.

"Love you, sissy." He lets go finally, backing up into the kitchen as we walk out the front door.

The car is idling in the drive. I approach and open the door for Kenna.

"Levi? Airport?" The driver confirms that I'm the correct passenger.

"Yes." I slide in next to her after placing the bags in the trunk.

We ride in silence for a few minutes. I tap on my phone, entering her information to confirm the ticket purchase.

"Did you bring your ID?" I ask.

She nods. I wonder why she hasn't asked where we're going or what's wrong with my sister, but I choose not to volunteer the information. I don't know how much I can share without my voice cracking.

"Did you tell your parents you were leaving?"

"Yes, of course. They were out on a breakfast date. I called them while I was packing. My dad is going to have my car sent back to OTU."

I'm curious about how they felt about her leaving, knowing her grandmother is in poor health.

You owe her an explanation.

"Remember how I told you that I haven't seen my sister since...I was about twelve." She doesn't respond, inadvertently giving me the courage to continue. "She ran away from home... or was kicked out—I'm not sure which. I hired a private investigator to find her and...he did."

The driver pulls the car up to the departing gate. I open the door and get out, retrieving our bags from the trunk.

"What's our flight number?"

I give her the information, and we go through the short line, choosing to keep our bags with us.

Once we clear security and start walking toward the gate, Kenna speaks again. "California?"

"Yes. I just found out that's where she's been living." I don't mention the drug charges, prostitution, or the fact that she's currently behind bars.

We get to the gate right as the passengers are lining up to board.

"My dad would freak out if he knew how late we were." Kenna shakes her head.

I laugh nervously. "I'm a little panicked, to be honest. I haven't seen her in a long time."

Her head flips around from observing the planes rolling down the runway.

"Well, I'm sure she will be happy to see you've grown up and gotten so handsome." She winks at me as she hands her boarding pass to the flight attendant.

Once we walk through and board the plane, I start to get anxious twinges in my gut. I haven't seen Sarah in years. She's a completely different person now. I have some money saved up to bail her out, but if she's involved too deeply in the serious things Samuel told me about, I have no idea if I'll truly be able to help her.

I'm shifting in my seat, trying to find a comfortable position in the small space.

"Would you stop? What's wrong?" Kenna is relaxed, her head resting on the seat as she looks at me.

"I'm not sure what we'll find in San Francisco. Are you okay with that?" I look down at the dingy aircraft flooring.

I feel the warmth of her hand reaching over to wrap around my fingers. I grip hers tightly, my chest squeezing.

"Whatever we find, I'll be with you."

31

Kenna

I've never smelled anything like the police station in downtown San Francisco. It reminds me of my parents' vacation home freezer that went out and sat for three months with old food in it.

"Isn't it weird how certain smells can unlock memories you thought you'd forgotten?" I whisper to Levi as we wait to speak to the woman at the front desk.

His lips curve up slightly. He reaches for my hand. I love the way he holds it, like he needs me here. I don't know how to feel about our relationship status, but all I know is, right now, I love Levi, and I want to be here for him. If it were my sister, I would need him by my side.

"Next."

We step up to the woman.

"Hello. I'm here to get my sister out. Sarah Taylor." His voice is strong and confident, but he squeezes my hand tighter.

She smacks her gum as she types on her computer. "Too late. She was released an hour ago."

We both stare at her for a moment. I glance up at Levi, whose jaw is clenched.

"Why?" he asks.

She shrugs, sipping on a can of Coke. "Overcrowding. Nonviolent offenders get out early when we need space for the dangerous ones."

"So, you think we could get her address? This is her brother, and he's really worried." I attempt my sweet and innocent smile, but the woman only frowns.

She taps her long nails on the desk. "Kids, you look young and healthy. I'm sorry your sister is mixed up in that life, but it would be best for you to go on home. Even good intentions can't help addicts." I catch a glimpse of sympathy in her dark eyes before she shouts over us, "Next!"

I tug on Levi's hand, leading him out of the station. Once we exit, I breathe a gulp of fresh air in through my mouth.

He doesn't say anything as we walk for a few minutes down the street. His legs are longer than mine, and I almost have to jog to keep up with him. A chill runs over my arms. It's the middle of summer. In Texas, we'd be sweating with a walk like this in the late afternoon, but here, it feels like an early morning in late fall.

"Levi, where are we going?"

My voice seems to bring him back from wherever his mind was, and his steps slow as he looks at me.

"I have to find her." He stops completely, letting go of my hand as he runs his fingers through his dark waves.

"Okay. Let's get a hotel—somewhere safe—and think about our next move." I look around at the filthy streets.

There's one establishment still open, but the sign is blinking with a failing lightbulb. Homeless people seem to be the only ones in the immediate area. We're clearly not from around here, considering I'm still in my white sundress and we're both glowing with health.

Levi seems to finally register our surroundings. He takes a step closer to me, wrapping his muscular arm around my waist and pulling me close.

"Let me order an Uber." He pulls out his phone. "I'm sorry I brought you here. I'll get you to a safe place."

In less than two minutes, a car pulls up to us. The driver confirms our identity before unlocking the door. He doesn't speak to us, driving through the city without looking at the GPS.

Once we start getting into a part of the city that looks better kept up, the tension in my shoulders relaxes. Levi doesn't speak until we reach the hotel. My heart is aching for him, and I don't know how to help the situation. I feel completely powerless.

"Holiday Inn was the only name I could think of. It has four stars. Is that okay?"

I nod. "This is great." I've never stayed in one, but it looks modest and clean from the outside.

The driver waits for us to grab our bags, and we walk into the hotel to get a room.

"Two rooms, please," Levi tells the pink-haired man at the front desk.

"Can we just get two beds, maybe?" I don't feel safe at all in this city, even in a locked hotel room.

I need to be close to Levi. There's an inexplicable, invisible tug on my heart to comfort him. Tiny warning bells are going off in my heart that this is a dangerous move, but I shove it out of the forefront of my mind.

"We only have two rooms available, and they both only have one bed," the clerk says. He hasn't taken his eyes off of Levi, looking him up and down with approval.

"That's fine. We just need one," I blurt out before Levi can say anything.

The man gives us our key cards, directing us to the fourth floor. Once in the elevator, Levi lets out a long sigh.

I reach for him, wrapping my fingers around his forearm. I wish I could offer him some hope, but I really don't know what to say.

How do you find someone in a city this size with only a name to go by?

He pulls out his phone, typing something into it. The elevator doors open. We find our room easily. Thankfully, it's clean even if the decor is ten years out of date. My eyes stray to the one bed I insisted was okay. I didn't plan on letting anything happen besides sleep, but as soon as the door clicks shut behind us, I'm already changing my mind.

My gutter-directed thoughts are interrupted by his phone ringing.

He answers it immediately. "Rogers?"

I go into the bathroom. I've needed to pee since we left the police station. After I come back out, he's off the phone, sitting on the bed with his head bent down. I walk up to him, sitting down and rubbing my hand over the back of his neck.

"Bad news?"

He doesn't respond, only nods his head.

"I'm sorry," I whisper, continuing to massage him.

Several minutes tick by before he sits up farther, turning to stare at me with his bright-blue eyes. They look into mine for a moment before dropping to my lips. He stares, waiting for me to give him permission. Our chests rise and fall in sync, the moment stretching on as we determine if we're going to move in the direction we both desperately want to. He takes my lack of denying him as the green light.

He leans forward, pressing a kiss to my mouth. I sink into him instantly, needing to comfort him in whatever way I possibly can.

The room is silent, aside from the brushing of our bodies against the fabric of the comforter. as I move to straddle his lap. I nibble on his bottom lip, and he sucks it inside his mouth roughly.

I'm still upset about his deception, but my ability to stay angry with him isn't possible when he's clearly in so much pain.

He needs this. He needs me.

My fingers curl into his hair as our tongues slide over each other. I pull back slightly to look at him. He reaches his hand up into my hair, grabbing it and pulling me back down to his mouth.

He controls our pace, kissing and sucking on my mouth like it's giving him life. I feel him growing hard under me. I slowly push on his chest, climbing off of him so I can kneel down between his legs. I undo the button of his jeans. He lifts up and helps me tug them down over his hips with his underwear.

He inhales sharply when I make contact with his skin. I know I'm the only girl to ever do this to him. His fingers are curled into a tight fist around the comforter, his mouth dropped open. There's something dominant about my position, even though I'm on my knees. He's at my mercy, and I've never felt so empowered.

It doesn't take me long to bring him to the end. He tries to pull away, but I keep my lips wrapped around him. I hold his gaze until he's finished.

I stand up, going into the bathroom to spit and rinse my mouth out. When I return, he's pulled his jeans up.

I sit by him, and he wraps his arms around me.

"I don't think anything else could've made this day bearable."

Laughter bubbles out of me. I tip my face up toward him. "I'm, like, starving. Can we order a pizza and watch a movie?"

He nods, leaning down to press a kiss to my forehead. "Anything you want, love."

32

Levi

One Year Earlier

My father's hand is white on the steering wheel as we drive home from church. The hum of the engine is the only sound. My eyes are on the road ahead, illuminated by the headlights in the dark.

My parents don't say a word as we pull up to the pale-blue house I've grown up in. We get out, walking inside, one by one. I'm thankful to see my mother's back retreating into the bedroom.

My dad goes to the kitchen sink, grabs a glass from the cabinet, and fills it up with tap water. He chugs it, sucking in a hiss of air when it's gone.

"I don't know who you think you were back there, but you will never speak to me that way again." The unspoken threat in his tone is as clear to me as the glass in his hand.

I plant my feet. "I'm going with them. It's not your decision."

He raises his hand high in the air, swinging it down swiftly, and the glass shatters inside the porcelain sink.

Three-year-old me would have cried.

Five-year-old me would have run away.

Eight-year-old me would have flinched.

But by age ten, I realized that silence was the safest response. No outward reaction, just like my mother has modeled. We would just give him whatever he wanted, and he'd respond by only destroying a few more things before storming out of the room.

But I'm nineteen years old now. My three best friends asked their parents tonight at the prayer meeting for their blessing to go to college at Ole Tex. I asked, too, knowing my father would have to keep up the pretense of being a reasonable, loving man by agreeing to seek God's heart on the issue.

His reaction was exactly what I expected, if only a little less dramatic.

"You are my son. I will not watch both of my children go into the world and live a life of sin and rebellion."

I'll look exactly like him in twenty-five years, and I know I'll despise every time I have to look at myself in the mirror from now until then.

"I've already applied and been accepted. If you want me to leave now, I will." I don't mention the full ride I was offered based on my perfect scores on the SAT and ACT tests. I've already been in contact with the online tutoring program I plan to work for to support myself and to find Sarah.

My father takes a step toward me, but instead of cowering, I stand up straighter.

"You're just like her, just like your bitch sister. I know she wasn't mine, but now, I'm thinking you aren't either. You're both bastards, the offspring of only God knows who. This whole town knows your mother is a whore. I've been a good man, raising you as my own son, and this is how you repay me?"

Once, when I was little, I asked my mother if he really was my and Sarah's father. I would hear him screaming at her to tell him the truth of whose kids we really were, but I could never hear her quiet response. She held me in her arms and sobbed as she explained that we were both his kids, but he would never believe it. He was convinced she slept with countless different men, even though she'd always been faithful.

"If he ever asks you who your real dad is, you just tell him it's him and you love him so much. Tell him you want to be just like him when you grow up. He'll like that."

"But I don't want to be like him when I grow up, Mama."

"Shh, I know that, and you shouldn't be anything like him. We just have to tell him that, so he doesn't hurt us."

"You don't deserve anything you have. You're a cruel, evil man. You're nothing like a man of God should be, nothing like Pastor Dean, Silas's dad, says Jesus was. You'll go to hell if you don't give up your sins, but I'm not going to stay here for the rest of my life and be the puppet you want me to be."

I can see his chest rising and falling faster and faster. His skin gets redder, eyes growing dark. My shoulders harden as I prepare for the blow. This is the first time I've stood up to him and might be the first time he hits me.

He lunges forward with his fist, but I raise my arm to block the blow. He's strong, and it hurts like hell. I grunt as I shove him back from me. His big body crashes into the kitchen counter.

"Boy, if you don't want me to kill you, you'd better cut this shit out."

He comes for me again, this time punching at my chest. He lands the punch, but I don't let myself make a sound. The satisfied smirk on his lips fades. He takes a step back, gearing up to hit me again.

All the rage and fear that has been churning inside of me since I was a child builds up and becomes impossible to hold in. I attack him, lunging forward with my fist raised high. I unleash it on him, pounding his face over and over again. Blood begins to spurt out of him before I realize that I'm stronger than I ever knew before. I finally step back, standing up on shaking legs. He doesn't move, and for a moment, I think I might have killed him.

It's shocking how little that thought affects me.

He finally moves a tiny bit, his eyes squinting open as he raises a hand to wipe the blood away from him.

"I'm leaving, and you will never see me again."

The hardest part is knowing that my mother won't come with me, even after I beg her to.

Present Day

The coffee hut Samuel Rogers wanted us to meet him at is seven blocks away. I carry Kenna's and my bag in one hand, so I can hold her hand in my other one. I don't know if she's here because she forgives me and wants to call off the annulment or for moral support. I'm hoping it's both. We had sex twice last night in the hotel room, and she let me use my mouth on her, which is becoming my new favorite thing. I want to taste her again right now, just thinking about it.

"So this guy is the private investigator?" she asks as we halt at a crosswalk.

"Yes." I lead the way over the asphalt as the light blinks for us to walk.

"And he found Sarah?"

"Yes." I don't mention that I made the money to do it by tutoring students. I don't want to bring up the topic of my deception toward Kenna or the fact that her father's generous bonus is what gave me enough money to send Samuel to San Francisco.

We arrive at the coffee shop and find a table inside. I've never met Mr. Rogers, so I'm not sure how I'll know who he is. We order coffees and a scone for Kenna. We're both content to silently observe the other patrons instead of talk. I should be taking this moment to try and win her back, but all I can dwell on is finding Sarah.

After a few minutes, a man enters the café, wearing a black baseball cap and a gray hoodie. He's nothing like what I pictured. He's in his early forties, and he looks like he takes good care of himself. He walks right up to our table and takes out a chair to sit in.

"If you want to meet her, we have to go now."

Kenna looks at me with wide eyes as we stand.

"What's the rush?" I ask. My hands grow clammy as we leave the coffee shop and follow Samuel.

"They make them leave the shelter by nine on Sundays for cleaning."

My stomach falls to the sidewalk under my feet. *Sarah is sleeping in a shelter?!*

Heat begins to travel up my neck as I think about my father's abuse. His cruelty made our home a miserable place to live. Even though I was heartbroken when she left, I never blamed her for it.

Now, my sister is at rock bottom, clearly struggling to survive in the world on her own.

"How long has she been living in the shelter?"

Samuel has led us to a parking garage. He goes in first. I let Kenna go behind him, so I can walk behind her. This city isn't safe for any woman, especially one who looks like Kenna.

"About three months, I'd say. That was when her boyfriend kicked her out."

He takes us up to a black Toyota Impala. He climbs into the driver's seat.

I open the back door, letting Kenna slide in ahead of me. I toss our bags in the trunk before following her in. She's wearing long black leggings today and a cropped white hoodie, allowing a sliver of tan stomach to peek out.

Her green eyes find mine once we're inside the car. She reaches over, interlacing our fingers. I exhale slightly, once again thankful that she's here with me through this ordeal.

We don't speak anymore as he drives us back into the slums of San Fran. It's visibly more impoverished on this side of town. I find myself wondering what causes people to become homeless and hit rock bottom.

Are a lot of them abused as children, like Sarah was? Is it drugs?

I want to help them all, but I know it's impossible. I'm here for Sarah. She's the one I need to focus on.

Every second of the drive, we pass people who need help. One woman has three kids in tow, all holding on to a rope she has tied around her waist. Walking behind her is a bent-over man pushing a grocery cart with a dog inside, along with random knickknacks that must be all he owns in this world. Right past the man with the grocery cart is a thin woman with a stroller that looks like one wheel has been replaced with a mismatched one, causing it to tilt slightly to the right side. She's skin and bones, her greasy hair knotted on top of her head.

Samuel suddenly cuts to the left side of the road, and my body crashes into Kenna. My face ends up in the crease of her collarbone and jawline. I inhale her cherry-vanilla perfume before pulling away.

He opens the door to the car, and Kenna does the same. I follow her out on her side of the car to avoid the incoming traffic on the highway. Samuel approaches the woman with the baby.

When she looks up at him, I know.

"Sarah..." I whisper.

I see Kenna's head turn toward me slightly as I walk up to my sister. Samuel is speaking to her in hushed tones. She glances my way with familiar, startled blue eyes.

Her mouth forms an O. She tilts her head back, and I realize that I'm much bigger than I was the last time I saw her.

"Sarah." My eyes fill with tears that I attempt to blink away.

Hers do the same. She's taken aback, frozen with recollection and uncertainty of how to move forward.

"Levi?" Her voice is recognizable immediately.

I step forward to engulf her in a hug. At first, she doesn't return it. She simply stands still, frail and weak in my arms.

Then, she stretches herself around me, tugging me in and accepting the hug and me along with it.

"Little brother...you're not so little anymore."

"You're tiny." I'm sure it's not the right thing to say, but she laughs anyway.

"What are you doing here?" She pulls back from me, wiping the tears from her hollow cheek with a tattooed hand.

She doesn't look well, not at all like the girl I grew up with.

"I've been looking for you." I watch her eyes shift from me to Samuel, Kenna, and back to me.

"Who are they?"

I take a step back. "This is a private investigator, Samuel Rogers. And this is Kenna Davis. She's—"

To my surprise, Kenna cuts me off. "I'm his wife. I'm so happy to meet you, Sarah." She extends a hand.

Sarah looks down at it like it might bite her. "You got married? Aren't you, like, eighteen?"

"I'm twenty, but yes, I got married." Mentioning the unintentional, drunken part of the process seems irrelevant at the moment.

She barks out a laugh. "Wow, I wouldn't have guessed it, but congrats."

The stroller starts to cry. Wait, no, the baby inside the stroller is crying. As Sarah reaches in to lift out a tiny, red-faced baby, I realize belatedly that she is a mother.

"Sarah, is this your baby?"

She wraps the baby up in a small blue blanket, tucking him in close to her chest. "Yes, he's mine. His name is...well, it's Levi, actually. Levi Junior, so LJ."

She blinks up at me, attempting to calm the child by rocking him side to side.

My chest squeezes. "He's...his name is..."

She smiles briefly before her face creases with frustration from his crying. "Ugh, please fucking stop! I don't know what he wants. He cries all the time for no reason."

I flinch at her language while speaking to her baby. His face is cherry red as he wails. She swings him side to side even faster.

"Um, would you like me to give it a try?" Kenna speaks up beside me.

I hold my breath until Sarah nods. She hands LJ over, and Kenna lifts him up over her shoulder as she begins to sing softly into his ear. His cries abate almost instantly.

"Sarah." I turn back to my sister.

Her eyes lift up to mine as she reaches into the stroller for a tube of lipstick. She's still beautiful, but her skin has lost its healthy, youthful glow and been replaced by a dark tan and the clear sign of malnourishment.

"Yes, brother?" She puckers her lips as she applies the dark-red color to her lips, using a hand mirror.

"I wanted to see if I could take you to lunch." I blurt out the words, unsure of how else to offer her help without sounding like I think she definitely needs it right now.

She perks up. "Oh shit, of course. Sal's Sushi? I've been in the mood for some sushi." She rubs her hands together.

The baby has started to cry again. I look over to Kenna, who is rubbing his back.

"Do you have a bottle I could try to give him?" she asks Sarah.

Sarah waves her off. "At the restaurant. I'm starving."

Red flags immediately fly through my mind, but I assume Sal's Sushi is close by. Samuel has been silently standing by for the entire exchange, but he leaps into action by opening the car door. Sarah slides in. I'm about to follow her and offer Kenna the front when she tugs on my arm.

"What about the car seat?" Kenna whispers low in my ear.

I look over at Sarah, who is settled into the backseat and trying to get Samuel to change the radio station.

"Hey, Sarah, do you have a car seat?" I ask her.

She looks over at me and shrugs before turning forward again. I look back at Kenna, who clutches Levi closer to her chest.

"We can't go anywhere without it. It's not safe."

I nod, knowing she's right. I'm pulling out my phone to search for the nearest store that might have one when she touches my arm.

"Look, the stroller is two pieces. The top disconnects, I think."

I look up to see her pointing at a red lever on the back side of the stroller. I pull up on it, and the seat part lifts off. She smiles at me as I turn the seat toward her. She gently places Levi inside, but he wails as soon as she does it.

"Oh, baby, it's okay. We'll be there soon."

Something strange happens to me as her voice goes from the usual high-pitched Kenna to a soothing motherly tone. My skin gets a little hotter, and I feel the urge to pull her close and kiss her right.

Sarah calls from inside the car, "Let's go. I'm starving!"

33

Kenna

I've always wanted to be a mom. It's been my dream since my little brother was born. I remember holding him in my arms, envisioning having my own kids one day to love and cuddle and guide through life.

Then the accident happened. My fingers find the faded scar on my side, tracing over the jagged lines. The doctor said it would be a miracle if I could ever conceive after the damage done to my reproductive organs. There was so much scar tissue a year later that they had to remove my fallopian tubes. I was seventeen, and I cried for three weeks.

"Janie said she fed him, but who knows? I'm gonna ask the waiter for a cup of tap water." Sarah signals to the waitress.

LJ has been crying since before we arrived at the restaurant. I've been standing up and gently bouncing him, but when Sarah says that he could be hungry, I feel my stomach starting to churn.

We've been with them for over an hour, and she's just now mentioning this?

"Who is Janie?" Levi asks, signaling the waitress. She either doesn't see him or ignores him altogether.

"Oh, she's kind of my roommate. She took care of LJ while I was locked up."

I tense up again. *What does she mean by "kind of" her roommate?*

It's just the four of us. Samuel let us borrow his rental car and disappeared into the streets of San Francisco. He said he would be back in touch tomorrow.

Sarah shrugs as she stuffs a roll of sushi in her mouth. "We live together when we're both out. While I was locked up, she was letting Sheila stay there, which is why I was stuck in the shelter, but now that Sheila is in the tank, my room is empty. She and Janie work downtown a lot. I prefer The Stretch."

I look down at LJ, who has finally stopped crying. His eyes are drifting closed.

"What's The Stretch?" Levi asks.

Sarah laughs, her hoarse smoker's voice carrying through the restaurant. "Oh, baby bro. Still so innocent. It's the hotspot in San Fran. It's where the boys go when they get a shipment. Where the boys go is where girls like me go." She winks, taking a sip of the third screwdriver she's ordered.

My skin is tingling with nerves at the thought of having to turn LJ over to her. She's his mother, so I know I don't have a choice.

Is she fit to be a mother? I almost feel guilty for thinking it.

I look down at Levi. His eyes are on Sarah, shoulders tense.

"Do you...do you need some help, Sarah? I came here to help you. You and LJ could come back with us and—"

She holds up a hand, her pretty face growing harsh. "Fuck no. I'll never move back to Texas. Fuck that state. Fuck those conservative assholes. Do you realize how many abortions I wouldn't have been able to get if I lived there? LJ wasn't even supposed to be born, but I was locked up and got too far into the pregnancy. The later ones hurt way worse. Anyway, fuck the red states."

Tears spring to my eyes at her open admission that she doesn't want her son. I clutch him tighter, resolving to take him home with me even if she protests. I look around, thinking I could sneak out with him right now...

You can't do that to Levi.

Levi places his big hands on the table, curling them into fists. "Okay, well...is there anything I can do for you here? I could connect you with a better women's shelter, one that would be safe for you...and LJ."

The waitress comes by with the check. Levi takes out his card and hands it to her. Sarah smiles.

"I don't need any help. Janie and I take turns with the landlord, so he gives us a good rate. I like having my own space. I could use a few extra bills, though. If you have them to spare." She looks up at me holding the baby. "For diapers and shit like that."

I turn to Levi, pleading with him with my eyes. His gaze meets mine for a moment before he nods. I release a breath, praying he understands what I'm trying to communicate.

She can't take him. He's not safe with her. I will not be silent about this. I'm not above kidnapping to keep a child safe from his own mother.

Sarah lounges back against the chair. She's wearing a hot-pink tank top, her black bra poking out the front. Her tiny shorts show her ass cheeks when she walks.

"I don't have any cash on me right now. Why don't we go to the store after this to stock you up on baby stuff? I never got to buy you a baby gift, and I'd like to." Levi takes the receipt and his card when the waitress returns with it.

Sarah's eyes narrow at him. I assume she wanted the money for something else, but I can't be sure. Surely she's on state benefits to help her buy diapers and formula.

"Well, you could, but I don't want you to miss your flight. A gift card would work." She smiles again, reaching a hand over to pat his arm. "I'm so glad you came to see me. It's been too long, but I'm also just exhausted. I never sleep well in lockup."

The longer this exchange goes on, the more my stomach twists. LJ starts to stir in my arms. I reach a hand out to pat his little head, rocking back and forth.

"We don't have a flight booked yet," Levi says. He leans back in his chair, a calm smile on his lips. "What if Kenna and I took LJ for the night to give you a break? We can go get whatever he needs at the store, and I'll make sure to get a gift card for anything we forget. You can take care of errands or catch up on sleep. We can meet back up for breakfast tomorrow morning. Does that sound okay?"

Sarah studies him for a second. Her eyes move up to me, and I attempt a warm smile as I rock LJ. I think I might crack under her inspection, but she slowly nods before starting to smile.

"Sure, okay. I do have some shit I need to do."

"I'm just telling you right now, I don't care if she's your sister. She's getting this baby back over my dead body." My voice is shaky.

We're checking out at the closest grocery store, and LJ has screamed almost the entire time. The people around us are staring speculatively as we bag up hundreds of dollars' worth of diapers, wipes, formula, bottles, pacis, a playpen, and baby-boy clothes.

We got everything we could possibly need and more.

Levi swipes his debit card. His expression is hard, jaw clenched. He looks down at his screaming nephew. I'm tearing open the package of pacifiers as hot tears build up in my eyes.

"I know you're hungry, little guy. We're going as fast as we can," I say to him as I push the pacifier into his little mouth.

He starts sucking immediately, calming for a moment. I'm afraid as soon as he realizes it's not giving him milk, he won't want it. Levi throws the last bag into our cart before we rush out of the store. We make it to the car in the now-dark parking lot before LJ starts to wail again.

I'm crying now, too, trying to reassure him. Levi is throwing bags into the car, sifting through them to find the bottles, formula, and gallon of water.

"How much do I put in?" His voice sounds strained. I can't decipher if it's anger, panic, or a little of both.

"It should say on the side of the can." I crawl into the rental car.

Another few agonizing seconds of infant screams pass before Levi has a bottle made.

"Don't we have to heat it up?" His blue eyes search mine as he shakes it.

"No, it's fine. Let me have it."

He hands it over, and I place the nipple into LJ's open mouth. He begins to suck viciously. Hot tears roll down my cheeks as I press my forehead to his.

God, please give us a way to keep this baby from that monster.

34

Levi

I don't know how the girl I grew up with turned into the woman sitting in the booth across from me. Her face was once round and youthful, and even though she's still beautiful, her sunken cheekbones and slightly yellowing teeth indicate the hard life she's been living. She's dressed similarly to her outfit yesterday, but this time, the lacy black top shows her midriff. The short denim skirt looks to be made for a young teen girl, not a grown woman. She hobbled in on red stilts twenty minutes late after I watched her smoke a cigarette outside the door.

"Kenna stayed at the hotel with LJ. He didn't sleep much, so I didn't think we should wake him this morning."

"Your girlfriend sure is a hottie. She's got that *rich bitch* look down." She winks at me.

The waiter stops by to take Sarah's drink order.

"Chocolate milkshake." She turns to me. "Trying to gain a few pounds, so the girls will bring in a little more business. What are you doing these days to earn a living? I know a girl like that expects you to send your little babies to private school and all."

I sit up a little straighter, my blood beginning to heat. I'm about ready to put my long-lost sister in her place for speaking about Kenna like that. Then I remember her son and how I can't screw this up.

"I'm a tutor. Actually, Kenna and I are married. She's my wife."

Sarah barks out a laugh. "Oh shit, I forgot. I bet Mom and Pops sure are proud as shit. The silent golden boy landed him a nice, perfect little girl." She shakes her head.

I shift my weight in the booth. "Sarah...do you want to talk about why you left? I never...they never told me what happened to you." I swallow, hoping it's not the wrong thing to say.

The waiter sets down her milkshake, and she takes a long slurp before answering, "Pops basically kicked me out. Caught me sneaking out one night to meet a boy I had been emailing from that homeschoolers website." She pauses, her eyes growing distant. "You know, come to think of it, it could've been a sixty-year-old perv for all I know. Anyway, Pop said he'd kill me if he ever caught me trying to leave again. He could make it look like an accident if he wanted to, blah, blah, blah. I figured I'd rather get raped by a stranger while hitchhiking somewhere far as fuck away than murdered by my own father."

I gape at my sister, my heart pounding in my ears. I believe every word of the tragic story.

She's telling it like it's not about her. She's floating above, looking down at the seventeen-year-old girl who was abused and ran away in fear of her life. Since then, the world hasn't been a kind place. I ache for her, but I also want to kick my younger self for being too afraid to do anything to help her.

"Oh shit, don't look at me like that. I'm *bueno* now. Life wasn't even that fucking hard until I gave birth. Shit hurt. And babies are expensive. You always gotta remember to feed them and shit."

She's slurping down the milkshake. The waiter returns to take our order.

"Pancakes, extra butter. Can you bring the biggest order of bacon you have, sugar?" She winks at him, and he blushes as he turns his pimpled face toward me.

"I'm okay, thanks."

He walks away, and I turn back to face my sister. "Sarah, I wanted to talk to you about that. You're out here, all alone. I can't leave you, knowing that you don't have any help or a support system. Raising a baby on your own can't be easy, and I want to be here for you. I need to be here for you."

For a brief moment, I see a spark of vulnerability in her eyes.

Then it's replaced with amusement.

"Baby brother, you're sweet, but look at you. You're all smart and handsome. San Francisco is not the place for innocents. You and your little wifey don't belong here. I run with the big boys, okay? It's not your thing." She tosses her hair behind her shoulder, smiling at a stranger I don't want to turn to face.

I curl my hands into fists under the table. I have no idea how my flighty, unpredictable sister will respond to my next words. But I have no choice but to say them. I send a prayer up for the power of persuasion and a bit of luck because I'm going to need it.

"Then let me help you from a distance." I inhale, gripping the edge of the bench. "Let me take LJ for a while."

Time stands still.

She blinks at me, her mouth gaping. Painful silence engulfs us.

I finally swallow over the lump and continue on. "I know you're doing your best, but...I could help for a little bit. Like you said, babies are really hard, but I can't even imagine how hard it is for you as a single mom. I make pretty good money. Kenna could stay home to take care of him. You'd be able to save up money, work more, get to a place in your life with a bit more stability, and...we'd bring him back as soon as you're ready."

I hold my breath, waiting for her response. She keeps staring at me silently as the waiter brings her a plate of pancakes and bacon. She slowly starts to cover them in butter before finally opening her mouth to speak.

"I...I don't know what to say. What would you tell people? That he was yours?"

I sit back slightly, a bit of relief pouring over me that she didn't stand up and demand that we give him back right away. Kenna was right. I needed to do this alone—without her and LJ here.

Sarah always craved independence. She doesn't care what people think of her, but being restricted is her worst nightmare.

"I could tell them whatever you'd like. That he's family and we're helping out or...that he's mine, if you'd want me to do that." I lean forward again, placing my elbows on the table. "Sarah, I feel like all my life I've failed you as a brother. I wasn't there for you when...you needed help and someone to share the burdens you were facing. Now I have a chance to do that. You're a single mother. This wasn't in your life plan. I'd love to have the chance to step in and try to make up for my failure to help you the last time I saw you in need. Please, please allow me to do this. It can be on your terms, whatever those might be."

She's pouring syrup over the plate. When it's swimming in the sugar, she cuts off a big bite and sticks it in her mouth. She watches me as she chews. I take a sip of my cold, black coffee.

"They asked me at the hospital if I wanted to look into adoption. I thought about it...but then he was so tiny and red. I had this moment where I remembered when Mom gave birth to you in our house. It felt like forever before the midwife finally carried you out into the living room. I held you in my skinny arms on that old, checkered sofa." Her blue eyes have grown distant. "He looked exactly like you—I mean, the spitting image. People would definitely believe it if you said he was yours." She takes another big bite of pancake.

My skin is crawling with nerves. *Does this mean she won't do it?* She was offered a way out before and didn't take it.

I slump back in my seat.

"So, what did you say? What was her response? How did it end?" Kenna's voice is higher-pitched than normal. She's got LJ tucked in close to her chest, and I can hear his little snores.

She's taken on a new level of beauty since we came to San Francisco. I never imagined it would be possible for her to level up in attractiveness. Her emerald eyes are looking at me like I hold the answers to any problem we might face.

"I asked her if we could help her out by taking LJ for a while, so she could get her life in order." I reach over to brush my hand over his soft, tiny head. "And she agreed."

"Flight 257 is now boarding. Please do not leave any bags unattended."

We both stand, and I reach around Kenna to swing the backpack diaper bag we bought for LJ over my shoulder.

"I just...I can't believe she agreed. Do you think she'll want him back, like, right away?"

We file in line with the other passengers, my arms loaded down with our luggage.

"I don't know what to expect from her. She's my sister, but this is the first time I've seen her in...eight years. She's changed."

In truth, she's nearly unrecognizable to me, both physically and emotionally. If I hadn't hired a private investigator to find her, I don't know if I would have believed she was the girl I grew up with.

We finally board the plane, finding our seats near the middle. Kenna takes the aisle with LJ while I squeeze near the window.

"I wonder how we can do things legally. Will we be able to take him to the doctor if he gets sick? We need, like, his birth certificate or something."

"Samuel is still there. He has a lawyer friend who is drawing up a contract for Sarah to sign, giving us temporary legal-guardian rights. I hope she's willing to do it. I told him to explain to her that we would need it in an emergency situation, just like a nanny or a babysitter would for parents going on a trip."

The airplane moves down the runway. LJ stirs for a moment as we lift into the air, but he doesn't wake up. I turn to face Kenna once the aircraft levels out and my ears stop popping.

"How are you going to feel when we have to give him back?" I whisper the words, worried someone around us will think we're kidnappers.

She turns to face me, her head leaning back against the seat. "How do you know we'll have to?"

I reach up to brush a blonde curl out of her eyes. My hand continues down to rest over hers, holding my nephew close to her chest. "I don't know at all what to expect. Until I have the signed guardian papers, I don't want to get my hopes too high."

We haven't even discussed adopting LJ. I see a spark in her eyes, confirming what I know we were both thinking. Her eyes begin to water.

"What if she wants him back, though?" Her voice is a hoarse whisper, and the sound goes straight to my heart.

"We'll face it when it comes." I squeeze her hand under mine. "Together."

35

Kenna

I hold LJ closer to my chest and inhale his fresh baby scent. The smell of a clean baby is the most potent shot of serotonin in the universe. He stirs slightly, his little chin wet with drool as he sleeps soundly.

It's been a week since we brought him home from California. I've practically moved in with Levi, but I saw a glimpse on his phone of a house search in the area. My heart nearly pounded out of my chest. I never brought it up to him.

My mind has been wandering. Some nights, I wake up in a cold sweat, clammy hands shaking as I rub LJ's back in his bed. I turn on his white noise machine, so he doesn't hear every little bump and noise we make.

She's going to come and take him back. She'll take him, and we won't be able to stop her.

I don't know how I got here so quickly. I never imagined I'd feel this way about someone else's child. Somehow, I've grown attached to him far too soon.

I've cried every day. The only things keeping me sane are my frantic prayers and Levi's steady reassurance that we will get through this.

"Whatever happens, we will survive this. Even if she wants him back, if she's still in a bad place, I won't stop trying until he's ours."

I trust him, but I'm still begging God for a miracle.

We've sunk into a bit of a routine where I take care of LJ during the days I don't have class, while Levi works as a tutor for the students taking summer classes on opposite days. He does some in-person meetings and some over the internet, but he usually goes to the library, where he doesn't have to worry about LJ's crying or my singing lullabies.

I glance up at the clock to see that it's nearing five p.m. I wanted to make tacos for dinner, so I take an already-sleeping LJ into the bedroom and lay him down in his bed. I catch a whiff of my own body odor and nearly have to hold my breath.

Mom life has truly snuck up on me. I never knew if I would get to experience this part of life. I go into the bathroom and strip down before turning on the shower. It must have been two —no, three—days since the last time I bathed myself. I have crusted baby spit-up on my pants, and I don't think I've worn makeup since we got back to Texas.

"It's no wonder Levi hasn't made a single move on me," I mumble to myself.

It's not for lack of me wanting him to. Since we've gotten back and he's shown nothing but a desire to save LJ, care for me, and help his sister, I cannot stop looking at him like...like I always used to look at him. The more time that passes since the big *tutor deception* scandal came out, the more I feel like I overreacted.

Meeting Sarah and hearing more about their upbringing and the intensity of his toxic family life have made me realize that he could truly have been too afraid to tell me the truth about who he was.

Would I have told him had the roles been reversed?

Yes, but being honest and forthcoming has always worked well for me in life. He hasn't had the same experience. What matters more is how he's responded since the revelation. He hasn't tried to hide, excuse, or downplay it. He hasn't attempted any forms of manipulation or gaslighting to make me think he was innocent, and it was somehow my fault.

Those things alone make me want to forgive him and tell him right now, tonight, that I want to be together for real again.

I step into the spray of the warm water, sighing indulgently at the relief the water brings to my tired body. It's not like I've done much of anything physical, but I'm emotionally drained with all the stress and worrying. A release is what I need, a mental break from this fear and uncertainty.

A noise sounds from the bedroom, a light tapping on the door.

"Come in," I call out quietly.

I'm already nervous about him being back. My head is in a space where I'm ready to ask him to join me under the shower for some mutual stress relief.

"Kenna?" Levi says through the door.

"Come in, so you don't wake him up."

The door finally starts to creak open. I'm frantically scrubbing my extremities with my loofah in case he actually decides to join me.

"Hey, sorry, just wanted to see if you want me to start dinner or if you feel like going out."

I debate my response for a few seconds. If I answer right away, he'll probably leave.

Flash him. The thought intrudes suddenly in my brain, a distant memory resurfacing of the first time he saw me naked, completely by accident. *Or just calmly ask him to join you, like a normal person.*

I've never been very normal. In a moment of boldness, I shove the shower curtain to the side, exposing my soapy, wet body to the cold air and his shocked face.

Time isn't real to us. It could be ten minutes, could be three seconds. All I really know is that his gaze burns down over me before he slowly begins to walk toward me. It's a small bathroom, so it only takes about three steps before he lands directly in front of me. My nipples have puckered at the touch of cold air.

He's always been a man of few words.

"Do you forgive me?" He barely manages to force himself to make eye contact with me.

I nearly start crying right then. I can't believe I've been denying how stupid, crazy in love with this man that I am.

"I want to tell you something first." I inhale a deep breath, not looking at him as I speak. "You know how I have these scars on my side?"

I see him nod in the corner of my eye. My fingers reach up to trace the familiar, jagged skin. "I can't... I won't be able to get pregnant...ever." My lungs freeze, waiting.

A few endless moments pass, the water from the showerhead the only sound. I have no idea how he'll take this news. We've both grown to love LJ. Parenthood has been a joyful, natural evolution of our relationship.

He's still fully clothed, but he takes another step toward me. The spray of the water is misting him now. He allows his blue eyes to melt down my body then, his lips parting as he slowly takes me all in.

His hands begin to unbutton his slacks. "You put every woman in the world to shame with your beauty."

I suck in a breath, my eyes locked on the work his hands are doing. They've moved to the zipper now.

"I think about you...far too much. Your body is the epitome of female anatomical perfection."

I reach my hands up to grab my breasts as I hold on to every one of his words. He freezes, watching me closely.

"I need you to touch me." My legs are quivering with need.

He drops his pants down, reaching up to pull his gray polo over his head. "I could stare into your emerald eyes for all of eternity and never tire of the color." He stares at me, his tongue reaching out to wet his bottom lip. "Even if it was only you and I...and we could never have kids—I want you—forever."

He slowly removes his boxers. I try to keep looking at his face, but my eyes betray me when they drop lower. His admittance of wanting me, even with my internal flaws, turns me on like nothing I've ever experienced before.

How have I waited so long for this? This man is my literal husband, and I've been depriving myself of pure, good, delicious bedtime activities. *He is mine.*

"Get in." I sound slightly feral.

He pulls off his glasses and sets them on the sink before stepping under the hot stream of water. I immediately wrap my arms around his neck. He closes the curtain before finding my waist with his large, manly hands.

"You're impossible to resist," he says in a deep voice.

My breasts are pressed up against him. The hair on his chest causes my nipples to tingle.

"You've done pretty well the past week." *I'm not upset about it at all.*

A smirk touches his lips. "You were mad at me. I was waiting for you to hopefully forgive me."

"I would have appreciated some kisses, even while trying to find the forgiveness in my heart that I have now extended to you."

His eyes are the darkest shade of blue I've ever seen, almost indigo. I let my eyes drift closed as he leans his face down toward my neck and plants a kiss against my jawline.

"You"—he moves slightly lower to the place between my neck and collarbone to press his wet tongue down on my pulse —"will..."

I jerk at the contact, a shiver running down my thighs. One of my hands reaches to grip his arm near the bicep, the other moving to rest against his abs. He's firm beneath my fingers, and I bask in the fact that I get to reap the benefits of his slavery to the gym.

"Never"—his hand moves around to my backside, squeezing just hard enough—"go..."

I press my breasts into his chest, the water slicking our skin and heightening every nerve.

"Without"—his lips are still trailing down, only inches from my nipple now—"my kisses..."

I suck in again as he makes contact, the feeling of his warm tongue shooting through me to the space between my legs.

"Again." He reaches the hand that isn't gripping my butt around to rub against my aching center.

My body is tense with need and desire, and he doesn't disappoint me, like so many before have. I press my face against his chest, enjoying each swipe of his thumb across my sensitive skin. He takes his sweet, leisurely time to listen to gasps, moans, and the slight increase in my breathing before my body releases and I breathe out his name.

"Levi..." I pulse for a few seconds, giving all of me up to him.

He's nearly holding my entire body weight up at this point. I'm half-slacked against the shower wall, half-relaxed in his arms. I blink up at him, tilting my head back with a smile.

"I cannot believe you made me wait *so* long for that."

He gives me a *cat who ate the canary* grin, leaning forward as he speaks. "It's barely been a week, Kens."

I reach down between us, grabbing his very ready thickness, while licking my lips in anticipation for what comes next. His eyes actually roll back into his head as he leans his big, muscled body into me.

"*Barely* two weeks, hm?"

He smiles, but it only lasts a moment before it's cut off with a groan of pure desire. He only allows me to touch him for a few seconds before taking over again.

He pushes my back up against the cold tiles, lifting my legs up and settling them around his hips. Both of his arms hold me up, and I love the look and feel of his muscled shoulders, activated with the effort. His movements are slow at first, and we both need to take a few seconds to catch our breath before he begins to increase his speed.

He's careful and rough with me simultaneously. The shower is tiny, but we make it work. He knocks over a shampoo bottle when he lifts his leg up to rest his foot on the side, and we both freeze.

The spray of the water is the only sound for the next five seconds. We sigh in relief when we don't hear crying, and he continues even faster.

My hands trail up from his shoulders to reach around and grip his neck. He dips his head down, our lips sealing together. We kiss for a few seconds before I drag my teeth down over his bottom lip.

It's like his body is possessed; he's a man starved for me. I'm his only way home, the water in the desert that he's been wandering in. And he's never done this before with anyone else.

His teeth sink into my lip this time, and I taste the saltiness of my blood seconds after the sting of pain. Surprisingly, that burst of pain is what sends me over the edge and floods my body with ecstasy.

My legs squeeze together, and my arms grip him tighter. He follows me, jerking his body for a few blissful moments.

We're breathless as we slowly peel ourselves away from each other. The water is still running over us, even though it's starting to cool. The timing couldn't have been more perfect.

I'm about to step out of the shower when he stops me with his thumb on my lips. The very same thumb that...

"Did I hurt you?" His voice is tinged with concern.

I smile up at him. "I liked it."

He doesn't seem to know quite how to process that. He blinks at me for another few seconds before I reach up to grab his hand, planting a kiss on his open palm. I open the shower curtain and step out just in time to hear LJ starting to cry.

36

Levi

It's early fall. LJ is wrapped in a blue-and-yellow gingham fleece blanket. I can't help but smile down at him as I push the stroller through the crunching leaves on the sidewalk.

Kenna's arm is looped around mine. She sighs contentedly. I look over at her, amazed as always at how beautiful her green eyes are in the morning sunlight.

"What is it?" I ask.

She leans her head on my shoulder, a smile touching her lips. "I'm just happy—that's all."

My heart jumps inside my chest at her words, and I realize that making her happy feels like all I ever want to accomplish in life.

"I'm happy too." I hesitate, taking in a few long breaths before I continue. "This is the happiest I've ever been."

Her hand tightens on my inner arm. She lifts her blonde head up. "Oh, Levi, me too."

LJ coos in the stroller, spit-up dribbling down his little chin. I stop walking as Kenna leans forward to wipe it away with a burp cloth. She tucks his blanket closer around him even though there's barely a chill in the October morning air.

"You are so handsome, aren't you? Do you want to get out and let me hold you?" She reaches up under his arms to lift him up.

There's a park bench a few steps away. We walk and sit down, and I roll the stroller beside us and lock the wheels.

"How was your quiz yesterday?"

"I got an eighty-seven."

I cross my foot over my knee. "That's good. Do you feel like the material is making sense?"

She nods. "I do. I think I could have done a little better if LJ hadn't woken up at midnight and again at three a.m."

My hand moves around to massage the base of her neck. "I'm sorry he kept you up. I tried to rock him, but he was fussing a lot, no matter what."

"I've wondered if his formula is bothering his stomach. The pediatrician said it might. We should switch to another brand, something organic."

I nod, smiling at how much she's embraced the role of motherhood even though there's a very real possibility that she won't get to keep the child she loves so dearly.

"That's a great idea. We can stop on the way home to get some."

By home, I mean the apartment we're renting on campus. Dan and Silas moved into their own place in the same building at the start of the semester so that Kenna could live with me and LJ. No one has pressed us for details even though it's been almost three months since my nephew "came to visit us."

She sits back against the bench, and I wrap my arm around her shoulders. LJ's eyes are heavy as he lies in the crook of her elbow.

"Have I mentioned that you make a beautiful wife and mother?" I murmur next to her ear. I didn't really think about it before it came out, but no truer words have ever been spoken.

She turns her face up to me, and I see that her eyes are misting. "I would give anything for this to never, ever change." Her voice is barely above a whisper. "Have you heard anything?"

A few feet away, two pigeons are pecking the ground, most likely feasting on some discarded breadcrumbs. Streams of sunshine pour through the canopy of orange and crimson leaves above our heads. A few walkers are milling about the park, but it still feels intimate, where we are sitting. The day couldn't be more ideal if Thomas Kinkade had brushed it to life on a canvas.

"She's...I asked Samuel to check on her whereabouts, and he said she's partying as much as ever." I swallow over the mass in my throat. "Still doing drugs, but no more charges other than a public indecency one that she miraculously wasn't put in jail for." My fingers toy with a strand of her curly, long hair. "I think I might go see her to talk about...the adoption."

Kenna stares at me for a few moments. She doesn't respond right away. Her fingers are tracing LJ's tiny ear. He seems to have fallen completely asleep, his rosebud little lips parted slightly.

"I don't...I don't know if we should anymore."

My pulse increases. I know she loves LJ, but maybe she's having second thoughts. We haven't even had a real conversation about whether or not she still wants to get an annulment. I know it needs to happen, but I was hoping I'd get the chance to prove how much I love her first.

"Well, if you've changed your mind, I understand." It's a lie. I don't understand.

She wipes away a tear that dripped down her cheek. "I'm just afraid, Levi. I'm afraid of loving him too much and her showing up one day, demanding him back. If we just don't bring it up, maybe..." She squeezes him tighter to her chest.

Realization washes over me. She doesn't want to love him and lose him. I pull her shoulders closer against my chest. I feel a burst of relief at her confession.

"I'm afraid too. But now that she sees how much easier her life is without having to take care of a baby, maybe she'll be more willing to sign the papers. I'm going to talk to her, but first..." I inhale, brushing my fingers over her damp cheek.

"But first...what?"

"First, I want to ask you something important." I shift my weight off of the bench, my knee connecting with the sidewalk. "I planned something really special. I was going to get a babysitter." I reach into my jeans pocket, feeling the cold stone against my fingertips.

Kenna moves her body, adjusting LJ in her arms. Her brow is creased in confusion.

She has no idea.

I'm on one knee, the other brushing against her leg. My sweaty fingers almost drop the ring. I grip it harder. "You got up this morning and said you wanted to take the walk, so I canceled on Harley and Adam watching LJ for us."

She still looks perplexed at my stance. "Okay..."

"I just feel like...now is the time."

The diamond glints in the light. Kenna's gaze drops down to my hands. She gasps, covering her mouth with her hand.

My words rush out. I'm unable to keep them on my tongue any longer. "I bought it before you asked for the annulment. I've been carrying it around in my pocket everywhere. I thought

I might do it on the Golden Gate Bridge, but then...we got LJ. I've thought about it a hundred times ever since we woke up, already married in Vegas. You deserve a real engagement ring, a wedding, the white dress, all the things. I want to spend the rest of my days giving you all of me and so much more. I want to prove that I'll never lie, never deceive, never do anything to hurt you. I love you, McKenna Davis." My voice chokes up. "I love you with every emotion I possess. I love the way the light shows every shade of green in your eyes. I love your laughter in quiet theaters. I love how you always tell the corniest jokes. I love your midnight snacking habits and the fact that you're still teaching me new things about the female anatomy every time we make love. I. Love. You." I take a moment to breathe, watching her bottom lip quiver. "Please be a family with me and LJ for the rest of forever."

The planet has stopped orbiting around the sun. Right here and now, it's only us and this day. Only our hearts beating, our lives suspended in a moment that will forever change us, depending on what she says. She can still walk away from this—from us—if she chooses. I want her to choose to stay, not be forced into it because LJ needs a good mother and we accidentally got married in a drunken haze.

She opens her mouth. "I—"

A phone ringing pierces the air. It's loud and obnoxious, completely destroying the moment. I reach into my back pocket, frustrated when I can't reach the silence button. I pull it out and press it forcefully.

Then I freeze.

"It's her. It's Sarah."

My eyes meet Kenna's as I swipe to answer the phone. "Hello?"

"I want him back! *I want my baby.*"

My heart is in my throat for the next twelve hours. I mindlessly get on a red-eye flight to San Francisco at eight p.m. It's cold on the flight, but I forgot to bring a jacket. Goose bumps form on my arms. I don't know if it's from the chill or my nerves.

She wants him back. She's going to take him. She can't take him.

I had no choice but to leave Kenna in a sobbing heap on the sofa. Harley, Adam, and Dan were there to comfort and care for her and LJ, but I still feel a queasiness in the pit of my stomach.

Going alone back to California was my decision. I have no idea how Sarah will react, but I couldn't convince myself to bring LJ with me on this trip.

Over the phone, my sister sounded beyond distraught. She also wasn't making much sense. After her initial demands for LJ to be brought back immediately, she started mumbling, slurring her words, and crying. I tried to talk to her and calm her down, but she wouldn't have any of it.

My last report from Samuel said that she is strung out most of the time. Even after my suggestions for rehab and offers to pay for it—even though I could barely afford the staggering sum of the facility—Sarah refused any of my help.

She does want money. One thing she constantly asks me for is cash. For a while, I sent her gift cards to grocery stores and fast-food places until I was told by Samuel that she was most likely trading them for drugs.

Last week, I refused to send her any more "help" unless she agreed to rehab for a minimum of six months.

I'd find a way to pay for it. I'd call my mother or my grandparents I haven't seen in years because my father didn't get along with them. I'd find a way even if I had to work three jobs.

That's when she got desperate. All this time, she's never even asked about LJ. Sometimes, I think she's forgotten he exists and that he's her son.

After my last phone call with her when she demanded cash or more gift cards and I refused, I didn't know what to expect from her. I kept all of this from Kenna because I knew she'd worry, panic, and stress about it to the point of not sleeping and eating. That's what I've been doing, and there's no reason for both of us to suffer.

Sarah is clearly an addict in need of serious therapy and rehab.

How do you help someone who refuses to be helped?

My back aches as the plane finally starts to descend. I was stuck in a middle seat due to my late purchase of the ticket. My shoulders stretch wider than the small airline's seat back, so I spent the entire three hours trying to hunch over and make myself smaller.

I stand up after the front rows begin to file out. It's late, but as I walk through the airport, I decide I'm not getting a hotel just to lie in bed, awake, anxious, and stressed out.

When I get through the smelly crowds of weary travelers and the overpriced food, I wave down a yellow taxi. The driver enters the address I give him on his GPS while chattering about his last passengers. Apparently, three scantily clad young ladies were in his backseat a few minutes before he picked me up.

"I took 'em to this fancy house, man, a mansion. They were dressed in tiny little skirts and all that. There's probably some glitter back there on the seat. Sorry about that."

I don't respond because I don't know how to. My knee bounces as we get closer to the destination.

The words I'm going to say when I get there keep rolling through my mind, but they never sound right.

Sarah, you need help. Let me help you.

If you ever want him back, you have to go to rehab. You can't be a mother and a drug addict. I won't let you.

Sarah, I love you so much. Please, let me take care of you.

Our life was bad, Sarah. I know it was. Our dad was a prick who oppressed you with his rules and cruelty. Please don't let him ruin the rest of your life. You can have a better life than this. There is so much more than this.

When I get there and see her gaunt face, it won't matter what I planned to say. Words always get caught in my throat, ever since I learned that staying silent and invisible kept me off the radar.

Now, it's not an option for me. I have to speak. I have to stand up for what's right. I have to be bold and loud. I won't back down from this fight. Even if I have to take my sister to court to get her son taken into the custody of the system.

I'll do whatever is necessary to protect my nephew. And I'll do what I must to save Sarah from herself.

"We're here, bro."

The deep-red brick building is to the left, illuminated by too few streetlights. I pay the taxi driver before stepping out of the car with my backpack. One set of clothes and a few toiletries are all I brought, but if I can avoid staying overnight, I will.

Sarah's apartment is on the third floor. Random people are loitering around in the parking lot and in the stairway of the complex. Even with my size, the fact that I'm alone without a weapon makes the hair on my neck stand up. This is the kind of place you could disappear inside of and no one would know where to look for you.

My knuckles connect with Sarah's door a few times before it swings open.

A girl with neon-pink hair and a matching sports bra says, "What?! I told you fucks to—oh." Her gaze moves over me as a knowing smirk touches her lips. "Well, I had no idea Sarah was getting such *elite* customers these days. Be honest. Is she doing it pro bono just because you're hot?"

She steps aside, leaving the door open in a silent invitation. I follow her into the apartment. It's dark, with mismatched furniture scattered around. The coffee table is littered with takeout boxes and beer cans. The entire apartment smells like cheap perfume, old food, and skunk.

A pang of guilt pierces my stomach.

I should have tried harder to help her.

My sister's condition is worse than I realized. I knew she was partying and wasting her life, but this place makes her situation appear far more dire.

"Where is Sarah?"

The pink-haired girl is lighting a cigarette. "First door on the left. She's pretty high. Her last customer was one of the big boys on the strip. Always brings favors. You get bored in there, mine's on the right." She winks at me before plopping down on the grungy sofa.

I hesitate. I want to ask her if she's okay, if she needs help, how she got in this place. My instincts are screaming at me to take them both somewhere far away from here. She's someone's daughter, someone's sister.

You have to help Sarah first.

My feet finally move toward the hall. I knock gently on the door. "Sarah, it's Levi."

No response.

I wait another few moments before knocking louder. "Sarah, can I come in?"

A memory flashes in my brain from when we were kids. My father took a sledgehammer to the headlights of my mom's car when she came home a few hours later than he expected. It was dark outside, and the sound of him smashing the front end of her Honda could be heard inside my room at the back of the house. I ran down the hall to Sarah's door. I knocked so many times, begging her to let me in. She finally answered the door, eyes red from crying. She let me come in, but she wouldn't let me sleep in her bed. Even on the hard floor with no blanket or pillows, I was thankful to be with someone.

I shake my head to bring myself back to reality. "Sarah! I'm coming in."

The knob isn't locked. I twist it open, spreading some light into the darkness. There's a lump on the bed, almost too small to be a full-grown adult. In the corner, I see a small bassinet, now overflowing with stilettos and tall boots.

I approach the bed and reach out a hand toward her. She's on her back, mouth open as she sleeps. The rise and fall of her chest are slow and steady. She looks more innocent like this, closer to resembling the girl I once knew than the last time I saw her.

After looking around the room, I set my backpack against the wall and settle back against it. Sleep probably won't come for me, but watching over her is all I want to do right now.

Tonight, I'll keep her safe.

37

Kenna

My mother handled it quite well when I asked her if she could babysit for me while I attended a funeral. I told her over the phone that I had been keeping Levi's nephew for the past three months and the only reason I didn't tell her was because I thought we'd have to give him back.

Her car pulls up in the parking lot of the on-campus housing. My dad gets out first, followed by my mom. My brother must have stayed behind with his best friend's family. My grandmother is doing better. I've actually been able to FaceTime with her lately and chat about old times with Lia. She seems to be more aware of herself when I've spoken to her.

I watch from the balcony of the second floor as they walk up. My dad is holding two duffel bags.

Once they knock on the door, I swing it open with a sob already caught in my throat.

"Hi." A tear slides down my cheek.

LJ decides to let his lungs loose at the exact same time, wailing loudly in my arms. As usual, I cry harder when he starts.

"Oh my goodness! Sweetheart, let me see that baby." My mother sweeps in, taking LJ from me as my father wraps me up in his arms.

I let out all my frustration, tears, and the stress of keeping it together for the past two days on my own. I cry away the anxiety and fear that have gripped me since I got the phone call from Samuel Rogers, the private investigator, telling me there would be a funeral in San Francisco and that's all the information I could get right now.

Harley and Adam have stopped by every day to check on me, but it wasn't until this morning that I woke up and realized I had to come clean to my parents.

"I have to tell you something." I push back, wiping under my eyes with the back of my hand. I don't waste any time spilling the story. "I got married in Las Vegas. Then we went to see his sister, and she had this baby. She...he needed us. So we took him home. He's been here with us for three months now, and I love him more than anything. Both of them."

"Honey, slow down." My mother's face is white. She's finally gotten LJ to stop crying.

My dad is still standing close to me, but he takes a step back so he can look at my face. "Start over, Kenna. Whose baby is this?"

"It's his sister's."

"Whose sister's?" my mom says.

"My husband's!" I hiccup, trying to take a deep breath.

"Honey, who is your husband?" Dad speaks up again.

I exhale slowly. "My tutor...Levi. The one I brought home when I came to see Grandma."

Their mouths form twin Os. They look from me to each other and back again.

"I got married in Vegas. It was a stupid, drunken mistake. I'd liked him for forever, and he finally admitted he liked me too. I didn't even know he was Mr. Taylor! It's romantic if you really think about it, but when I first found out, I was so mad. When we came to visit, we weren't even together—well, we were married, but—"

"Kenna." My father holds his hand up. "Where is Levi now?"

I feel the tears beginning to well up again. "He went to San Francisco to help her, but—" I start sobbing. My whole body shakes with the effort, and I know it's the pent-up emotions I've been holding in all this time.

The door bursts open from behind me. I turn back to see who it is, and my heart leaps inside my chest. I fling myself around his neck, still crying. He looks exhausted, like he hasn't slept in days.

"Baby? What's wrong? Why are you crying?" Levi is supporting most of my body weight. He brushes my hair back with one hand, the other curled around my waist.

I finally get myself under control again before leaning back. My lips connect with his jawline as I press a kiss over his stubble. "Don't ever leave me again—*ever*."

His eyes are misting as he leans forward to kiss me on the corner of my mouth. "Never," he whispers.

As I turn back around, I see that my mother's eyes are wet too. My dad just looks confused.

"Can we please get an explanation now? Are you two married?" My mom's eyes are wide.

I nod, opening my mouth to explain before I realize Levi is about to. He takes my hand.

"Yes, sir, we are married. It was an accident. I wasn't sure if Kenna wanted to...stay together, but after we decided to, I planned to come talk to you. I wish I'd had time to do it right by you the first time. We got caught up when my sister needed us to take my nephew. She..." He swallows, trying to continue.

I squeeze his hand. My voice softens. "She passed away two days ago. Levi had gone to see her, and she overdosed. He didn't know it, and she died in her sleep. Then he contacted a funeral home and the CPS system in California, and he was trying to locate their parents—who have completely disappeared—when I called you in panic mode. I'm so afraid someone is going to show up and try to take LJ from us."

My mom steps closer to reach out a hand and rest it on my forearm. "Oh, honey, that's awful. Why have his parents disappeared? I wish you had called us sooner, when all this began. I can't imagine what it felt like to bear these burdens on your own. We...understand what it's like to be young and in love. Don't we, dear?"

I shake my head, whispering, "I don't know what happened."

My dad's expression softens slightly. He hasn't moved any closer to us, but I see his shoulders droop down a bit. "I'm sorry for your loss, son. We lost a daughter when Kenna was in high school. Were you able to contact your family?"

He nods. "My mother's best friend from my hometown was able to give me her phone number. I stopped hearing from her several months ago, and I've been so caught up in everything that I forgot to keep checking in. She left my dad because he was...difficult to live with. Apparently, he was stalking her pretty bad at first. She's safe now, but hearing about my sister... wasn't easy."

My mom starts to cry then. Memories of Lia must be resurfacing. I take LJ from her, realizing by the smell that he needs a diaper change.

"I'm going to clean him up." I step into the bedroom, where the diapers and wipes are, and lay him on the bed.

The door opens and shuts behind me.

"Hey." His voice is noticeably weaker now that we're alone.

He's been through hell in the past few days, probably worse than I have. Once I finish cleaning up LJ, I lay him on his belly on his baby blanket in the middle of the room. He rolls over immediately, smiling to himself. His pediatrician said he was slightly behind for his age, probably because he hadn't been given adequate time out of his crib and car seat to move around, but he's catching up quickly.

Strong arms wrap around me from behind. Levi's lips press to the side of my neck, his warm breath tingling the sensitive part of my skin over my pulse. His big, firm body is pressed up against my back.

Nothing in the world brings me a sense of peace like his arms holding me. I can feel his heart beating a little too quickly. The longer we stay like this, the more his heart rate gradually begins to slow down.

"You have no idea how badly I've needed this." His hoarse voice rumbles through me.

My arms reach back and around to grab the back of his neck. He slowly twirls my body around while still holding me. My eyes meet his blue ones, all the turmoil in their depths reaching out to crush my heart.

"I would give anything to take away your pain, my love. I'm so sorry..."

His mouth comes down to press against mine. It's a hard, deliberate kiss. He's desperate to feel something other than his pain, and I'll gladly give him what he needs. He sucks my bottom lip roughly, swiping his tongue across it. His hands are greedy, kneading my ass.

We can't go much further since LJ is in here, awake, and my parents are in the living room. He seems to realize this when the baby starts making babbling noises.

Levi gives me one last lengthy kiss before coming up for air. His lips are red. "I needed that. Thank you. Can we...pick this up where we left off later?" He bends down to pick LJ up off the floor, hugging him close to his chest.

"Of course."

"You should pack...if you want to come with me to the funeral."

I nod. "I do. I'll get a bag together. When are we leaving?"

"We should be on our way to the airport right now."

38

Levi

I wouldn't have survived traveling back to California without Kenna by my side.

There's no way I could have made it back into a taxi and made small talk with the driver again.

Even more unlikely to have happened would be me going to a hotel and getting any sleep at all.

I'm existing outside of myself, feigning indifference to the storm of emotions that seem to be swirling within me.

My wife seems to understand that I need to take her in the shower, underneath me on the bed, and then again on top of me. We trade off sleeping and having sex throughout the night.

She's life to me in the dark. I feel numb to everything but her. We hardly speak, but she holds me and lets me touch her.

I wouldn't make it through till morning without touching her. By the time the clock says six, I'm ready for more, but I know she must be sore, so I don't initiate it.

We get to the funeral home at eight. My mother is waiting, but no one else bothers to come. She looks better than I expected, even though her eyes are red with tears.

"Mama." I crush her small frame to my chest. We hold each other for a long time.

I let myself cry for my sister and the pain we all suffered at my father's hand together, now only remembered by my mother and me.

When we finally separate, the hired minister beckons us to enter a small room with rows of orange cushioned pews. As we walk up, I see the urn that Sarah's ashes are in.

The service is brief. The man who never knew Sarah gives a short message about life, death, and the full circle humans supposedly make on this earth. I tune him out, instead focusing on my own guilt over the fact that I was asleep in her bedroom when she died.

The coroner's report stated that even if she had been taken to the hospital, she still would have died. The drugs had caused her to have liver failure. She had taken heroin, but it had been laced with an unknown toxic substance.

Once the service is over, the three of us turn to leave with the urn. My mother thanks the minister, and we walk out together.

"Who is the beautiful young lady you brought with you, Levi?" She turns her shiny blue eyes toward Kenna.

"This is my wife, Kenna Mae Davis Taylor."

My mom's eyes widen. She chokes out, "Pleased to meet you, dear. You are lovely." She covers her mouth with her hand as more tears fall.

Kenna rushes forward, drawing her into a hug. "I'm so pleased to meet you too. Your son is the best man I could've ever dreamed of."

They hold each other for a few long moments, both sniffling.

I reach around to lay a hand on my mom's shoulder. "Mom, there's someone else I want you to meet. He's in Texas."

Four Weeks Later

"You never said yes."

"Um, sir, you never asked!" Kenna giggles as she stuffs a grape into her mouth.

"Well, I've been wanting to for a very long time now."

"Not as long as I've been waiting, *Mr. T.*"

I groan, pulling her face down to kiss me. Her mouth is sweet from the grape juice, and it reminds me of another part of her that's equally sweet and delicious.

I'm lying with my head in her lap as she sits cross-legged on a picnic blanket. The sun has already set, and a few stars are poking through the night sky. We're staying the night at Harley and Adam's winery. They insisted on us taking the guest room in their old farmhouse for our little weekend getaway. LJ is having some bonding time with my mom back at our apartment.

The state of California awarded Kenna and me custody almost immediately. After learning that we had been caring for LJ for months and conducting a home evaluation, they gladly relinquished the responsibility of yet another orphan with drug-overdosed parents. He didn't have any record of a father on his birth certificate.

"We've technically been married for six months, and you still haven't legally changed your name. Do you even want to become Mrs. Taylor?" For the first time in weeks, I can't stop smiling.

"Even though I haven't legally changed it, if it's changed on Instagram, it still counts."

I laugh out loud before sitting up. I get up on one knee, digging in my pocket once again.

"McKenna Mae Davis, please check your phone."

Her brows scrunch together. She reaches over to the side, finding her phone. She swipes the screen open.

"I don't—" Her voice cuts off as a slow smile spreads across her lips. She doesn't move for a full ten seconds. She bites into her lip, slowly shaking her head. "Oh. My. Gosh."

She turns the phone screen toward me as she covers her mouth with her hand.

> **From:** Mr. Taylor
>
> **To:** McKenna Mae
>
> Ms. Mae,
>
> I have an important question to ask you.
>
> Your answer will affect all my future plans and happiness.
>
> Will you do me the honor of becoming my wife?
>
> Please consider your response carefully, because my whole heart is at stake.
>
> Sincerely,
>
> Mr. T

She begins tapping on the screen for a few minutes, biting down into her lip with a smile.

> **From:** McKenna Mae
>
> **To:** Mr. Taylor
>
> Mr. T,

YES, YES, YES!

Yours always and forever,

Kenna Taylor

Epilogue
Kenna

Two Years Later

"Give Daddy his present. Here, LJ, give this one to Daddy." I hand him the little box concealed in shiny red wrapping paper with a white bow.

He holds it in his chubby hands, smiling as he runs to Levi sitting on the edge of the fireplace. We're all dressed in matching plaid pajamas for our first Christmas Eve in our own home. Levi adjusts his glasses and smiles at LJ as he hands over the gift.

"Thanks, buddy. You want to help me open it?"

He's the hottest dad I've ever seen in my entire life.

I lift up my phone to take a video. LJ tears at the wrapping paper. His face is pure joy as he looks from me back to Levi with a grin. They finally have the wrapping paper off to reveal a basic brown box.

Levi looks up at me with a question in his gaze. "What do you think it is, LJ?"

"What do you think it is, Daddy?"

He smiles wider, eyes sweeping over me suggestively. I don't expect him to guess, simply because I just found out a few days ago and I begged the social worker not to tell him. Keeping it in has nearly killed me.

He lets LJ take off the lid to reveal two tiny white onesies. I capture the moment forever on my phone, the moment where Levi's face registers what this means.

His smile drops. His lips part. If I were closer, I'd bet I could see his pulse increase. Bright-blue eyes meet my gaze, and I can see from my space on the sofa that he's already about to cry.

LJ lost interest in the little clothes almost immediately and is attempting to stuff the crumpled wrapping paper inside the box. Levi stands up slowly, gripping the fabric in his big hands. He walks over to me, each step making my smile grow.

"Are you surprised?" I ask.

He doesn't respond. He drops down on his knees to the space between my legs. He leans forward to press his face right up to my chest, inhaling as he does so. His lips kiss over the fabric of my pajamas.

"I hope it's a girl," he says.

My face hurts from smiling too much. "You know there are two onesies, right?"

He lifts his head. "Two?"

I nod, reaching for the onesies he's holding. "Twins. She's due in four weeks, but they'll probably come sooner."

His lips slowly curve into a grin, and I sigh in relief. Adopting one baby is a big step. Doubling that number is quite ambitious.

"Did the mother already choose us?" His brow furrows. He reaches for my hands, intertwining our fingers as he leans down to kiss my knuckles.

"Yes...she's sixteen. They told me that she wanted a younger couple, and she liked that we've already adopted once before."

He nods. LJ walks over to us, chewing on a wad of red paper. I dig it out of his mouth before pulling him up to sit on my lap. Levi sits beside me, wrapping his arms around my shoulders and holding us close.

"If one is a girl, I think we should name her Sariah."

"Sariah? Like...Sarah and Lia?"

He nods. "It means princess of the Lord. And she's definitely going to be my little princess."

My heart might actually explode when I get the chance to watch him love on our baby girl. With as much as he already spoils me and LJ, I cannot fathom the level of spoiling Sariah would get.

"What if one is a boy?"

He grins, leaning his forehead against LJ's. "I was thinking Davis."

"My dad would love that." I lean back against his arm, closing my eyes. I can already picture them toddling around our home with LJ.

"What does my wife think about it?"

I smile, hugging LJ closer to me. "I love it, and I love you."

THE END

Also by MJ

Falling For Temptation is book one in the Good Ol' Boys Series. Here is the link to the book on Amazon.

The tattooed vixen in my first college class is everything I shouldn't crave if I want to stay on the straight and narrow path.

My family expects me to find a sweet, innocent girl. Harley Kain's questionable past and skin-baring clothing definitely don't fit the bill.

I think she might be the temptress my momma prayed I would resist, but I can't look away. All I want is to get an Agriculture degree and go back to the cornstalks and dirt. It's the only life I've ever known, and I'm perfectly content on the farm.

Until I see her.

She's guarded, but my protective instincts kick into overdrive when I find out she's been walking home alone at night. When she finally confides in me, I start to realize the dangerous life she's running from.

I want to protect her. I want to do more than that. But if I give in to my overwhelming desire for her, I'll be throwing away my future. My family will never approve.

Even if I am willing to sacrifice it all and fall for temptation, convincing Harley she's worthy of love could be impossible.

Scan to see it on Amazon.

BIG SHOT is book one in the Keep Your Secrets Series. It's a romantic comedy suspense story with a billionaire boss, quirky heroine, the injured damsel trope, a badass best friend, and a taste of the classic office romance. It follows the story of a billionaire Navy SEAL and a girl who never expected to be thrust into a world with secret agents and foreign spies. Go here to see it on Amazon.

Kate
THIS IS NOT YOUR ROUTINE ROM-COM.
I mean, it's close. I can see why you'd think that.

It started with the usual. I got fired and cheated on in the span of two hours.

I wanted to forget my troubles with the sexy stranger at the bar, so yes, I approached him. And yes, he definitely made me forget my pathetic life that night.

Until three days later when I was officially introduced to said stranger—as his new assistant.

The real twist?

He thinks I was sent here to kill him.

I wasn't—of course. It was all a big mix-up involving bourbon, supermodels, and government secrets labeled CLASSIFIED.

I've never even held a gun before, but apparently I give off Russian spy vibes.

I'm not the girl who grew up craving excitement.

Masked men breaking into my apartment and trying to kill me was never in my five year plan, but if we survive, maybe I can convince Mr. Big Shot to make me a part of his.

Luke

I've never been fooled by an enemy agent—until her.

Scan to see it on Amazon.

Keep Your Ring is book two in the Keep Your Secrets Series. It's releasing in September 2022. It's a enemies-to-lovers romantic comedy suspense. The best reader experience will be to start with book one **BIG SHOT**.

Fallon
I never should have said I DO to my brother's worst enemy.

When my brother told me that my husband murdered my ex-boyfriend, I was—furious. I've always heard that marriage was difficult, but I never expected to want to kill Garrison less than a month in.

When we said our vows, we promised forever.

After seeing my parent's marriage crumble to pieces, I'm determined not to be the one to break this promise.

Making him miserable beyond words and destroying every last shred of peace he possesses, however—that's my next vow.

Everything was going according to plan until the guy I brought home to piss off my husband ended up kidnapping me.

What is it with men these days? How hard is it for a girl to find a quick revenge hookup?

Anyway...I'm forgetting the point here.

If he would give up his feigning innocence act, things would be much easier. My defenses are starting to struggle the longer he holds out.

But I will NOT give in. I might take physical breaks a few times, on the deck of our yacht, on our NYC penthouse rooftop...but NOT in my heart.

Garrison
The thing is, I never stopped loving Fallon—but hate is a much more visceral sensation.

Pre-order this book here.

Scan to see it on Amazon.

About Author & Links

Mj adores when a fictional man is humbled by a feisty woman who he never anticipated.

She began telling love stories when they kept morphing out of her fevered soul, craving a place to rest.

Writing is her natural state of mind, whether it be in the drive-through line or near the calming lake she lives down the road from.

She is a single mother from Texas and eternally indebted to her writing, which rescued her from the darkest place she'd ever been.

Mj's lifelong dream is to reside in a house by the sea.

You can connect with Mj via Instagram @mjarix_ or TikTok @mjarix.

You can email her at mjhendrixwrites@gmail.com.

Her website is www.mjhendrix.com. Go to the About Mj | Contact tab to sign up for new book alerts.

Scan to visit www.mjhendrix.com.

Acknowledgments

The hardest year of my life was the year I started writing novels.

In January 2021 I woke up from a dream, unable to stop my head from spinning with a fictional story. I had to write it. My mind wouldn't leave me alone until I did. I'm so glad I listened, because I found a true passion. That passion saved me from a dark and dangerous time.

Here's a fact. When someone is oppressed to the point of being unable to survive in their world, the mind takes over. It prevents the trauma from destroyed that person by blocking out the truth and creating a false reality.

Reading and writing fiction is absolutely vital for those whose reality is too intense and traumatic to cope with.

This is why I write. This why I share my stories.

Now for the thank you's to my team of bad bitches.

Thank you to Jovana, my invaluable, intelligent editor. (She didn't edit this section so pardon my horrific grammar and punctuation.)

Thank you to Misha, also a hero and the only reason my work is readable.

Thank you to my beta readers, Raeanna, Keri, and Ashley. You three are saints for even attempting to dissect something half-decent from my second draft.

Love all you queens.

Made in the USA
Monee, IL
10 September 2022

13700900R00204